A DETECTIVE INSPEC

BENEATH THE BODIES

NEW YORK TIMES #1 BESTSELLER **TONY LEE** WRITING AS

JACK GATLAND

Hooded Man
MEDIA
INSPIRATION • PRODUCTION • PUBLICATION

———————

Published by Hooded Man Media.

First Edition: March 2023

PRAISE FOR JACK GATLAND

'This is one of those books that will keep you up past your bedtime, as each chapter lures you into reading just one more.'

'This book was excellent! A great plot which kept you guessing until the end.'

'Couldn't put it down, fast paced with twists and turns.'

'The story was captivating, good plot, twists you never saw and really likeable characters. Can't wait for the next one!'

'I got sucked into this book from the very first page, thoroughly enjoyed it, can't wait for the next one.'

'Totally addictive. Thoroughly recommend.'

'Moves at a fast pace and carries you along with it.'

'Just couldn't put this book down, from the first page to the last one it kept you wondering what would happen next.'

Before LETTER FROM THE DEAD...
There was

LIQUIDATE
THE PROFITS

Learn the story of what *really* happened to DI Declan Walsh,
while at Mile End!

An EXCLUSIVE PREQUEL, completely free to anyone who
joins the Declan Walsh Reader's Club!

Join at bit.ly/jackgatlandVIP

COVERT ACTION

COUNTER ATTACK

STEALTH STRIKE

DAMIAN LUCAS BOOKS

THE LIONHEART CURSE

STANDALONE BOOKS

THE BOARDROOM

For Mum, who inspired me to write.

For Tracy, who inspires me to write.

CONTENTS

PROLOGUE

IF HE WAS BEING BRUTALLY HONEST, IT HADN'T BEEN THE BEST of days for Lance Mason. And that was before they found the body.

Mason had been the Verger for Temple Church in the City of London for a few years now. It wasn't the most taxing of jobs, and he found it strangely peaceful in the church, regardless of the constant thrum of tourists, all looking for the church used in "that Dan Brown movie." Which in some respects was true – the Templar Church of Temple Inn had been used in the novel *The Da Vinci Code* as one location where clues to the whereabouts of the Holy Grail were, and every Friday for a good couple of years during the heyday of the novel (and then the film), the Master of the Temple Church had given a talk to up to two hundred tourists a time on the "Da Vinci trail". But, at the same time, the story set inside the church was complete rubbish. Mason hadn't been connected to the church when they'd filmed there, but he'd heard stories while walking around the dominant feature of the church – the ten statues of knights that now lay on their backs on the floor in the centre of the circular nave – stories about how they wanted the statues moved, or the windows replaced for better lighting while filming, surprised that the walls weren't removable like real film sets.

Of course, these were stories told to him by people who'd had the stories passed to them, so the whole thing was likely a massive game of Chinese Whispers, but it didn't matter. Lance Mason wasn't a fan of the book's general idea, had never watched the film, and looked down on the people who came here looking for an imaginary conspiracy by an imaginary secret order, used in an imaginary story – whether it was in book form or film. And he was amused when, as they entered, they found glass cases surrounding many of the effigies. Mason was also tired of hearing these people knowledgeably explain to their friends, based on the information they'd received in that damned novel, that some of the Knights Templar effigies had their legs crossed at the ankles because they'd been to the Holy Land on a crusade. Mason had to actively restrain himself for pointing out this was complete bollocks, and that among academia, it was now accepted that such attribution was a "fanciful idea," to be more polite. But he understood how this was too romantic an idea to give up, as even before the book came out, Wordsworth, Dickens and Tennyson all made allusions to this – even if it was a sixteenth century stylistic form.

Standing in the middle of the circular Nave, the first part of the church built in 1185, and based on Jerusalem's *Church of the Holy Sepulchre,* where the Templar order began, Mason looked down at the effigies of knights surrounding him. Some of them still had sharp, defined features, while others had their faces melted by German incendiary bombs during World War Two, when the church had one of its many forced redesigns. These included a post-Great Fire of London one where it was refurbished by Christopher Wren, making extensive modifications to the interior, including the addition of an altar screen and the church's first organ. This lasted unto 1841 when Smirke and Burton "Charlottenised" it, a look that stayed until the aforementioned bombing of World War Two, and the subsequent rebuilding by the architect Walter Godfrey in the fifties.

Amusingly, Godfrey had found Wren's renovations had been held in storage after being removed in the nineteenth century, and they were returned to their positions. Which meant that the church he stood in *still* wasn't close to the one the Templars once stood in.

The knocking at the door shook him out of his thoughts; he'd been waiting for it, but the solace of the church always allowed his mind to drift. Pulling himself out of his thoughts and walking to the south side door, he pulled out his keys, unlocking and opening it to reveal a young woman with dyed-black hair in a Barbour coat. It was early February, the snow from earlier that week was still visible in the shadows where the sun hadn't reached it, and it was bitterly cold.

Too cold for just a Barbour, that was for sure.

'Mister Mason?' she asked, holding out a hand. 'I'm Jean Darblay. We spoke about the recital?'

Mason took the hand, shaking it before letting go and stepping to the side, allowing her to enter the church. She seemed too young for such an old name, but they usually went around in circles. His nephew had just announced his new son was named Winston ... the poor bastard.

'Sorry, it's still cold in here,' he explained. 'We close at four usually, and we only keep the heating on if there's a performance in the evening.'

Jean graciously entered, patting her hands against her arms as she did so.

'I find it bracing,' she smiled. 'I'm just glad you were happy to meet me at this time of night, as I couldn't get into London before seven.'

Mason nodded. He wanted to say how this was a massive pain in the arse for him, and how he'd much rather be home watching *Happy Valley* or something on catch-up TV, but he decided it was better to simply allow her to look around, take some measurements and then get on with it. She'd called – or, rather, the company she worked for called – to book the space for a private, corporate recital around Easter, but had needed to "scope the location" first. Mason had bitten his tongue at this, knowing she could easily watch one of a dozen videos on the church available on YouTube, and save herself the time and hassle of a trip.

Or, rather, save *Mason* the time and hassle of a trip.

'Wow,' she said, finally looking around the church as she walked into the circular Nave. 'It's certainly something, isn't it?'

Mason nodded again, even adding a 'mmm' noise to the response.

Jean smiled, looking upwards.

'This was where Robert Langdon stood, right?' she asked. 'In the film?'

Mason groaned inwardly, realising this now wasn't some kind of location visit, but was likely a fan using an event to give herself private access.

'Yes, I believe so,' he said, motioning her towards the other end of the church. 'If we can, I'd like to show you the main Chancel, as we find that facing back to the Nave shows a better visual layout of most events, with the audience in the pews, facing to the sides while the makeshift stages are held between these pillars.'

'Sure, sure,' Jean walked over to Mason, but noted him glancing back at the door. 'Are you okay?'

Mason forced a smile in return.

'Sorry,' he replied. 'We had some issues here this morning before I arrived. The police had a report of someone seen in the church last night, so an officer came in and had a look around. They didn't find anything, but at the same time they'd asked Louise – that's the woman who opens up – to step out, just in case there was someone inside.'

Jean now hugged her sides as she looked around.

'But they didn't find someone, right?'

'No.'

'How easy is it to get in?' Jean asked. 'Because we'd be leaving expensive equipment in here during the run.'

'It's not easy at all,' Mason said tartly, his professionalism insulted by this. 'Only a couple of us have keys, and you have to be trusted to get them.'

To emphasise this, he rattled the keys on his chain.

'Anyway, there was nobody here, so it was probably someone having a laugh,' Mason finished. 'The barristers in Middle Temple are always taking the piss. And we had a tour this afternoon, and nobody saw anyone hiding here or upstairs.'

'Upstairs?' Jean frowned, her eyebrows knotting. 'There's an upstairs here?'

'More an upper gallery, a clerestory around the top of the Nave to add more light in,' Mason waved at the circular walls behind them. 'There's a door to the right that leads you up there.'

'Could I have a look?' Jean made a hopeful expression, as

if this would sway Mason. But, as it was, Mason had by now accepted this had turned into some kind of tour, and nodded.

'The door's open,' he said, walking over to the stained wooden door embedded into the stone. 'We often have exhibitions in the gallery.'

Opening the door, he allowed Jean through first, nodding towards the stone steps to the side, climbing up, and following the steps around to the right.

'Be careful, they're quite steep,' he said, but he needn't have bothered, as Jean started up the steps two at a time.

Sighing, he followed her, but stopped around halfway up the staircase, as his visitor had paused beside a curved wooden door embedded into the external wall.

'What's this?' she asked.

That, Mason thought to himself with a smile, *is a thing not mentioned in the bloody Da Vinci Code.*

'Ah, I'm not sure I should talk about that,' he replied, partly for theatrics, but also because the place gave him an uncomfortable feeling. 'This is – well, it *was* – the penitential cell.'

'The what cell?' Jean pulled at the door, but found it locked.

'Penitential,' Mason repeated. 'This small room, only four-feet-six-inches long, and two-feet-six-inches wide, confined the disobedient and unholy brothers of the Temple, forced to endure severe penance with solitary confinement; in a room you couldn't sit or lie down within.'

It was more theatrical than he intended, but it gave the desired effect, as Jean now stared in morbid curiosity at the door.

'Wow,' she said. 'That's harsh.'

'It's more than harsh, it could be fatal,' Mason said, his

professional pride dented by the response. 'They locked away Walter Bachelor in there for eight weeks, and left him to starve to death after disobeying the Master.'

'Eight weeks,' Jean couldn't take her eyes off the door. 'I know it's a little cheeky, but ... could I have a look inside?'

Mason pursed his lips.

'I need to point out, this punishment was likely a Templar thing, and nothing to do with the organised Church of the time—'

'Yeah, yeah, I get that,' Jean looked down at him. 'Please?'

Sighing, Mason walked up beside her and, from his jangling keychain, he pulled a key from the others, inserting it into the lock and twisting, the solid click from within announcing the door was now open.

'All yours,' he said, stepping back down.

Jean took a deep breath, nodded, and then opened the door, peering into the darkened room.

And she *screamed*.

It wasn't an "oh I had a fright" kind of sound, this was guttural terror, and Mason immediately caught her as she stumbled back into his arms, stammering as she pointed into the room.

Moving carefully past her, Mason looked through the door to see what had scared Jean so.

Someone had wedged a body against the wall in a half-sitting, half-standing pose.

It was male, and the body had been dead for a very long time, now barely more than a skeleton, cleaned of all detritus apart from one scrap of decomposed skin holding wisps of brown hair onto the scalp, the bones still connected some-how, unseen within the clothing. The skeleton was wearing a suit, shirt and tie, with black patent-leather brogues on its feet, the hands still crossed over its chest, even though it was no longer in the prone position it had likely been in for years.

The entire vision was decades old, apart from one thing; a piece of card, written on in pen, and placed around the body's neck by a piece of string.

WEIGHED AND FOUND WANTING

Mason didn't stare any longer, instead he closed the door again, locking it quickly, as if expecting the long-dead man to clamber out of the penitential cell and stalk them down the stairs.

'That's ... that's not part of the tour, is it?' Jean whispered nervously.

'No, Miss Darblay,' Mason admitted, pulling out a mobile phone and already calling the police as he spoke. 'That most certainly isn't.'

'And that's not been in there for decades?'

Mason shook his head.

'That wasn't even in here yesterday,' he replied as he turned his attention to the phone. 'Hello? Police, please. I want to report a—'

He paused.

'Actually, I don't know what the hell to call it, but it definitely needs you guys to come and have a look.'

THE PROTESTERS HAD PRETTY MUCH FINISHED AT ST PAUL'S Cathedral by the time PC Charlotte – better known as "Charlie" – Mainsworth started her shift.

She wasn't even sure why they were protesting; all she knew when she arrived was it was mainly students, probably protesting climate change or something, and for some unknown-to-her reason, they'd chosen St Paul's as their place to speak out.

Mainsworth didn't care, either. She'd had a stinking hangover all day, the product of her cousin's twenty-fifth birthday party the previous night. Why she couldn't have waited until the weekend before going all-in on destroying as many brain cells as she could, Mainsworth had no idea. But, as the loyal relative, she'd gone along for the ride, even though she was on duty the following day.

She was probably still over the limit when she clocked on earlier that day, but it wasn't the first time.

Mainsworth was a stocky woman, short, but muscular with it. She'd been called "dense" at Hendon while training, and it was a nickname that had carried on through her career, in Mile End and in Thames Valley. But this wasn't because of her intelligence, it was more because she had a density higher than most coppers around her. While they were light like aluminium, she was dense like lead. It also helped her out when she was playing rugby, as nobody had yet managed to better her on the pitch, even at her age. In fact, when she was playing defence, she actually had to reduce her power a little, as she was pretty capable of concussing even the best players.

She hadn't always been that way though, and when she was a teenager she had been much slimmer. She was a definite catch back then. Her mum had been the same way, though her dad was lithe and slim, the type of man who'd fly away in a gust of wind.

Mainsworth didn't see her dad much. And she hadn't seen her mum since her thirtieth birthday.

That had been the day Mum had passed away.

She'd hoped it hadn't been *personal.*

Shaking her head to blow away the dark memories, she winced as the headache now returned in force. Sitting back for the moment, groaning, she cricked her neck, rotating her head around as if hoping some click would magically remove the pain.

'You need some pain killers?' It was a male voice, young with it. Thinking it was another protestor, or someone coming to try to argue an arrest, Mainsworth placed her "game face" on, and turned to face—

Another copper.

He was young, around ten, maybe fifteen years younger, so in his mid-twenties. He was a little taller, but also a little slimmer, with blond hair in a centre parting; the "curtains" style she remembered from the nineties had returned, and he looked like he was growing it out, maybe to hide the scar on his eyebrow that made him look like a wannabe rapper.

His uniform was slightly different to hers, though. For a start, even though their fluorescent jackets were similar, his buttons were silver, not the gold of the City of London police. Her forage cap – the peaked hat she wore – was banded with red and white dicing, with a gold badge on the front, while his was black and white dicing, his badge as silver as his buttons.

Met police, then, she decided.

'Aren't you a bit out of your jurisdiction?' she mocked, nodding at St Paul's. 'Or are you taking confession?'

The officer smiled.

'Just passing through,' he said, holding a hand out. 'PC

Dixon.'

'Mainsworth.'

Dixon looked around the street as he pulled his hand from hers.

'Heard this got rough earlier,' he said. 'Paints being thrown around or something?'

'Possibly, I wasn't here then,' Mainsworth admitted, looking over to where Dixon was looking, embarrassed to admit she hadn't even considered asking why there were coloured paint marks on the pavement. 'Only got here an hour back. Was sorting a domestic in Blackfriars before that.'

Dixon nodded at this.

'Headache been there all day?'

'How do you know I've got a headache?' Mainsworth eyed him suspiciously.

In response, Dixon tapped his vest.

'I'm a copper,' he said. 'I followed the clues. And you looked in pain.'

'Oh, so you Met boys are all Columbo now?' Mainsworth joked. She was enjoying the back and forth, and Dixon was a good-looking man, even if he was almost half her age. Although, she was still in her thirties, just about; it wasn't *that* much of a stretch.

And it wasn't the *first* time she'd had an affair where the age difference was noticeable.

'Yeah, my head's killing me,' she admitted. 'Too many vodka cranberries last night.'

'I've got paracetamol in the squad car,' Dixon nodded over at Ave Maria Lane, leading off the Main Street. 'It's just up there. If you want some?'

Oh, I definitely want some, Mainsworth thought wickedly to herself. He had a look, something that was familiar to her, which gave him an attractiveness she couldn't deny – but she couldn't quite place it.

Looking back at the remnants of the protest, she weighed up the options in her head. On one side, she'd be leaving her post. On the other side, a chance to end the rest of the shift pain-free was worth it.

'How far up?'

'Literally by Amen Court,' Dixon replied, already moving that way. 'I only came here because I needed to pick something up.'

He nodded at the crowd still outside the church.

'But that's become a little trickier right now. I'll do it later. But if you want the tablet, it's in my first aid kit.'

'Why?' Mainsworth asked, unwittingly following the officer as he headed away from the cordon. 'I mean, it's just a headache. You could just aim me at the nearest chemist.'

'Dunno,' Dixon admitted. 'Maybe I was hoping to spend some time with you, convince you I'm a nice guy?'

'And why would you want to do that?' Mainsworth was now walking beside Dixon as they walked onto Ave Maria Lane.

'Because I'd have a better chance of asking you out for a drink that way,' Dixon grinned, flirting openly, walking over to a blue Peugeot 5008. 'Ignore the lack of police branding, I borrowed one of the detective's cars.'

Mainsworth paused.

'Your CID allows you to drive their cars?'

'Sure,' Dixon frowned. 'For quick tasks, anyway. Yours don't?'

'Ours are a little ... eccentric,' Mainsworth smiled. 'I'm Temple Inn.'

'Ah, the *Last Chance Saloon*? I've heard of you,' Dixon

opened up the back of the car, now rummaging around in a green first aid box. 'You're under Monroe, right? And Walsh Junior?'

Mainsworth had never heard DI Walsh named as "Walsh Junior" before, but it was no secret that his father had been a high-ranking copper. Her mum had even known him back in the day, and had probably even mentioned him, but she'd never cared to pay attention, really.

'I'm not under them, but yeah, they're there,' she said. 'You know a lot for a Met boy.'

'I'm full of surprises, Charlie,' Dixon said ... but then stopped rummaging.

'Shit,' he said. 'You didn't tell me your first name, did you?'

PC Charlie Mainsworth took half a step back from Dixon, realising she'd walked into an empty street at night with an effective stranger.

'Who the hell are—' she started, but she didn't get any further, as PC Dixon spun around, a syringe in his hand, slamming the needle into her neck, pushing what was inside it deep into her bloodstream. As she staggered back, clutching at her neck, unable to speak, her throat paralysed, he walked quickly over to her, catching her as she stumbled, walking her to the car and, as she eventually passed out, rolling her into the boot of the vehicle, closing it behind her.

Climbing into the driver's seat and tossing his cap to the seat beside him, PC Dixon started the Peugeot 5008 and, checking quickly in the mirror to make sure nobody had witnessed the abduction, he drove off northwards, towards Smithfield and the A40.

1

A NIGHT AT THE OPERA

DECLAN DIDN'T KNOW EXACTLY WHAT TO EXPECT FROM THE evening, but the one thing he *hadn't* expected to be doing when out on the town with a billionaire, was watching an opera.

If he was brutally honest, he hadn't really wanted to go out in the first place. He'd only met Eden Storm a couple of times the previous summer, and at the time Eden had made it perfectly clear he was interested in dating Anjli Kapoor, which made the night ahead a little awkward. Because when Eden was last on the scene Anjli was single. Now Declan and Anjli had been a couple for a good few months.

However, just because they were together right now, didn't mean they'd be together forever, and Declan had been worrying for a while now that he wasn't making enough of an effort in the relationship. It might even have been mentioned to him by a couple of people. And now, with Eden Storm appearing out of the blue and inviting them both on a "double date", things seemed mighty suspicious.

There was also the niggling fact Eden was a far better

catch than Declan, too. His dyed white hair from the previous year was now jet-black, although still spiked, with each tip immaculately styled. He was tanned and toned, looking a good five years younger than his thirty-five years, which meant he looked a good decade younger than Declan. A billionaire tech entrepreneur, with his rock-star father's millions and back catalogue added to his late mother's pharmaceutical inheritance, Eden's electric, solar powered car company *Edisun* was still making waves in the tech journals – well, this was according to Billy, who was the only person in the department reading these things – and Eden was being touted as the next Elon Musk.

Which was a poisoned chalice considering the *first* Elon Musk.

He was wearing a black leather jacket, white shirt and blue jeans. Recalling a conversation he'd had with Billy once about Eden's style choices, Declan assumed once more that Eden's shirt alone cost more than Declan's suit.

He was also being extraordinarily nice which always made Declan suspicious.

Eden had contacted Anjli around a week back – even though she'd turned him down the previous year, they'd still kept in touch, the detective sergeant and the billionaire. She'd received a message saying he was in town with his new girlfriend, was only around for a couple of days, and did they want to do something exciting. Anjli had asked Declan if he wanted to go, and although he wanted nothing less in the world as the very thought of spending the evening in Eden's company as he dazzled Anjli with tales of his good-looking-ness, and rich-guyness gave him mild acid reflux and nausea, Declan could see she really wanted to meet up.

And, there was a little amusement deep down, when

Declan saw the jealousy that Billy Fitzwarren, only *minorly* rich compared to Eden Storm, showed when he heard about the "double date".

They had settled the plan through a woman named Amanda, who was apparently Eden's "life", and by that Declan meant the woman who held every part of Eden's entire existence together; the "Pepper Pots" PA to his Tony Stark. Eden had taken Declan and Anjli to the Royal Albert Hall, where, in "Box 57", a four-person private box, they would drink champagne, eat expensive food and watch the Strasbourg Philharmonic Orchestra perform Mozart's *Don Giovanni.*

Declan didn't know many operas, but he knew this one, purely because he'd watched the movie *Amadeus* a lifetime ago, and this was an opera lampooned in it. For some reason, he'd believed the ghost that appeared was Mozart's father, but now, based on what had happened in the first act, he wasn't too sure.

In fact, he wasn't sure about anything anymore.

They'd arrived late – a car theft outside St Bride's Church had taken up their afternoon – and had only just got to the box before the show started. The box itself was narrow and claustrophobic, if Declan was being honest, with a very strong red theme going on: deep-red painted walls, a thick red carpet leading to red and gold seats, and a red curtain to pull across behind you. Even the table, beside the wall and filled with food and drink, including several bottles of wine and champagne, was covered in a red tablecloth.

Eden was there, expensive as ever, being tactful enough not to glance at the incredibly expensive Rolex on his wrist to remind Declan of his lateness. Instead, he'd introduced both Declan and Anjli to Dominique Lacroix, his super-model girlfriend, wearing a "little black number" that made her look as if she'd walked off a red carpet to be here, and offered them both champagne, apologising that *the box staff didn't have Guinness up here*, but pointing out that *he was sure they could get a pint sent up.*

Declan's back had gone up at this, wondering if Eden had been mocking his more working-class status, a pint over champagne and all that, but he realised this was Eden being Eden, a man who wanted to make sure his guests enjoyed their night.

Declan and Anjli both took a glass of champagne as the show began; Declan grabbing a piece of warmed sourdough bread and butter from the side table to chew on, as they settled into their seats, sitting slightly above Eden and Dominique as they watched the performance on a stage slightly to their right. And, thankfully for Declan, there were small flat areas on the back wall either side where, as the cast sang their Italian lines, the same lines, but translated into English, appeared by the magic of some sort of screen projector.

Declan hadn't been to a live opera before, regardless of the whole "box" experience, and he found it ... interesting. He wasn't sure if he'd understand the opera itself, but he found, after a little while, it was like watching a movie with subtitles.

And singing.

And being live.

After what felt like a few minutes, but was actually over an hour, the first act finished, with the villainous Don Giovanni escaping his three, unmasked judges, and Declan found himself rising with many of the others, applauding enthusiastically, to Anjli's amusement.

And then the break had begun and, as the audience shifted in their seats, Eden rose from his own chair, nodding to the back of the box.

'We have time for a snack now,' he said, holding out a hand to show the table at the rear beside the door that entered the box. 'Turkey roulade with apricot stuffing, pigs in blankets, seasonal vegetables, dauphinoise potatoes, red wine sauce, and a Confit duck leg, braised red cabbage, new potatoes and peppercorn sauce.'

Declan looked at the small bowls on the table, and his stomach growled.

'And there are dessert canapes coming, too,' Eden smiled, his American accent faint, but still there. 'I hope you don't mind, but I asked for the Christmas menu for us, as I like that more.'

Declan smiled. *Of course Eden Storm could get whatever menu he wanted.*

'I'm surprised we're not in the Royal Box,' he quipped. 'This seems a little small, less grandiose for you.'

Eden grinned, motioning for Declan to join him at the front of the box. Walking down the steps, nodding at Dominique as she passed back into the rear of the box with Anjli, Eden motioned for Declan to lean over the edge of the red velvet trim, looking down onto the box below. There, about five inches below the lip, was a stone crown, the gold paint and white pearls now fading.

'We're in the box above,' Eden smiled. 'It's pretty much as close as you can get to the view without being in it.'

He peered over.

'There are people in there, but I don't think it's royals,' he added. 'They give the seats out to their staff when they don't attend.'

Declan nodded at this.

'Billy's family has a box at the O2,' he replied. 'The staff get seats by lottery.'

'Similar thing, most likely,' Eden agreed.

Declan laughed, looking around the box, and the surrounding ones on either side. The location of the box was nestled within a horseshoe-shaped row that seemed to travel three quarters of the hall's circumference, each one a narrow sliver, a wedge filled with people. It was quite cramped, with the two seats in each row almost next to the seats in the adjoining boxes, with only a narrow, red-felt barrier providing privacy.

'I have to say, I didn't expect you to be so close to the normal people,' he gently mocked. 'No security, either.'

'You think I need security?' Eden raised an eyebrow. 'Just because I have money doesn't mean I'm not like everyone else.'

'The first time we met, you flew us to a crime scene in your private helicopter,' Declan replied. 'And you offered to take Anjli to Paris for lunch. I don't know anyone else who'd do that.'

'If I hadn't flown you in my helicopter, you wouldn't have caught a killer,' Eden countered.

'True,' Declan shrugged. 'But you're still a little exposed here.'

'You think?'

With his back to the edge of the box, and facing inwards, Eden considered the words, nodded, and then clapped his hands twice.

It was like a magic trick; although most of the Royal Albert Hall stayed the same, the three boxes on either side of them, each with two couples in, suddenly froze in place, like the most surreal game of "statues" Declan had ever played.

'I wasn't sitting next to strangers,' Eden replied calmly. 'I'm not that stupid. At every point, I knew who was with me. And I bought out the three boxes on either side of this one, just so I could have privacy.'

He looked at both sides of the box as he grinned, clapping his hands a second time.

'Guys, that was spectacular,' he exclaimed. 'Enjoy the rest of the show, and thanks.'

Declan watched the other boxes return to their conversations, each one filled with laughter. One woman on his right, the woman who'd been sitting to the side of Eden, but in the box beside him, gave Declan a cheeky wink before turning to her friends.

'That's Amanda,' Eden nodded to her in thanks. 'She's the one you spoke to who arranged this.'

'Why?' Declan was actually getting annoyed here. 'What, so all of this was just to show off? So you could go "look at me, aren't I important," or something similar?'

'Actually, it was the opposite,' Eden's smile faded now. 'I knew if I just took a single box, paparazzi and news outlets would buy the boxes beside, just on the off-chance they could grab a photo, or learn why I, the technology-billionaire son of an eighties music legend would have a night out with two detectives.'

He nodded across the stalls, over to the boxes on the opposite side.

'My security, the ones you were worried about, are all over there, taking telephoto lenses off photographers,' he sighed. 'As they do every night.'

'So why do it?' Declan asked. 'Why become a target for them?'

'Because if I didn't, it'd mean they'd won,' Eden replied sadly. 'And I'd become a recluse. I'm not ready to have my life controlled just yet.'

He pulled a small black book out of his jacket, holding it up as if it was a holy item.

'You putting Anjli in your little black book?' Declan didn't mean to say the words, but he'd been thinking it since he arrived. This whole thing wasn't for Declan, he was pretty sure about that. Instead, it was for Anjli, currently enjoying dessert canapes with a supermodel.

'She's already in it,' Eden held up a hand to stop Declan from replying. 'Because this is my *bullet journal.* My life, as much as Amanda there controls it; this is where all my ideas come, and are written in. You were engrossed in the opera, but if you hadn't been, you'd have seen me pull this out and take notes throughout the whole thing. I find doing things like this, things that I'm not that much a fan of, gives my brain a chance to refocus on other things.'

He looked down at the book in his hand.

'My father had one of these,' he said. 'Musicians call them cookbooks, a storage place for songwriters to throw snippets of lyrics when they come to mind. It's the same as a commonplace book for writers, or the notebook you write in when speaking to a witness.'

Declan didn't mean to, but he unconsciously touched the notebook in his inside jacket pocket.

If Eden noticed this, he didn't comment, still staring at the book in his hand.

'Fun fact, the term "little black book" comes from history, when people kept track of kings in these,' he said. 'That then changed when Henry the Eighth kept a literal black book where the names of people who were sinful were written. His black book was a way of keeping a record of who should be punished for their sinful ways.'

'So it's not about sex?'

'Oh, it's very much linked to sex,' Eden smiled. 'In the mid-Eighteenth century, Samuel Derrick conspired with Jack Harris, the "Pimp General of all England" to create an annual guide to London's prostitutes and their specialities. It was hundreds of names long and was known as "Harris's List of Covent-Garden Ladies." A copy of which is quite rare. This, however, is my "second brain." If I was to lose it …'

He let the sentence hang as he looked out over the auditorium.

'Seems strange that a man so interlinked with tech goes analogue when taking notes.'

'Can't hack a book,' Eden grinned as he placed it back into his jacket. 'The point I was making was if I listened to everyone, I'd never go out. My life would be repetitive, I'd become the same and anyone I was with … well, they'd become the same. Or, they'd wither on the vine.'

Eden was looking at Dominique as he spoke, and Declan frowned as he followed the gaze, because there was every chance he was staring at Anjli instead.

'If you don't like opera, why bring us here?' Declan asked, watching Anjli. 'We could have gone anywhere, done anything.'

'Anjli,' Eden explained. 'She said to Amanda your favourite thing in the world was a night at the opera.'

'Yeah, but not this,' Declan almost laughed. 'She meant "A Night At The Opera," the album by Queen.'

Eden opened his mouth in surprise, closed it, and then laughed.

'Well, this is awkward,' he said, as the mood between the two men lifted.

'Seriously, though,' Declan pressed. 'Why the night out? And don't tell me you wanted to show off your new girlfriend, because you've spoken more to your fake audience member assistant tonight than you have her.'

Eden looked up at the Royal Albert Hall's ceiling and sighed.

'What are your intentions with Anjli?' he eventually asked.

'My intentions?' Declan was half-expecting the question, but it still threw him. 'What the hell do you mean by that?'

Finally, the mask was taken off, as were the gloves, as Eden squared up to face Declan.

'I've had a long chance to look deep into myself,' he explained. 'Therapy following the antics of last June notwithstanding, I realised that with everything I have, I was missing something.'

He looked up at the two women.

'Something maybe Anjli Kapoor could offer,' he finished.

'If I recall, you already asked, and she turned you down.'

'Oh, you're right, she did,' Eden nodded. 'And now, with hindsight, I see she did this because she was in love with you, but didn't know it.'

Declan looked up at Anjli who, seeing him watching, held up one of the dessert pots.

'These are great,' she said. 'Try the limoncello snowballs.'

Declan smiled.

'I'm lucky,' he whispered.

'Yeah, you are,' Eden replied, and there was a hint of

sullenness in his voice, as Declan realised this was something he couldn't, with all his money, buy. 'But watching you, I'm not seeing a couple that are happy.'

Declan froze at this. He'd been worrying about this since Christmas, watching his colleagues prepare for weddings while he and Anjli coasted along. He'd said at the time they were "finding their feet", but to be honest, he was scared.

A year ago, he'd almost rekindled a relationship with Kendis Taylor, ending with a one-night stand before she was brutally murdered. A year before that, he'd split from Liz, his wife of many years, after she decided she wanted someone who didn't put the force above her.

At the time, he'd understood this, but in a matter of days she was about to marry DCI Henry Farrow, his onetime boss, and someone who was more a workaholic than he was.

Which meant it wasn't his workload loyalty that had broken up his marriage.

It was him.

He'd had this in his head for the last month; should he really move on with Anjli, or was he stopping her from living her life? He was scared to move forward, looking back at his previous failures, the "curse" he seemed to have – even his most recent crush before Anjli, Theresa Martinez, turned out to be a murderer – and wondering if she'd be better off without him.

But Eden Storm, the good looking, younger, more stylish, more exciting billionaire standing beside him, telling him effectively to *move aside and let someone else dance with Anjli?* That stirred something primal inside him.

'Tell me what you see,' he said, holding his anger back, keeping his voice calm.

'I see two housemates,' Eden replied calmly, objectively

even. 'Who made a jump into something bigger, but now both regret it.'

Declan took a deep breath, letting it out slowly as he considered the statement.

'And you get this how?' he asked carefully. 'Did Anjli mention this?'

'No, but I have eyes, and I've spoken to her now and then. And I saw the moment you arrived there were problems.'

Declan nodded, looking around.

'So all this was to take Anjli from me?'

For the first time in the conversation Eden looked surprised.

'God no!' he said. 'I wasn't asking so I could take a shot! I did that and she turned me down. All this was supposed to be for you, to give you something fun and exciting to do with her – although that didn't go as planned – so you could enjoy a date night for once.'

'You don't think I enjoy date night?'

Eden stared deeply into Declan's eyes, almost as if searching for an answer.

'No, Declan,' he answered sadly. 'I don't think you enjoy much of anything anymore.'

Declan went to reply, but then stopped.

He was right.

'So how do I fix this?' he asked.

'She deserves better,' Eden looked out across the auditorium. 'So be better. I like Anjli, as a friend. She keeps me grounded when we talk, mainly because she doesn't see me like other people.'

'An arrogant billionaire?'

'Touché,' Eden smiled. 'I'll put my cards on the table,

Declan. If you broke up, I'd risk another chance at winning her, even though I don't usually return to a failed project.'

'Anjli's a failed project now?' Declan smiled back, finding something he could use. 'That doesn't seem very hearts and flowers, now. Very... business like.'

'I learned from the best,' Eden shrugged. 'You.'

Declan winced, accepting the comment.

'You might think I'm business like in my relationship, but it's complicated, and to be frank, none of your business,' he replied. 'When you're solving cases, looking at dead bodies together, it does kill the romance slightly.'

He leant in closer.

'But don't mistake compartmentalising for coldness,' he finished. 'I'd do anything for her.'

'Good to hear—' Eden started, but stopped as Declan's phone buzzed. Looking up at Anjli, he saw her phone had done the same, and that was never good.

'Sorry,' he said, pulling the phone out and checking the message.

It was from Monroe.

Get your arse to Temple Church now.

Declan returned his gaze to Anjli, who looked down at him, nodding.

'Sorry, Eden, but duty calls,' Declan said, placing the phone away and shaking Eden's already outstretched hand. 'I appreciate everything you did here, I really do, but Anjli and me? That's between us. And, if I'm honest I can't work it out myself, so I have no hope of explaining it to someone else.'

'Don't get complacent,' Eden smiled as he spoke, but the message was ominous. 'She's out of your league, and if you keep taking her for granted, one day she'll realise it. And I'll be waiting.'

Declan nodded. 'And as for you, can I give you some advice?' he said, stretching as he looked around the boxes. 'You're not here with your supermodel, even though she sat next to you for the first Act. You've smiled more with your PA than you have with her. Maybe you should consider your *own* workplace relationship?'

Eden's eyes widened, and Declan grinned. For all his billions and his blue sky visioning, Eden Storm was just like everyone else, unaware of what was right under his nose.

'I'm Tony Stark,' he whispered, almost in realisation.

Declan didn't answer this, instead walking up the steps and into the small room, glancing at the remaining food and feeling the rumbling of his hungry stomach, annoyed he had eaten nothing before talking to Eden.

'You get the same text from Monroe?' Anjli asked, nodding at the phone.

Declan nodded.

'I could go, if you want,' he suggested. 'You stay here, enjoy yourself, I'll call if we need you?'

'I'm fine,' Anjli walked over to Eden, giving him a quick hug before nodding farewell to Dominique. 'Let's go.'

Walking out of the box and heading for the stairs, Anjli couldn't help herself, and laughed.

'God, he knows how to pick them,' she said. 'Dominique spent the entire time talking about her work as a hand model, while he stared sadly at his assistant. I'm guessing you saw that too?'

She gave a roguish grin at Declan as she paused on the steps.

'And what were you boys talking about?' she asked.

'Operas, and Queen,' Declan lied. 'And the fact Eden Storm bought out half a dozen boxes just so he could have privacy.'

'It's a totally different life,' Anjli continued down the stairs, but Declan reached out, pausing her.

'It could be your life if you wanted,' he replied. 'Eden still pines over you.'

'You breaking up with me?' Anjli turned to face Declan now.

'God no,' Declan stammered. 'It's just I know I'm—'

'A bloody idiot,' Anjli kissed Declan before turning away and hurrying down the stairs. 'Come on, let's see what the miserable old Scot has for us.'

2

CHURCH SERVICED

IT TOOK HALF AN HOUR TO GET TO TEMPLE INN FROM THE Royal Albert Hall, and the journey had been tense. Anjli could tell something had happened between Declan and Eden, and while Declan was making light of the whole situation, there was definitely something bothering him.

Arriving back at the Temple Inn Crime Unit, it was only a five-minute walk to the church itself, nestled in the middle of the Inns of Court, and surrounded by taller buildings, including the Inner Temple itself.

PC Esme Cooper was on duty outside, the "do not cross" cordon crossing both sides of the plaza outside the church. Seeing them approach, she motioned for a couple of the onlookers, likely to be paparazzi or reporters, to move aside and let the detectives through.

'Cordons?' Declan narrowed his eyes as they passed under the crime scene tape. 'It's that bad?'

'It's the location more than the crime, Guv,' Cooper replied as she nodded over to the church's entrance. 'Knights Templar, Da Vinci Code, secret conspiracies, all that sort of stuff. I've already had two of these eejits asking if Robert Langdon was on the case.'

'Eejits?' Declan smiled. 'That's very DCI Monroe of you.'

'Yeah, sorry,' Cooper blushed. 'I can't stop saying it.'

'Is the boss in there?' Declan stopped at the door.

'Yes, and Doctor Marcos and Sergeant De'Geer,' Cooper replied, before hesitantly and uncomfortably adding, 'and DC Fitzwarren.'

Declan snuck a glance at Anjli as the name was spoken.

'How is he?'

Cooper shrugged.

'Same as usual,' she said. 'You'll see.'

Declan nodded and sighed, not really wanting that conversation. Since Billy had arrested his own boyfriend on murder charges, leading to a whole mess of things that ended with Andrade Estrada taking witness protection and disappearing from Billy's life forever, Billy had been a little ... *different*.

'What's the case?' Anjli asked. 'Monroe didn't say anything.'

'He wants it to be a surprise,' Cooper nodded at the door with her head. 'It's definitely not one of the normal ones.'

COOPER HADN'T BEEN WRONG IN HER STATEMENT. AS DECLAN and Anjli walked into the church, they found it abuzz with forensics officers as DCI Alex Monroe, his white hair and beard standing him out from the younger officers, noted their arrival and grinned.

'Sorry for destroying your double date with a billionaire,' he said, his Glaswegian twang more pronounced than usual as he peered out past them and into the courtyard. 'He didn't give you a lift, did he? I didn't hear the helicopter.'

'We caught a cab,' Declan replied, stone-faced, determined to rob any fun from Monroe's ribbing. 'We missed the second act, though, so you owe us that.'

'Aye, I'll warm up my throat muscles and give you a wee tune later,' Monroe turned and was already walking to the middle of the church. 'Until then, we have a mystery for you.'

In the middle of the church, and spread out onto a blue tarpaulin, laid along the aisle that led to the altar, was a body. Or, as Declan looked down at it, more a skeleton welded together and stuck into a black suit.

'Jesus,' he muttered.

'Not quite,' Monroe replied dryly. 'Although he's in the building, so to speak.'

'How long's he been in here?' Anjli asked, looking around. 'Surely not since …' she left the end of the comment hanging, choosing instead to swallow.

'Don't be idiots,' Monroe growled. 'They only found it today.'

He turned away from the body, and the CSI examining it, and pointed at a wooden door.

'Body was found a couple of hours ago in a small blocked-off cell up there,' he said. 'Don't ask what I mean by cell, we'll end up being here all day. Let's just say there's a little room that didn't have a skeleton in a suit inside it yesterday, but which had a skeleton in a suit inside it today.'

'Who found it?' Declan asked.

'Verger for the church was showing a prospective client around,' Monroe read from his notes. 'She wanted to book the church for a recital or something, but he thought she wanted a sneaky peek about. Looks like she got more than she bargained for.'

He scrolled down the list.

'Woman's name is Jean Darblay, Verger's name is Lance Mason.'

'Lance?' Declan raised an eyebrow. 'Not many Lance's seen around these days. Apart from that guy in *The Last Starfighter* and *Jaws Three*. Lance Guest.'

'I'll have you know Lance was a very common name, once upon a time,' Monroe straightened as he spoke. 'Many people were named it. In medieval times, people named their sons Lance, a lot.'

He paused, grinning, waiting for a response.

'You get it, aye?' he patted Declan's arm. 'Lancelot?'

'It says here that Lance is also a nickname for Lawrence,' Anjli was reading from her phone, ignoring her boss's joke.

'You just did that to ruin my joke,' Monroe complained.

At this, Anjli grinned.

'It's what I live for, Guv,' she said. 'So I'm guessing if he's the Verger, then this Mister Mason would have seen the body earlier in the day? Maybe while doing rounds?'

'Actually, no,' Monroe returned to the notes. 'The penitential cell isn't opened—'

'The *what?*' Anjli and Declan both spoke as one.

'I told you not to ask,' Monroe looked up. 'You've made me lose my place. It's a small room that they dumped Templars in. A stupidly small solitary cell. Although it had windows and you could call to people in the Nave. So maybe not, then.'

Sergeant Morten De'Geer, emerging from the wooden door and pulling off his gloves, saw the others and, ducking so his immense Viking frame didn't smack his head against the lintel, walked over.

'Verger said that a police officer came in earlier today as someone had called the police last night claiming they could see lights in the windows.'

'Do we have a name for the witness?'

De'Geer shook his head.

'And we don't even have the report that was called in,' he said, and the irritation was obvious in his voice. 'We would have been closest, so it had to come to us. But it was gone midnight, so it would have been a Desk Sergeant taking the note and passing it on to be looked at.'

'Who was on duty last night?'

'Mastakin, but he reckons nobody called.'

De'Geer scratched at his beard.

'I suppose it could have been Bishopsgate or one of the other City units that took the call, but either way, apparently this morning an officer from Temple Inn came in to do a secondary search.'

'Do we know who?'

'Again, no,' De'Geer was frustrated at being unable to answer. 'The Verger's asked the woman who opened up, a Louise Straw, to come back to us, but she's at bell ringing and probably hasn't checked her messages yet. She's the one who could tell us, as apparently he pissed her off when he told everyone to get out in case there was someone dangerous in the church.'

'Seems a fair request,' Declan shrugged. 'Especially if there's a concern.'

'Well, apparently it was a male officer, and he checked about for ten minutes, came back out, said there was nobody around and it was a prank. When Louise questioned him on it, he started telling her if she didn't back off he'd arrest her for wasting police time, even though she wasn't the one who called.'

'Sounds like a keeper,' Monroe grumbled. 'I'd like to know his name when you get it.'

'I'll be bollocking him first, boss,' De'Geer replied curtly. 'Sergeant's privilege.'

He went to speak, paused, and then looked over at the main entrance.

'One thing Mister Mason *did* say was that Miss Straw was a little confused, as when the officer left he had a folded-up black bag under his arm, which she was sure wasn't with him when he entered.'

'Curiouser and curiouser,' Declan mused as, from the door, Doctor Rosanna Marcos emerged. She was in a long, padded winter coat and a jumper, pulling the latex gloves off and running her hands through her frizzy, dark hair as she motioned for the group to come over to her.

'What's the problem?' Anjli asked as they arrived.

'Nothing,' Doctor Marcos gave a little apologetic shrug. 'I just didn't want to walk over to you, so I decided to see if you'd come over to me.'

Monroe let out an exasperated gasp.

'My soon-to-be wife, ladies and gentlemen,' he said with mock sadness. 'So, what do you have for us?'

'Well, whoever placed this body in the cell took it from the grave,' Doctor Marcos started, looking across the church at the skeleton in the suit. 'The clothing is twenty years out of date, and the threads aren't scuffed. It wasn't a new suit when it was originally worn, but it was looked after.'

She considered this.

'I think whoever this was, they were laid to rest around

two decades ago, judging by the state of decay, and that at some point they were removed from the grave and placed in the church, still in the suit they were buried in. Which was impressive.'

'How could they be placed like that, though?' Anjli enquired. 'Surely skeletons just collapse in a pile of bones, so having them in a suit—'

'Usually, you'd be right,' Doctor Marcos nodded, interrupting. 'But in this case, whoever took the body from wherever it was interred spent a lot of time making sure it was connected back together again.'

She tapped at her own joints as she explained.

'From what I can work out, they removed the clothes, which probably wasn't that difficult considering the fact that the bones would have just fallen out, anyway. And then, arranging them together like a jigsaw puzzle, they replaced them in the correct positions, before attaching them with wires, glue and small welds to make effectively what you'd see in a medical skeleton.'

Declan nodded, understanding what Doctor Marcos meant. She even had one of these in her office, the ones that sort of hung around on a moveable pole and jangled a little when they were touched.

'Anyway, once they created a workable skeleton, they then redressed it in the original clothes and brought it here. Impressive work.'

'Doesn't sound so impressive,' Anjli frowned. 'What am I missing?'

'Gunk,' Doctor Monroe smiled. 'When the body first decomposes, all the liquids seep out. Although the funeral directors would have used embalming fluid to preserve the body and slow the decomposition process, mainly by dehydrating and hardening tissue, slowing down bacterial putrefaction by killing existing bacteria. However, the effects only last a few weeks.'

She nodded back at the body.

'The body would have been cleaned and drained of all fluids, including blood in the venous system, but as it decayed, there would have been ... seepage. And with nowhere else to go, it would have dried into the clothes, hardening them slightly. I have some photos of putrefaction on my phone if anyone—'

'That'll be fine,' Declan swallowed, for the first time that evening feeling grateful he'd only eaten a small piece of bread at the Royal Albert Hall. 'So the clothes would have been stiff, and the body harder to put back in than get out. Gotcha.'

'Do we have any idea how they brought it in?' Anjli was writing in her notebook as she asked. 'I'm guessing a skeleton like this isn't exactly hard to hide?'

'Well, one interesting thing about the skeleton, and we'll have to make sure I'm correct here, is it looks like there were three junction points in the revised skeletal structure,' Doctor Marcos replied. 'And by that, what I mean is they've glued it and welded in the metal bolts, everything I mentioned earlier, to keep it together – but then they've built it into three parts.'

She tapped at Monroe as she explained each part of the body.

'The upper torso has a connector to the lower torso and hip joint, and there's a similar one around the clavicle and neck. What this means is that you could effectively take it apart, and carry the pieces separately like a Christmas tree, until you need it whole, at which point you click them together again, and then open out all the limbs.'

'Are you actually likening this body to a Christmas tree?' Monroe looked horrified.

'Well, I mean it doesn't exactly have lights and tinsel and things like that,' Doctor Marcos argued. 'But the base idea is the same. I'd have to look more into this tonight when I get a chance to properly look over the body. I'll have a better idea for you tomorrow morning.'

'Do we have an ID for the body?' Declan asked.

At this, Doctor Marcos shook her head.

'We're still waiting,' she explained. 'As soon as we came in, we took a piece of DNA for sampling. Luckily, there was a piece attached to the skull.'

Pausing for a moment, Doctor Marcos stared at the body in the middle of the church, her eyes narrowing.

'Too convenient, to be perfectly honest,' she added. 'The entire skeleton feels like it's been scrubbed to leave the bones nice and pristine. But there's one patch of skin, one patch of hair on the temple that wasn't removed – almost as if the person doing this *wanted* us to check the DNA.'

'If you go to all this work, there has to be a reason,' Monroe mused. 'Maybe they wanted to sign their work some- how, by giving us a way to identify this?'

'If they wanted it identified, they made it bloody difficult,' Doctor Marcos looked at De'Geer. 'Sergeant Viking here has more details.'

De'Geer cleared his throat, nonplussed by the nickname.

'No wallet, no identification,' he started. 'That wasn't too surprising though, if this was, as theorised, a buried body it wouldn't have either, as you rarely have wallets or identifica- tion when you bury someone.'

Declan nodded, writing this down.

'Not a great start then,' he commented.

'Well, it's not all bad,' De'Geer gave a small smile. 'We did find a couple of things. Inside the suit's jacket, pinned to the material, was a dry cleaning tag which hadn't been removed. The chances are they dry cleaned the suit before placing it on the body, and just never took the tag off on the inside, or didn't notice it.'

'Did it have a name?'

'Not for the body, but it had a dry cleaner's address and number, and the name on it was a funeral director, so I've sent that off to be checked into.'

'Undertakers probably dry cleaned the suit before dressing the body,' Monroe added. 'Could be a long shot. It's going to be at least twenty years old, so the chances are the dry cleaners might not even exist anymore, and the undertakers might be gone as well.'

'So we won't know who this body is until we get a DNA match, or a hit from the suit place,' Anjli muttered. 'Great.'

'There were some other things I can tell you about,' Doctor Marcos nodded to another forensics officer, taking an iPad from her and reading the screen. 'The body was stabbed in the chest.'

'Cause of death, perhaps?' Declan noted the fact down.

Doctor Marcos shrugged, however.

'Honestly? I couldn't answer that until I look closer. But, there are knife cuts to the ribs, and a lateral or anterolateral stab could do this as the blade passed between the ribs, maybe clipping them as it went straight to the heart.'

She shrugged.

'Although I haven't really had a good chance to investigate it fully,' she admitted. 'There's every chance they nicked a rib while they were connecting the body back together. But I can also tell you that whoever this is had a contusion on the right temple, possibly an old wound that was fixed later.'

De'Geer took over now.

'When we get the body back to the table, we'll provide an accurate charting of the teeth and fillings still in the skull to compare with dental records of missing persons—'

'Still in the skull?' Monroe held up a hand. 'I was under the assumption teeth didn't fall out of a skull?'

'I meant the ones that are real,' De'Geer looked briefly at Doctor Marcos, as if unsure he was explaining correctly. 'When giving a cursory examination, we saw that the two front teeth of the skull are fake, and placed in at a later date.'

Monroe, hearing this, froze in the spot, stroking his beard as he turned back to Doctor Marcos.

'So, let me get this right,' he said. 'You're telling me this person, when they were alive, was stabbed in the chest, had a serious wound to the head at some point in their life, and had their two front teeth knocked out?'

'That's about right,' Doctor Marcos frowned back at Monroe as he paced, glancing back at the body as he did so.

'Do you have an age?'

'Roughly? We can't be sure until we properly check, but I'd say probably mid-thirties to forties.'

'And they died twenty years ago ...' Monroe was stroking his beard as he thought aloud to himself, before his eyes widened in revelation. 'Mary, mother of Jesus, I think I know who this is!'

Monroe looked up at the door that led to the upper level.

'And you said it was found in what was called the penitential cell?'

'Yes,' De'Geer read from his own notes now. 'A cell that

was made for people who were unholy, blasphemous, and evil.'

'I think it's a copper,' Monroe whispered. 'I think this is the body of Detective Sergeant Arthur Snider. He was attacked two years before his death, a violent attack during a raid that left him with a broken skull on his right side – and he died after being stabbed while trying to arrest a drug dealer.'

He looked up at the ceiling briefly.

'I also know he had his teeth knocked out at the front of his mouth,' he finished.

'How did that happen?' Declan asked.

'Because I was the one who did it,' Monroe admitted. 'Your dad knew him too. You might even have met him over the years. He wasn't part of the team, but he was in our orbit.'

He looked at De'Geer.

'Find out where he was buried, and then get someone down to the churchyard. See if his grave has been damaged in any way? And compare your DNA sample to anything we have for him; he should have something on record.'

'There's something else,' De'Geer added. 'He had a note around his neck. It said "Weighed and found wanting."'

'Well, that's not bloody ominous at all,' Monroe grumbled.

At this point, the door they'd been staring at opened, and Detective Constable Billy Fitzwarren walked into the room. Usually dapper in a three-piece bespoke suit, this Billy was different. His clothes were mismatched and crumpled, his hair – usually on point and styled – had grown out and was straggly, and there was a slight dusting of five o'clock shadow on his chin.

'Got anything?' Monroe asked as he approached.

'Nothing upstairs,' Billy replied. 'Although one of the officers reckons the front door, or whatever you call that bloody thing at the end of the church, in the round part, had been opened within the last couple of days.'

'And how did they work that out?' Monroe raised an eyebrow.

As a response, Billy shrugged.

'I don't know,' he said. 'It's dry inside, but there are markings and dirty scuffs on the floor over there, as if somebody had walked in from the outside this morning after it rained.'

He looked back to the door at the end of the church, the opposite end to the altar.

'So I think what's probably happened is the officer that came in opened the door this morning to check if someone could have got in or out, saw nothing and came back in.'

'Or they went over there and opened the doors so they could bring a bag of bones in,' Declan suggested.

'Plausible, keep on with it,' Monroe nodded, the curt motion stating this conversation was over as he turned and walked off with Doctor Marcos. De'Geer was discussing churchyards on the phone, and now only Billy, Declan and Anjli stood together in the centre of the church.

'How you doing?' Declan asked.

'I'm fine,' Billy replied with the tone of a man who really didn't want to be having this conversation.

'You sure?' Declan continued. 'You don't *look* fine.'

'What, because I'm wearing a crumpled suit?' Billy snapped back, to Declan's surprise. 'Because I look unshaven? I'm sorry, Guv, I didn't realise you had dibs on that look.'

Before Declan, surprised at the outburst could reply, Billy walked off.

'It's been a month since they put Andrade in witness relocation,' Declan muttered. 'I was hoping he'd be over it by now.'

'He loved him,' Anjli replied sadly. 'Billy was trying to work out how to spend the rest of his life with him. To have to arrest him, and then see him leave, never to be seen again, not even in a phone call or a Christmas card ...'

Sighing and nodding as he stared after Billy, Declan eventually looked back at Anjli.

'I get that,' he replied. 'It would kill me if I lost—'

Realising where he was going with this, he stopped, clearing his throat.

'Anyway, so what should we do now?' he asked.

'There's not a lot we can do,' Anjli placed her notebook back into her pocket. 'CSI has checked the scene, and the witnesses have been interviewed and gone. We know it might be a copper, so I'm gonna wander back to the unit and see if I can find anything else on Snider.'

Declan nodded.

'I'll come with you,' he said, glancing back at Billy. 'This place is a little too gloomy for me right now.'

And, with the skeletal remains of a possible onetime DS Snider being carefully placed into a body bag for transportation, Declan and Anjli left the church and headed back to the office.

NIGHT CALLS

They hadn't stayed at the office for long; the chances of any fresh revelations on the body appearing before dawn were minimal, and so after an hour of checking files, Declan suggested they call it a night and they drove back to Hurley.

The drive had been quiet, mainly, each of them deep in their own thoughts, but as they drove along the M4, Anjli turned to Declan, while he was driving.

'Did you know him?' she asked.

'Who?'

'The dead guy. Snider. If it is Snider, that is.'

Declan considered the question as he reached their turn off, indicating left.

'I think I met him when I was a kid,' he replied. 'Around fourteen, maybe? I can't remember much about him. I know Dad wasn't happy when he turned up at our door. That was about it.'

'Why would someone do that,' Anjli said softly. 'Sorry, not turning up on your doorstep, I mean digging up, doing all that stuff and placing him in a cell, just to send a message? And who's the message to?'

Declan didn't have an answer, and simply shrugged.

'Hopefully, we'll find out tomorrow,' he said.

Anjli glanced at her phone on her lap, as it lit up. She still hadn't turned it off vibrate since the opera.

'Monroe?' Declan asked, still watching the road.

'Eden Storm,' Anjli smiled. 'Making sure we're okay—'

'*You're* okay,' Declan muttered.

'*We're* okay,' Anjli snapped, tired of whatever this was. 'He's sent it to you as well, but as you're driving and your coat's on the back seat, you probably didn't hear it. He sent a photo. Apparently he bumped into The Rock at some party after the opera. You know, that wrestler film-star guy.'

She looked over at Declan.

'Now, do you want to tell me what the hell's going on with you?'

Declan let out a breath he hadn't realised he'd been holding.

'Eden still likes you,' he replied. 'Like, *really* likes you.'

'And you think I don't know this?' Anjli laughed. 'Declan, I'm a detective. I solve crimes with clues. And Eden's clues have been super blatant.'

She trailed off, her eyes widening.

'You think I *like* him?' she said. 'Is this still that bloody worry you had after the opera? I thought you were okay with it.'

'I am,' Declan replied. 'And I'm over the moon you chose to be with me. But then I see these billionaires going for you, and I think you could have a better life.'

'Hold on, "these billionaires?" You think there's more than one?' Anjli was actually chuckling now. 'You bloody idiot. It's you I love. God knows why, but you're not getting rid of me that easily.'

Declan nodded, a smile creeping onto his face.

'That's good,' he said. 'And I love you too.'

'Damn right you do,' Anjli looked out of the passenger window. 'I'm outstanding.'

Declan went to reply, but instead just let the smile broaden. And, for the first time that night, he didn't know why he was worried.

'He knew your dad, right?' Anjli asked suddenly, returning Declan to the present. 'I mean, if your dad wasn't happy to see him.'

'Eden?'

'No, you bloody fool. Snider.'

'I think they worked together, sure,' Declan nodded. 'But I couldn't tell you when or how.'

'But your dad could,' Anjli smiled. 'We still have his files, remember?'

Declan groaned a little, more irritated at himself than anything else, for forgetting the treasure trove they had in the Hurley house he'd inherited when Patrick Walsh had passed away. For all of Patrick's career, he'd kept detailed notes of his cases – it was one of the ways the Victoria Davies case had been solved, and how Kendis Taylor had come back into his life, as his father had contacted her about turning his stories into a memoir. As it was, he never completed this because of being murdered, not by one of the many people he'd put away, but in a car accident arranged by the daughter of a serial killer who'd been discovered by Patrick, one that had spent years as a friend of the family.

'If Snider was in any case with Dad, it'll be in the file,' he said. 'Looks like we'll be up for a while tonight.'

'Searching through musty old files rather than celebrity parties,' Anjli grinned. 'You definitely know the way to a woman's heart, Declan Walsh.'

Declan smiled, but internally, he was concerned. The last time he'd gone through his father's notes, he'd realised Patrick Walsh wasn't the shining knight he'd always held him up to be, and had his darker, slightly corrupt side, as had his then DS, Alex Monroe.

Declan hoped, if he was being honest, that Arthur Snider was someone his father had forgotten to keep notes on.

Because if he had, Declan was worried about what he'd find.

It was close to midnight when Monroe walked into the *Blind Beggar* pub in Whitechapel.

He hadn't wanted to meet here. The pub wasn't the one he remembered from his earlier days on the beat – a "spit and sawdust" pub for locals – but was now a trendy, louder pub, building on its Kray Twins connection and serving London-priced drinks to a younger generation. It was brash, noisy, and the most indiscreet place you could possibly want to meet.

And that was probably why Harry Sullivan liked it.

Harry was a small, weasely man in his early seventies, although he looked a hundred and twenty. He'd been an informer for the police when Monroe first started, and had been his go-to contact for most of his time at Mile End – and some of his first year in Vauxhall, although his intelligence on anything south of the river was ropey, and Monroe had moved to other informants over the years.

He'd kept an eye on the man, though. Sullivan was an archive of valuable information; one of the few people left in Whitechapel to have actually shaken the Kray Twins' hands, rather than the wannabes who claimed they had, knowing there was no way they could be checked up on. And he had even had a stand up row with Eddie Richardson and lived to tell the tale, although the fact he was twelve at the time was probably the reason.

Harry Sullivan had been in Whitechapel and Mile End for all of his life, and was the heart and soul of the East End.

He was also incredibly treacherous.

As Monroe entered the pub, he saw it was party night – it was always party night, though – and he knew Sullivan wouldn't appreciate the noise. Walking up to the bar, taking his time to get through the three-day queue of people wanting to be served, he nodded to one of the bar staff, a young man in a black shirt, with what was probably a trendy hairstyle.

'Where's Harry Sullivan?' he asked, his voice struggling to be heard over the background noise without shouting.

In response, the barman looked Monroe up and down.

'Look, you gonna order a drink or what?' he asked, ignoring Monroe's question. 'It's a busy night, and I ain't got time for chats.'

Monroe sighed.

'What's your name, laddie?' he asked.

The barman frowned.

'What's it to do with you?'

Monroe pulled out his warrant card, waving it in front of the barman's face, taking a small amount of delight as he saw the young man pale a little.

'It makes it easier for the paperwork when I arrest you for being a wee scroat,' he growled. 'Harry Sullivan. Now.'

The barman looked caught, and Monroe felt stupid. Of course the barman would tell him to piss off – he was probably being paid to do so by Sullivan.

'Look, he's expecting me,' Monroe continued. 'DCI Monroe. Alex.'

The barman didn't seem too sure about this, but nodded towards the back of the pub.

'Far corner of the garden,' he said. 'Hope your coat's warm.'

Buying three whiskies, allowing one for the barman for his troubles, Monroe negotiated his way through the night-time crowds, and walked out into the side garden.

Harry Sullivan was sitting on his own, in the corner of the "smoker's area" of the garden, puffing away on his pipe as Monroe walked over, placing one glass down in front of him.

'Surprised you're being left alone,' he said as he sat facing the older man. 'It's a busy night and your table is prime real estate.'

'They know not to,' Harry replied, his voice a soft, raspy East End accent. 'They know I'll mash 'em if they do.'

'As in a fight?'

'Nah,' Sullivan grinned, showing a line of crooked, nicotine-stained teeth. 'To be honest, Ali, I don't rightly know what it means. I just know that a man in his seventies, growling at a teenager in *this* pub scares the piss out of them.'

Monroe allowed the nickname; there weren't many outside of Glasgow that were allowed to call him "Ali", and although he wasn't close to Sullivan, it was a term of endearment.

'You good?' he asked conversationally as Sullivan went to

drink the whisky, but the older man started to laugh, placing the glass down.

'Jesus, just ask the bloody question!' he exclaimed. 'What's all this small talk bollocks?'

'I'm trying to do better,' Monroe explained. 'I realise I've been a bit of ... well, a prick in the past. Probably with you.'

'Yeah, definitely with me,' Sullivan nodded slowly. 'Come on then, what's the problem?'

'Carmichael,' Monroe said, and the single word made Sullivan sit up.

'You sure you want to go back down that road?' he asked. 'I remember the fallout. I kept the hell away from it.'

'I think Arthur Snider has been dug up and put on display,' Monroe said, staring into his whisky before drinking the whole glass in one go. 'I think someone's hunting for it.'

'Ali, nobody's seen "it" for decades,' Sullivan looked around now, as if expecting someone to be listening to them. 'Snider took the location to his grave.'

'Aye, but what if that's why someone *returned* to the grave?' Monroe asked. 'If someone sniffs around the Carmichael case, some very nasty things could come out.'

Sullivan watched Monroe for a long, silent moment, the only noise that of the distant partying drinkers.

'This isn't about you, is it?' he eventually realised. 'This is about Patrick's lad.'

'He's had a tough year,' Monroe nodded. 'His dad dying, the whole realisation that he wasn't as white a knight as he believed, that I wasn't, even ...'

'He never learned about what was going on during the Carmichael fallout?'

'I made sure of it,' Monroe looked away, too ashamed to

catch Sullivan's eye now. 'He doesn't need to know what happened during the case.'

'He should be told, Ali,' Sullivan shook his head. 'I'd want to know. If he found out, he'd want to know too—'

'Well, *he is nae gonna find out!*' Monroe shouted, his Glaswegian accent coming out stronger as he replied. And then, as quickly, he brought himself under control.

'It was a bad time,' he muttered, staring into his glass. 'After the 7/7 bombing, things fell apart, but the year before that, it was worse. Me and Emilia? We weren't talking. To be honest, I think she was having an affair. I know Chloe Mainsworth was, and Patrick ...'

He sighed.

'Let's just say if the Carmichael case hadn't happened, then we would have lasted a little longer, but we would still have imploded. And Snider would still have been killed by a drug dealer.'

Sullivan watched Monroe for a few seconds before replying.

'You're not still going on with the lie, are you?' he smiled, a thin-lipped, humourless half-smile that made him look even more feral. 'The one where a drug dealer stabbed Snider, and not someone deliberately sent after him?'

'I go with what I know,' Monroe replied stoically. 'And Casey Smith admitted to it.'

'Of course he did, he was paid enough,' Sullivan held up a hand to stop Monroe's next protest. 'Probably by Paul Carmichael, too. He was a vicious bugger. And Snider had made a fool of him, whether or not it was legit. And don't tell me you never looked into it, Ali. We both know who sent Arthur Snider to hell, and it wasn't no teenager with a box cutter in his hand.'

Monroe stared hard at Sullivan, before pausing himself, looking around the beer garden.

'I should get another round in,' he said. 'Although it's stupidly expensive. That's what drinking in a historic location gives you, I suppose.'

'Yeah,' Sullivan grinned, happier now the tense moment had passed, and now with a sparkle in his eye. 'When I was a kid, you could go to a shop with just a pound, and come home with four comics, three chocolate bars, two packets of fags, a bag of crisps and a cold drink ...'

He waited a moment, letting the pause build for the punchline.

'Now? Now they have cameras everywhere,' he finished with a mock mournfulness.

Monroe chuckled. It was a poor joke, and an old joke, but currently, and in the mood he was in, it was a much-needed joke.

'Did you ever confirm who took the money?' he asked. 'Not the people who stole it, but the person who took it from them?'

'You mean you didn't?'

'Not funny,' Monroe shook his head. 'I always assumed it was Snider, but he did nothing out of the ordinary—'

'What, like buy an expensive, mid-life-crisis car?' Sullivan laughed. 'He had his own ways of supporting his mid-life crisis.'

'I'm serious,' Monroe went to lean back but remembered just in time he was on a bench. 'Two million is a lot, Harry. He wouldn't have been able to hide it. He was poor as dirt, and all the way until his death, he still struggled to pay his bills. And after his death, Laura never had enough money to look after Luke, so he didn't leave it to her.'

'Sure, he didn't leave it to his wife, but maybe he left it to his other lover?'

'She never seemed flush, either.'

'I had my theories, but they were never fleshed out,' Sullivan shrugged. 'I always thought it was Walsh.'

'Patrick? No, it wouldn't be him.'

'You sure, Ali?' Sullivan watched Monroe carefully. 'He had the motive, the time and the means to do it. And if Arthur Snider didn't steal Paul Carmichael's millions almost twenty years ago, and it wasn't you, your wife or Chloe Mainsworth ... then it had to be Patrick Walsh that ripped off the money, hid it from the authorities and lied to everyone he knew for the rest of his life.'

4

MISSING PERSONS

THE FOLLOWING MORNING, ANJLI AND DECLAN TOOK SEPARATE cars into the Temple Inn unit; not because of any arguments, but because they knew from previous cases that once one of these progressed, they'd end up all over the place, and waiting for a car share at the end of the day could be problematic.

They'd spent a good few hours checking through his father's notes, but had only found a handful of mentions. Snider hadn't been part of the team, but while Patrick Walsh and Alex Monroe were at Mile End the same time Derek Salmon had been around, Arthur's name had only occurred a couple of times.

However, confusingly, there was a space in the diary – a month, in early 2005, almost twenty years earlier, where nothing was written. This was unnatural for his usually fastidious father, and Declan made a mental note to speak to Monroe about this when they had a chance.

Billy was at his desk when they entered and gave a visible groan as he saw them arrive. Declan knew why, too – Billy was wearing the same clothes as he had the previous night, had most likely stayed there all evening, and probably intended to have a shower before the others arrived, but had allowed time to creep up on him.

'Late night?' Declan asked, pulling his coat off and hanging it over his chair.

'Is it still classed as night when it's eight in the morning?' Anjli added, walking over to Billy. 'You smell like a brewery. It's a bit early for drinking, isn't it?'

'Not if you haven't stopped,' Billy forced a smile. 'Then it's a very late in the day drink. The previous day.'

His smile faded as he looked at Declan.

'I'm not drunk,' he blurted. 'I had a few last night, but I came back here to check something, and I fell asleep at the desk. Hence the ...'

He trailed off, pointing at his clothes.

'That's okay, crumpled isn't just my thing, it can be yours too,' Declan deadpanned.

'Yeah, sorry about that, too,' Billy reddened. 'Wasn't a good day yesterday.'

'You know you could talk to us about it,' Declan said. 'Or, rather, speak to Anjli. She's better at it than me.'

He paused, mentally replaying Billy's earlier words.

'Why did you come back again?' he frowned, his eyebrows furrowing together as he looked back at Billy. 'Nothing would be arriving before this morning.'

'Another thing,' Billy nodded at the door, where a nervous PC Cooper stood waiting. 'Doing Esme a favour. Have a chat with her while I go shower.'

And, with a nod to Cooper, Billy rose and walked off towards the back door of the office, leading to the break room and the shower.

Declan glanced over at Cooper.

'Everything okay?' he asked.

'To be honest, I'm not sure,' Cooper blushed. 'I might be making a mountain out of a molehill, but I mentioned it to DC Fitzwarren, and he had a look for me, got nothing.'

'Okay, I'm going to need more,' Declan grumbled. 'I'm feeling like I missed an episode or something.'

'Sorry, yeah. Okay. There was a climate change protest in St Paul's yesterday afternoon,' Cooper explained. 'Some of our lads and lasses went over to help with the crowd control when it wound down later that evening. One of them hasn't come back.'

'What do you mean, one of them hasn't come back?' It was Anjli that spoke now, walking over. 'They've disappeared? They went AWOL and joined the protesters?'

At this, Cooper directed her answers to Anjli.

'Exactly what I said,' she replied. 'She went out around seven in the evening and joined a mixed City squad who were mainly just keeping the public from getting involved. The protest finished around seven-thirty, and once it was dispersed around half an hour later the coppers went back to their respective units, but St Paul's isn't exactly that far away from here, and she could have walked back in a matter of minutes. But she didn't.'

'You're sure?' Anjli replied. 'You would have been at Temple Church by then, maybe she came back and then left again?'

'I spoke to a couple of the other officers on the scene and they said she disappeared halfway through the clean-up section,' Cooper shook her head. 'She didn't even stay until the end.'

'Which officer are we talking about?' Declan asked now.

'PC Mainsworth. Charlotte.'

Declan looked at Anjli.

'Recognise the name?'

Anjli shook her head.

'We get a lot of new faces,' she replied. 'If she's new, we might not have placed face to surname.'

'She's quite new, sir,' Cooper also replied to Declan. 'She was a recent request to the unit by DCI Monroe.'

'Oh, she was, was she?' Declan smiled. 'Another broken bird to bring into his group. Well, I'm sure she's probably okay. Maybe she was ill or something. Monroe has his reasons for bringing us in, usually because we're too good to fire.'

Cooper considered this.

'I'm not sure she could be classed as that, sir,' she replied. 'And us uniforms are usually brought in because we're requested, not about to be fired, like...'

She left the statement hanging, and Declan winced a little at the unspoken "like you" in the comment.

She was right.

De'Geer had been brought across because he was good, likewise Cooper. Monroe hadn't deliberately pulled across uniforms in the same way he'd recruited Billy, Anjli, Declan and Doctor Marcos before, so this was a little out of the ordinary.

'She was complaining of a headache,' she continued uncertainly, as if trying to convince herself that everything was all right. 'I saw her earlier on, and she had a bit of a hangover.'

'What's your relationship with her? Friendly? Cordial?'

'She looked after me when I first started out as a copper in Slough,' Cooper pursed her lips, trying to work out how to tactfully explain what she wanted to say. 'She was about fifteen years older than me, a real career uniform.'

'And she was still a PC? Not a Sergeant?'

Cooper smiled awkwardly. 'Yeah. She's got her ... problems ... you see.'

'How'd you mean?'

'Well, one of the reasons she was brought across is because she was still working in Thames Valley after I left, and they were ... shall we say ... a little *unhappy* with her attitude.'

'She wasn't up to scratch,' Declan translated.

At this, however, Cooper held up her hands, shaking her head.

'She's a good copper, but she has demons,' she explained.

'A copper with demons? That's just right for Monroe's band of misfit toys,' Anjli grinned.

'Okay, well, call her home number,' Declan suggested. 'Send her a text message.'

'I've done all that, sir. She isn't replying,' Cooper shook her head. 'She doesn't do this usually. And I'm a little concerned. I even took a squad car over and knocked on her door, but nobody was there.'

'Hence why you asked Billy for help?'

'He said he could look at the CCTV, but I don't think he got far,' Cooper admitted. 'And yes, I know she said she had a headache or a migraine. And maybe she just took herself off. But, if she didn't ...'

'Then we've had a Temple Inn copper disappear at the same time we found another copper buried in a Temple Inn church,' Declan stroked his chin as he nodded. 'Maybe we *should* look a little more into this. Get someone to take a car right now, and go knock on her door again.'

'Thanks, Guv,' Cooper smiled and walked off, her mood lightened now her concern had been shared.

Anjli stared at Declan.

'What?'

Declan was already typing into his computer, accessing the HOLMES 2 network.

'If that body turns out to be Snider—'

'It is,' Anjli looked at her own screen. 'Rosanna Marcos sent us an email last night.'

Declan tapped on his keyboard.

'Arthur Snider was connected to DCI Monroe. PC Mainsworth was brought into the Unit by DCI Monroe,' he said, reading the screen. 'Her mother was in the force too, it seems, her name was ...'

He stopped, reading the screen.

'DC Chloe Mainsworth,' he said. 'Passed away almost ten years back, cancer.'

Anjli walked over, staring at the screen over Declan's shoulder.

'She was in the notes we read last night, and worked with Monroe,' she said, pointing. 'And with your dad.'

She walked back to her desk.

'That explains why her daughter's now in the unit,' she said, almost jokingly. 'Monroe does like bringing in the children of old colleagues.'

'"Weighed and found wanting,"' Declan intoned. 'That's what was on the note around the neck, right? It's personal. That's a judgement made on a dead man, so maybe Mainsworth's another judgement?'

Anjli was about to comment on this when the door opened to Monroe's office and the DCI peered out into the office.

'Billy finally gone to bed?' he asked.

'Shower.'

Monroe nodded.

'Briefing in ten, then.'

He ducked back into his office, and Declan looked at Anjli.

'Do you want to ask about Mainsworth, or shall I?'

Anjli pulled out a fifty pence piece.

'Toss for it,' she said with a smile, but Declan shook his head.

'Nuh-uh,' he said, taking the coin and placing it back in her jacket pocket. 'You know that trick, where you can tell the side before you reveal. And I don't let anyone toss a coin for me since the Red Reaper.'

Anjli puffed her cheeks out.

'Rock, paper, scissors?' she suggested.

IF CHARLIE MAINSWORTH'S HEADACHE HAD BEEN BAD THE evening she'd been abducted, it was nothing compared to the throbbing in her head right now.

She'd woken up in a sitting position, tied to a chair and set in the middle of what looked to be a crypt of some kind; brick walls on all sides and a lack of windows made this feel more spooky than it should. A wide open space with a low, arched brick ceiling, and alcoves along each side, each with their own wooden cell-door grille had terrified her, and Mainsworth had spent the first hour screaming for help and trying to remove her bonds, but they were as secure as the chair was.

There was a chance she was in some kind of bunker, she

considered, although bunkers were usually concrete and not brick, but even then she didn't know why she was there. She was still wearing her uniform, although her radio was gone.

So at least the little pervert hadn't done anything.

She sniffed, as a faint ammonia smell wafted around, and realised with a reddening of anger and embarrassment that while she'd been unconscious she'd pissed herself.

This started her screaming again until her hoarse throat gave out once more and the headache returned with a vengeance.

The room's lack of external light – a single bulb in the main space beyond the cell door bars being all that was given – meant she didn't know what time of day or night it was, but surely there had to be someone who could hear her.

She rocked back and forth on the chair again, but the metal legs were heavy, and bar a small amount of give, the chair wasn't going anywhere. And the zipties around her hands and feet were strengthened with tape, multiple ties attached to each limb. Whoever this prick was, he wasn't new to this. He knew what he was doing.

As if by magic, the man who took her, the supposed PC Dixon, emerged through the door at the end of the room. It was a wooden door, and even though she was at an angle to it, the corridor behind it was as dark and windowless as the room she was in; for the brief moment she could see through.

'Morning,' Dixon said warmly, a bottle of water in his hand. 'Sleep well?'

'Go to hell,' Mainsworth growled. 'What the hell is all this, anyway?'

She stopped as a thought, a memory, pushed its way back to the front of her mind.

'How did you know my name?' she asked.

Dixon paused, made a mouth-shrug with his lips and placed the bottle on a table beside the door in the shadows next to a cell and to that point unnoticed by the restrained police officer.

'I know a lot about you, Charlotte,' he said. 'I know you shouldn't be a police officer, how you're a disgrace to the badge, and how your mother was exactly the same.'

'Don't you dare speak about Mum like that,' Charlie snarled. 'You didn't know her.'

'I met her,' Dixon waggled a finger. 'Don't change my narrative.'

'Change your *what?*' Mainsworth was furious at the attitude of her jailer. 'Look, just let me go, yeah? We'll chalk this up as a joke. Nothing more to be said.'

'*No!*'

The shout echoed around the room as Dixon stared at Mainsworth, and for the first time in the subdued light, she could see the black trousers, white shirt and black tie weren't police issue; the shirt didn't have shoulder tags, for a start. And this made Dixon look more like an undertaker than a copper – a worrying thought.

'Do you think this is funny?' Dixon snapped. 'Your mother was weighed and found wanting, but she was cremated, wasn't she? And you're not dead ...'

He calmed himself down.

'Yet, anyway,' he finished ominously. And, this stated, he picked up the water bottle, walking over to Mainsworth.

'You'll be dehydrated,' he said, screwing off the top of the bottle. 'Here, have some water.'

Mainsworth took a couple of mouthfuls as Dixon aimed it at her mouth, letting the water flow gently. And then, nodding as she'd had enough, she closed her mouth as he took the bottle away—

Only to be splatted by the remnants of the water, a full mouth's worth, spat out at him.

'I don't want anything from you,' she said, struggling once more with the bindings. 'And when I get out, I'm gonna kill you.'

She screamed for help again, but it was cut short when Dixon backhanded her across the cheek, knocking her head back, the chair's solid base now allowing it to rock with the blow, making sure she took the full effect.

'Where's the money, Charlie?' he asked.

'What money?'

'Paul Carmichael's money,' Dixon snarled. 'I know it had to be you. It could only be you who took it from him.'

'I don't know what the hell you're talking about!' Charlie screamed out. 'What bloody money? Look at me! Do you think, if I was loaded, I'd still work as a sodding uniform?'

Dixon stared at her, the water bottle in his hand. And then, glancing around the brick room, looking up at the ceiling, he nodded quietly to himself.

'Do you know where you are, Charlotte?' he asked. 'No, of course you don't. These tunnels used to be part of a house of detention. A prison.'

He looked back at Charlie.

'That's where people like you deserve to be. Deserve to rot in.'

He shuddered, as if the thought was too much to consider right now.

'I'm going out,' he eventually said, tossing the water across the room, where it rolled to a stop, the remnants of the water within now draining out of the top of the overturned bottle and onto the floor. 'I'll bring you some lunch when I return. And then we'll have a chat about missing items stolen from the dead.'

'Just let me go!' Charlie Mainsworth screamed as Dixon turned and walked out of the room, closing the door behind him.

There was no sound of the door being locked; he didn't need to. Mainsworth was securely tied, and for the moment, completely under his control. She didn't know what he meant by "stolen items," either. *Something she'd nicked in her two decades of being a uniformed officer?* There were too many items there to count.

Alone in the room, somewhere far from any possible help, and locked down by a madman, PC Charlie Mainsworth started to gently sob to herself.

5

BRIEFING

'RIGHT THEN, SETTLE DOWN, WE HAVE A BUSY ONE HERE.'

Monroe stood beside the plasma screen at the front of the briefing room as he waited for the other officers to enter and settle down.

An exhausted Doctor Marcos, still in the clothes she wore the previous night, was standing beside him, while De'Geer sat at the back with PC Cooper.

Billy was on usual duty, laptop in front of him, the connection to the plasma screen showing on his own display, although his head, still damp from the shower was heavy, almost resting against the screen as he forced himself to drink strong coffee.

Rounding out the room were Declan and Anjli, in their normal seats, while Detective Superintendent Bullman, her short white hair slightly dishevelled, possibly because she too had been up all night, hovered near the door.

Monroe, noting everyone's attention, cleared his throat.

'So we have a strange one today,' he said, shaking his head. 'Usually we're solving murders so we can lay the victims to rest, but this time we're solving the mystery of one coming back.'

He looked at Billy.

Billy, in return, was still staring at the desk.

Monroe cleared his throat.

Billy, looking up and seeing everyone watching him, sighed audibly.

'The whole thing's connected,' he replied irritably. 'You could just tap the screen, rather than waiting for me.'

'But I want to wait for you to press the button, laddie,' Monroe said with no hint of humour. 'That way, I know you're still in the room. Not physically, but mentally.'

Billy sighed again and pressed a button; an image of a man in his thirties appeared on the screen.

'There, that wasn't too hard, was it?' Monroe said sweetly. But then he continued, his tone far darker now. 'So if you want to keep your job, I suggest you stop whatever victim-related martyr complex you have here, and get your wee arse into gear, aye?'

Suitably admonished, his tired face reddening, Billy nodded.

'Right then, where were we?' cordially again, Monroe looked to the screen. 'Ah yes, Detective Sergeant Arthur Snider.'

He looked at Doctor Marcos beside him to continue.

'We got confirmation around six this morning,' she replied. 'DNA matched. It's definitely Snider. And the police sent to the City of London Cemetery and Crematorium in Wanstead last night found a hole where his plot had been. But we'll get to that in a moment.'

'Arthur Snider was a pain in the backside most of the time, and he wasn't an angel,' Monroe continued. 'But he died in the line of duty. Which makes the theft of his body personal.'

There was a silent nod at this. Declan rose a hand.

'I met him when I was a kid,' he said. 'Though I didn't remember him. But last night I looked through Dad's files and found a handful of cases you'd been on together.'

'Oh aye?' Monroe replied, and Declan knew the tone was one of concern, as to what Patrick Walsh had said in the notes. 'You'd better explain a little for the new people in the room.'

Declan looked around to De'Geer and Cooper. The former had come onto the team just after the *Red Reaper* case, the latter a few months later, but neither had been around when Tom Marlowe, Monroe's "kind of" nephew had explained to Declan and the others the truth of their bosses' past.

'As you know, DCI Monroe used to be DI to my father's DCI back in the day, working the Victoria Davies case,' he explained. 'They were a team including then-DC Derek Salmon and DS Emilia Wintergreen.'

'The one that—' De'Geer started, but then stopped.

Seeing this, Monroe grinned. 'Aye, the one that was married to me and then one day disappeared when she took over an MI5 unit, effectively never existing, in career and marriage,' he said. 'That one.'

De'Geer shut up.

Declan took the opportunity to continue.

'Anyway, after the Davies case, Special Branch took the team and moved them to Mile End,' he continued. 'Mainly because after 9/11 there was a lot of fear that something similar would happen in London, so the police were doing a lot more proactive anti-terrorist work.'

He looked over at Monroe, who nodded at him to carry on.

'On their boss's orders, they were forced to work a little more off the books, be innovative, make deals with people like the Lucas Twins, all that.'

'Unfortunately, the undercover deals we were making to get into the scene became easier to swallow the more we did,' Monroe took over now. 'Patrick hated it, but I was used to the world. It felt more simple. And when Olivia Marlowe, our contact in Military Intelligence, died in 2005, Emilia – that's DS Wintergreen – moved into her role, and the whole thing was phased out.'

'How come?' Cooper, having not heard the tale before, asked.

'Because we were tasked with making sure 9/11 didn't happen in the UK, but then 7/7 happened, and we didn't see it coming,' Monroe muttered. 'Not Special Branch's greatest hour.'

There was a moment of silence. Declan almost felt bad for bringing it up.

'Anyway, what did you find, laddie?'

'A couple of years after you moved across to Mile End, you worked with Arthur Snider on a rape case, but found him to be less than professional – Dad's own words, from his notes. You had a falling out where you punched him in the face, taking out a tooth—'

'Two teeth,' Monroe held up two fingers.

'But the only other time we could find when you really worked together was a jewellery robbery in Stratford,' Declan continued. 'It was believed the Twins were behind it, but it was never proven. You claimed Snider had taken a bribe from them, through Danny Martin, their enforcer at the time, to keep them updated, and because of this, the case fell apart.'

'Aye, that's about right,' Monroe growled. 'Wee bastard let Johnny know we were coming for him. And he wasn't shy about admitting what he'd done, either. He would have been fired, too, if he hadn't died a year or two later. Drug dealer bust went wrong, and he was stabbed in the chest. Died on the way to hospital.'

He looked away, through the window.

'There was talk, after that, he'd been targeted and killed by the dealer, because he'd been trying to get a hold on to the lad's business. But it was left alone. He was a hero officer, dying in the line of duty. To find out otherwise would deny his wife his pension.'

He looked back at Declan.

'Anything else in the notes?'

Declan paused.

'There was a third time you seemed to work together, around early 2005, but the notes aren't there,' he explained.

'I don't remember a third time,' Monroe stroked at his beard. 'You sure?'

'He's on a manifest, so he definitely attended a meeting with your team, but that's all I have.'

'May have just been dropping something off. Anything else?'

Declan shook his head. That Arthur Snider was mentioned on a single sheet in a month that didn't exist in his father's usually fastidious notes was bad enough.

That Monroe didn't even want to check into it was suspicious as hell.

'No, Guv.'

'Right then,' Monroe straightened. 'As you all see, he was

an utter shite and a terrible police detective. But a detective he was. And because of this, we'll solve this bloody case. And, now we've character assassinated him enough, how about we return from the past and look at the present?'

Declan flushed at the mild berating. He knew that era of Monroe's past wasn't one he liked to see the curtain pulled back from. But anything that gave context was always important.

De'Geer stood up now, opening his notebook.

'Two nights ago, someone in Temple Inn apparently called the police about strange lights seen through the windows of Temple Church around one in the morning,' he explained. 'They thought it was burglars, using torches, and as the church wouldn't be in use at that time, the police sent a couple of officers to check, They arrived and found nothing to give the impression of forced entry, saw no lights and left, intending to return later.'

He checked his notes.

'This occurred yesterday around ten in the morning, when the church was opening for the tourists. Louise Straw, the woman running the welcome desk, was on duty when a solo officer arrived from Temple Inn, asking to have a check around, explaining about the call the previous night. He said there was a chance that someone could be in there still, and asked Louise and her assistant, Peg, to step outside while he gave it a once over.'

'Solo officer? That's not procedure,' Anjli muttered.

'So, he closed the door, had a look around and then about ten, maybe fifteen minutes later he came back out, told her there was nothing going on in there, and that they didn't appreciate having their time wasted. Even though it wasn't either of the women who'd made the call.'

'Do we know who this was?' Declan asked.

'That's the problem,' De'Geer looked up from his notes. 'Sergeant Mastakin was on graveyard shift two nights back, and nobody called in. Which meant he didn't send anyone to look, and therefore nobody was told to come along yesterday morning.'

'Could they have been Bishopsgate?' Billy asked from the computer.

'No, Louise is adamant the officer claimed he was from Temple Inn,' De'Geer replied. 'But she said there were a couple of discrepancies – first off he came out of the church with a black bag under his arm she hadn't seen him enter with, like a garment bag, folded up, but also that his cap was wrong. It had the black check banding rather than the City's red ones.'

'So he was Met police? Why tell her he was Temple Inn?'

De'Geer shrugged.

'That's where the confusions start,' he said. 'We spoke to Bishopsgate – in fact, we spoke to every unit in the City, and not one of them had a call two nights ago, nor did they send an officer to look into it the following morning.'

'And this officer found nothing?'

'No, and considering what was found later, this was a little surprising,' Monroe nodded at Billy, who reluctantly pressed a button. Now the screen showed the image of a human skeleton, wearing a black suit, and pressed into an enclosed stone space, a note hung around its neck. 'Our long dead DS Snider, back from the grave.'

'We checked into the gravesite, and three days ago, they had a team from the council arrive to exhume the grave,' Cooper now said. 'They had the correct paperwork, and they took the coffin away in a council van.'

'I'm guessing the council had no knowledge of this either?' Monroe asked.

In response, Cooper shook her head.

'No, Guv.'

'So the timeline is that three days ago someone takes Arthur Snider's body from the City Cemetery, where he's been for almost twenty years, and then two nights ago sneaks in with the body and dumps it in a cell?' Declan frowned. 'Is that enough time to do all the welding and scrubbing Doctor Marcos spoke of?'

At this, Doctor Marcos straightened from her position of tiredly slumping against the table.

'Not really,' she said. 'The bones were cleaned, apart from one patch to provide DNA evidence, and then welded and bolted into three pieces. This would have taken a while. I would have expected longer.'

'Maybe they had longer,' Bullman said from the door. 'Didn't you say something about the other door to the church?'

'Yes,' Doctor Marcos nodded. 'There were marks on the floor of the round part of the Nave that suggested the door at the end of the church had been opened and something pulled into the building. It'd rained the night before, but was dry outside.'

She tapped the screen, opening a folder and then clicking a photo file. Now an image of the church appeared.

'This is the porch,' she explained. 'The main tourist entrance is to the south, and open plan. This is covered, which meant it was still wet yesterday morning, as the sun hadn't got to it. We think the officer entered the church and, when the building was cleared of witnesses, he opened the door, which means there's every chance he pulled in a bag, and then closed it. He then took the bag up to the penitential cell, pulled the three pieces of secured skeleton out, attached them, and then left, rolling the bag up and placing it under his arm in the process.'

'The cell was locked, until Mister Mason opened it up yesterday evening, but it was a basic lock so easy to lock and unlock with the right tools,' De'Geer added. 'It could have been left there for days before someone saw it.'

'No, I think they'd have found a way to get it seen,' Monroe stroked at his beard. 'This was a message. And I just don't mean the one around his neck.'

'Weighed and found wanting,' De'Geer stated.

'The bastards who did this placed the body into a cell where prisoners, corrupt knights, blasphemers, heretics, all that were placed into, saying he was being judged. They said they were Temple Inn coppers when they could have said anywhere, and the victim had a past with me. Someone wanted *us* to see it.'

'Maybe we should look into the woman who was having the tour?' Anjli suggested. 'The Verger said it was her who asked to see the room.'

'Aye, do that,' Monroe nodded.

'Any prints on the body?'

'None,' Doctor Marcos replied. 'And the description of the officer we got was "young, white, and pretty." She wasn't great, eyesight wise.'

Monroe sighed, looking over at Cooper.

'Would you like to tell us of your side to this, too?' he asked. 'I understand you and the wee tired bairn there have been hunting a lost sheep.'

'Aye – I mean yes, Guv,' Cooper stood. 'I have a friend, she's a uniform, Charlie Mainsworth. She was Thames Valley police until a month back when she transferred here. She mentored me back when I started there, although it was more "watch what she does and do the complete opposite," if you know what I mean, but we'd kept in touch after I moved. But I knew she was having issues, drinking, and she was on the verge of being fired, and I mentioned my concerns to DCI Monroe here, who then stepped in, pulling her across.'

'I did this because I knew her mother,' Monroe explained. 'DC Chloe Mainsworth. She died a decade back, but I worked with her in Mile End when she came up from the uniforms herself. Knew Charlie too, a little, when she was a teenager.'

He looked at Declan.

'You met her a couple of times, too, but she was about three years younger than you, and you didn't like girls at the time.'

'Oh yes?' Billy winked at Declan.

'I mean he wasn't into girls *or* boys,' Monroe snapped irritably, and Billy, realising the opportunity for sport had faded, slumped tiredly back down, tapping on the laptop.

Monroe went to continue, but stopped, staring at the plasma screen. Billy had pulled up an image of Chloe Mainsworth now, placing it next to one of her daughter.

'Shite,' he whispered. 'Of course. This is a message for me. Both of them.'

'Guv?'

Monroe looked back at the briefing room.

'Chloe Mainsworth was an excellent officer,' he said as he rubbed at his chin. 'I think she may have even worked on the cases we had with Arthur Snider. We need to check that.'

'We should check where she was buried,' Anjli added. 'Make sure there's nothing missing.'

'No, she was cremated, I was at the ...' Monroe trailed off.

'Jesus,' he muttered. 'She can't be brought back, but her daughter can be punished in her stead.'

He motioned for Cooper to carry on.

'She went missing during yesterday's St Paul's protest,' she read from her notes. 'She's not the best for keeping time, and she'd complained of being hungover earlier, so people assumed she'd just nipped off to a pub, or gone somewhere for a crafty nap, but she didn't come back last night.'

She looked over to Billy, who, realising it was his turn, straightened.

'I started looking into this later in the evening,' he explained. 'Esme – PC Cooper – asked me to look into CCTV of the area, see if we could find anything.'

He tapped on his keyboard, and an image appeared, a grainy CCTV one, obviously zoomed in, the pixels large and blurry. It was of a female officer, standing by a cordon.

'I found her around eight pm, near Stationer's Court, to the west of St Paul's,' he carried on. 'She stood there for about fifteen minutes before this man spoke to her.'

On the screen, a second officer appeared, but the screen resolution was blurry. All that could be made out was that he was Caucasian, and male.

'They spoke for a couple of minutes, and then they walked down Ave Maria Lane,' Billy zoomed out of the image as the two officers walked off. 'Unfortunately, there're no cameras aimed at this section of the road that can give me a clear view. However, when an officer went looking for her two, maybe three minutes later, after she was seen as not being at her post and not answering her radio, she was nowhere to be seen.'

'That's right beside Amen Court, where Justice left his first body,' Anjli shuddered.

'Let's hope she's not a body yet, aye?' Monroe, seeing Cooper's worried expression, muttered. 'She's an officer of our unit and she's been abducted. She went missing around the same time as the body of Arthur Snider was discovered, so I'm guessing this isn't any kind of freak coincidence, and is instead a message for us. For me, even. And I'd like to work out what it means.'

As the others nodded, a phone outside in the office rang. Bullman quickly answered it, nodding and returning to the briefing room.

'Arthur Snider's son is here,' she said to Monroe. 'Wants to speak to you.'

Monroe groaned.

'Aye, we'll do that,' he said, nodding at Declan. 'You met Luke, right?'

'I think so,' Declan put his notebook away. 'Although I don't remember this Charlotte, so I probably won't remember Luke.'

'The rest of you, although this body is a mystery, he's not going anywhere soon,' Monroe barked. 'But we have a copper who's in danger, and I want all hands looking into this. DS Kapoor, take PC Cooper and go have a chat with Johnny Lucas. See if he knows anything that could link this sudden revenge spree. And someone check into that bloody woman in the church! Go! Go!'

As the others rose and started leaving the briefing room, Declan looked at Monroe.

'Interview room?'

'No, my office,' Monroe replied. 'He's probably found a

hole where his dad was. But I'd like to know how he knew to come here.'

And, as Monroe stormed out, Declan felt a chill travel down his spine, a feeling often referred to as "someone walked over my grave," and made a mental note to check his own father's place of rest before the day was over.

Because this was possibly only the beginning.

6

SONS OF FATHERS PASSED

LUKE SNIDER WAS A YOUNG MAN, NO MORE THAN TWENTY-three, maybe twenty-four years in age. Pale-blond hair in a centre parting, he was slim and, apart from a small cut across his right eyebrow – more likely a childhood scar than a deliberate razor cut created in the trendy style people often attempted – Declan would call "fresh faced." If it wasn't for the furious scowl upon his face, Declan might even have said Luke looked pleasant. Happy, even.

But the scowl put all of that away.

Monroe leant back in his chair, facing Luke as the younger man sat down across the desk from him, Declan to his side. Luke was in black trousers and a white-collared shirt, a pale-blue corduroy jacket over the top. It was supposed to be a more informal location than an interview room, but Declan wasn't sure if the ambiance was exactly right here for that.

'Luke, I'm surprised to see you,' Monroe started. 'It's a pleasant surprise, though—'

'Really?' Luke interrupted, his voice dripping with scorn. 'I thought you'd be expecting me.'

'Why would you think that?'

Luke reached into his jacket pocket and pulled out a piece of paper, placing it on the table.

As Declan leant closer to look at it, he saw it was actually a white business card with one word written on it.

MONROE

'Where did you find this?' he asked.

Luke sat back, turning to look at him now.

'It was found at the bottom of a hole – a hole where my father's body once was,' he replied.

Monroe shuffled uneasily in his chair at this.

'I'm guessing I probably shouldn't have put my finger-prints all over it, but I'm not a copper, so I don't think like you,' Luke said, turning back to Monroe as he spoke.

'Luke, we were going to call you today—'

'Were you? And tell me what?' Luke snarled, his emotions getting the better of him. 'Tell me what the hell's going on? Because currently, all I'm seeing is that someone's taken Dad's body, and they're using this to pass some kind of cryptic message to you.'

Monroe puffed out his cheeks, taking a moment before replying.

'Aye, we only found out about this earlier this morning,' he explained. 'Your father's body was taken from its place of rest three days ago.'

'Taken,' Luke nodded. 'That's a polite way of saying "ripped from the ground with no care how people would feel," isn't it?'

He forced himself to calm a little.

'So how did you find out about this?' he asked. 'And what's the note supposed to mean?'

'It means someone wanted to make sure I knew for certain this was a message for me,' Monroe replied, his tone clipped and flat. 'Last night, the body, still in its funeral attire, was found in Temple Church.'

'Wait, what do you mean it was found? It was laying in state?'

'Not exactly,' Declan, tiring of the attitude but understanding why Luke had it, interrupted. 'The remains had been placed in what was called the "penitential cell", where it was found by the Verger.'

'Nice,' Luke muttered sarcastically. 'And that's what, exactly? A place to put bad Templars?'

'Actually, you're pretty spot on there,' Monroe replied. 'It had—'

'So what are you doing about it?' Luke, ignoring Monroe, interrupted.

Monroe bristled at this, but hid his irritation at being stopped.

'We're hunting the people who did this,' he said. 'We have a description, we're looking into it. We *will* find who desecrated your father's grave.'

Luke nodded, his face was flushed with anger, but before he could reply, Declan leant closer.

'Luke, if you don't mind me saying, you seem angry,' he said softly.

'Really?' Luke was almost mocking in his response. 'More than someone who's learned that their father has been exhumed in the most violated way possible?'

Declan stared at Luke for a long moment before replying.

'Well, to be honest, yes,' he said.

Luke shrugged.

'Knowing I have to come down here and speak to you two doesn't exactly fill me with joy,' he said.

'Us two? Hold on, am I missing something? Have I wronged you?' Declan sat back at the comment. He understood the bitterness, but there was definitely something else going on. 'What exactly have we done here? We only just found out for certain the body was that of Arthur Snider, and we had no knowledge of the grave robbing before that.'

'Don't worry about it,' calming himself, Luke waved a dismissive hand. 'It's fine. When can I see the body?'

'It's being examined by our divisional surgeon at the moment,' Monroe straightened in his chair now. 'And if I'm being honest, laddie, I don't know if you'd want to see it. It's nothing more than a skeleton in a suit now.'

'I don't mean in real life, I'm guessing there are crime scene photos? I'd like to see them.'

Monroe stared at Luke.

'Are you sure?'

Luke nodded.

'I'll have to see it when I put the body back in the coffin,' he said. 'I thought this might help desensitise me.'

Monroe picked up his iPad, scrolling through images on it. Eventually, he found the picture Declan had seen earlier on the screen; one of the skeleton in a suit, placed against the wall of the penitential cell, a placard looped around his neck. Monroe turned it around to show the image, Luke taking the device from him and staring at the image for a long moment – a suit with a skull on top – before placing the iPad back onto the table, at no point giving away any emotional or physical reaction.

He either held it back very well, or he genuinely didn't care about it, Declan thought to himself as he watched the younger man sit back in the chair.

'When can we have the body back?' he now asked. 'We'd like to get him re-buried as quickly as possible.'

'We're looking to get it back to you as quick as we can—' Monroe started, but paused as Luke held a hand up.

'*Him,*' he hissed. 'The body is a him, not a bloody *it.* You've been calling him that since I arrived, and it's pissing me off. Don't you dare lessen my father. Not you, of all people.'

'Aye, sorry, yes,' Monroe nodded at this. 'We're looking to get *him* back to you as quickly as possible. We don't yet know why this was done, though, so we need to examine all avenues first.'

'Well, just look at the note on his chest,' Luke suggested, leaning back on the chair as he looked at Declan. '*Your* father may have been a perfect model of police procedures, but my father was a criminal. And the writer of the note knew it too.'

'Now come on, laddie—'

'My father would have been fired a dozen times if he'd lived,' Luke snapped back at Monroe. 'And you know that more than anyone.'

'Now come on, Luke, that's not fair—'

'*Tell me I'm wrong!*' Luke rose from the chair in anger. 'You, the man who punched him in the face so hard you knocked his teeth out! You think I haven't heard about that? I grew up in the East End, knowing all about my father. All I had was people telling me either my father was police scum, or that he was *corrupt* scum. They could never get their stories in line, but they always knew the punchline. And he was furious when you took his two teeth. Said the ladies all loved his smile, and how he had to have falsies drilled in to fix it.'

'I'm sure it wasn't easy—' Declan started, but stopped as Luke turned on him now.

'And what would you know?' he snarled. 'We met once, you and me. You were in the army or something, and it was at a wedding. I was seven years old, or around that. There you were, standing in the church, the hero in his uniform, dripping with medals, your high-ranking police dad beside you; I think it was shortly before you left the army and walked into a detective role without even trying. Must be great having friends in high places.'

Declan let Luke continue his angry rant – he knew this was grief more than anger talking.

'Now listen here,' Monroe rose to match Luke now, not getting the memo from Declan about grief. 'I'm sorry you're angry, but this isn't the place for a bloody therapy session, and your father's been long gone for years now. And you're not the only one in the room who's lost his father.'

Luke went to speak, thought better of it, and then took a deep breath.

'The difference between us,' he said calmly to Declan, 'is you had forty-odd years with your dad. Whereas mine died when I was a toddler.'

Declan didn't reply.

His anger rising again, Luke continued.

'You got to see your dad grow old, while all I saw was a photo. You got to speak to your dad every day, while I don't remember what he sounded like.'

He turned to Monroe now.

'Yeah, he lost his dad too, and I'm genuinely sorry for

him, nobody should go through that – but don't for one second think you can liken us both, Alex.'

If Monroe bristled at the use of his first name, he didn't show it as Luke now paced around the office.

'I know all about the mighty Declan Walsh,' he said, pulling off his jacket and placing it on the coat stand, over Monroe's, almost as if he was showing dominance in the room. 'Punching a priest, screwing over your own officers in Mile End, accused of terrorism, hunted for a dozen other things and still you stand, a serving officer. All these screwups, fixed on your behalf. Even the Prime Minister thinks you're awesome.'

'That's not how they happened,' Declan argued.

'Others think differently,' Luke muttered. 'Some still harbour resentment for bringing you onto cases, after you screwed their lives up.'

Declan went to reply, to ask what Luke meant by that, but before he could speak, Luke was off again.

'Do you want to know about my life?' he asked mockingly. 'I'll tell you about my life. My dad died when I was three. My mum didn't want kids like Dad did, and when I turned up, he was over the moon, but when he died, Mum was left with a pain in the neck son she never wanted, and a dead husband who cast such a shadow over her, that every time she went out onto the street, went shopping or travelled to work, people would look at her and go "that's the wife of Arthur Snider."'

He took a breath.

'But they didn't talk of him as the man who bravely died in the line of duty while fighting a knife-wielding criminal, but as the man who took money from the Twins. The man who helped the Seven Sisters come to power, the man who

helped the Simpsons take South London, the man that probably had an affair, and *that's* why he was killed.'

'Was he?' Monroe couldn't help himself.

Luke stared out of the window now, peering out across
the office as he continued, rubbing at his arm through the
shirt as he spoke.

'My father was a corrupt cop, and all of my life I've had
his shadow hanging over me,' he said sadly. 'I don't have the
happy memories you have of your fathers. I have sad memories. A toddler at a funeral. The various awkward meetings I
had with DCI Monroe throughout my childhood and teens,
when he would repeatedly turn up, whenever he could be
bothered to remember, or when his conscience finally
pricked enough at him to come and apologise again, for
something that had happened in relation to my dad. I even
looked at joining the force, you know – my dad had wanted
me to be a cop, just like your dad wanted you to be a cop, and
even though I knew it wasn't for me, I felt the pressure every
time I heard this from *him*.'

He pointed at Monroe here.

Declan nodded at this.

'I get that,' he said. 'The pressure on someone to fulfil—'

He stopped as Luke Snider started laughing.

'There was no pressure!' he exclaimed. 'I never had the
chance to feel the pressure! The moment I started my appli-
cation process, the first thing they said to me was, "oh,
you're the son of *that* Snider." They knew who I was, they
knew my family history, and as far as Hendon was
concerned, the apple didn't fall far from the tree. I walked
away, and you know, I was *over-bloody-joyed* at not following
through.'

He pointed at Declan.

'Your dad took money to look the other way, but I don't see them blocking your promotions.'

Declan went to reply to this, to argue the case for his father, but realised it wasn't worth doing – because Luke Snider was right. The difference, however, was that Arthur Snider had become too dependent on the money he made on the side.

'I understand this is difficult for you—' Monroe started.

'It's not difficult at all. It's annoying,' Luke shook his head, serious once more. 'It's annoying because I now have to re-bury the body of the man that fathered me. A man who, for all intents and purposes *wasn't* my father, nothing more than some bloke who lived in my house for the first three or four years of my life and then died, and a man who's caused me problems all my life.'

He sat back in the chair, and Declan gained the feeling this angry rant was finally beginning to spend itself out.

'My mum and me, we never got on,' he muttered. 'By the end, I wasn't even calling her Mum, and when I went to university, I never looked back. I never returned and never saw her socially again. It's all business with her, anyway.'

Monroe shifted in his chair as Luke seemed to deflate in his chair.

'I understand this isn't a moment you're looking forward to,' he said gently. 'But can you think of anybody who might have just cause, or *any* cause, to do this to your father's body?'

'Take a number and join the queue,' Luke shrugged. 'There's a list of people who hated my dad enough to do this. Paul Carmichael, but he's dead. Maybe his son, Peter? Never met the guy, but I'm sure he had an issue. The only question is why they've taken so long to do it.'

'There's a female police officer who's missing as well,'

Declan replied, perhaps a little too harshly, still smarting from the attack against his father. 'We think it might be connected to the case, and although asking this might be an inconvenience to you, it's a possible life or death situation to somebody else.'

'And I'm sorry for them,' Luke looked at Declan now, his face emotionless and blank. 'But this isn't my problem. This man you have, this skeleton connected with wires and bolts, that's not my father. That's some gruesome made up toy – someone's created a Meccano set with bone.'

He rose from his chair.

'I came to find out what was going on. I didn't come here to be part of your investigation, and I sure as hell didn't come here to reunite with my dad's old friends,' he said, looking over at Monroe. 'Because let's be honest, Alex. You and him were never friends.'

He looked at Declan now.

'And your dad wasn't friends with anybody,' he snapped. 'You intending to go see him soon?'

'What do you mean by that?' Declan straightened in the chair, sensing an argument, but Luke held up his hands in a shrugging motion.

'Well, they've dug mine up, maybe they'll dig yours up too,' he suggested. 'As I said, he wasn't exactly an angel, was he?'

'Now you listen here, laddie—' Monroe rose.

'No, Alex. I don't think I will,' Luke spun, his finger now pointing accusingly at Monroe. 'I know you did the same. You all did. You took your little pay-outs. Dad would tell Mum, and when I was older, she told me. I grew up knowing about it. And every time you turned up, offering some money, or apologising again, I knew it was because your guilty conscience wouldn't let you sleep at night. Did you take the lighter?'

'The lighter?' Monroe looked confused at this.

'Yeah, Dad's Zippo. I've got vague memories of it, hazy ones from when I was a kid, and Dad's friends – or at least the people who'd come to see Mum over the years, would mention it in passing. Never saw it after he died. Did you take it as some kind of twisted keepsake? I'd like it back if so.'

He looked at Declan.

'That goes for you too, if your Dad nicked it.'

'I never took that lighter, and neither did Patrick,' Monroe growled in response. 'Snider probably tossed it away, because he didn't even bloody well smoke.'

'And yet it's nowhere to be found,' Luke walked stiffly to the coat rack, fumbling for his coat, putting it on while heading to the door, all while holding his anger in check.

'While you're here, laddie, can you tell me where you were yesterday morning?' Monroe, no longer playing the sympathetic ear, asked.

'I'm a suspect?' Luke looked around.

'No, but at some point, we're going to have to look into everything, and the man we're looking for is a young man of your age and ethnicity,' Monroe replied.

Luke nodded at this.

'I was in the library. I'm sure I can find you witnesses. There was a coffee shop north of Farringdon station I had a coffee in. I'm sure my credit card receipts would show proof, so feel free to check,' he replied, more confident than Declan had expected.

He turned back to the door and opened it, but before he left, he spoke one last time.

'My dad was found wanting, weighed and judged,

according to that note around his neck,' he finished, hand holding the door handle. 'Good. Maybe now it'll be over. Let me know when I can bury him, or better still, just pass the body back to the council, and let them do it. I'm done here.'

And with that, Luke Snider left Monroe's office.

'Well, I think he took that quite well,' Monroe muttered as he watched Snider storm across the outside office and leave through the main doors.

'Something's wrong there,' Declan mused, following Monroe's gaze. 'That's more than an angry man. That wasn't a man furious at the death of his father, that was a man who was prepared for what he was going to see.'

Monroe's eyebrows creased together.

'What do you mean?'

Declan couldn't explain it, but the image of a skull in a suit, its only just-visible fingers popping out, came to his mind.

'I don't know,' he admitted. 'Everyone has a morbid curiosity, I get that. It's why, when someone tells you a mutual contact has died, you have to hold back the urge to ask *how*. But when he looked at that image, he didn't flinch.'

He sighed.

'I have a feeling Mister Snider knows more than he's letting on.'

'Aye, we'll be monitoring him,' Monroe leant back in his chair, stretching his back. 'And listen, don't you listen to his lies about your father.'

'Are they lies?' Declan rose now, the conversation with Luke over. 'Remember, I've read my father's notes. He wasn't an angel. And undercover or not, some things he did weren't right. And there's a massive chunk of missing notes, notes I'm sure were there when I first moved into the Hurley house. A month of them, all around this time. Any idea where they could be?'

'Are you asking if I took them?'

'It wouldn't be the first time you tried to hide something from me,' Declan shrugged. 'To keep my memories of my dad pure. I'm a big boy, Guv. I can take whatever I see or hear. So, if there's anything you want to say to me, or show me, you know where I am.'

And, nodding to Monroe, Declan left the office, fighting the urge to return to Hurley and check his father's grave.

7

ELECTION-HEARING

ANJLI HAD AVOIDED VISITING GLOBE TOWN FOR THE LAST FEW months, and if she was being brutally honest with herself, she hadn't missed the bad associations she had with the place.

There was a point when this was a daily occurrence for her while working at Mile End, and she'd often patrolled this area, until a fight with a domestic abuser had removed her from the unit and placed her in the Temple Inn "Last Chance Saloon" under Alexander Monroe.

'If you want, I can wait outside,' Cooper said as they stared at the Globe Town Boxing Club through the car's windscreen. 'I know what the people around here are like when they see a uniform.'

'Oh, I think you'll be fine,' Anjli smiled. 'Remember, he's legitimate now. Candidate for election and all that.'

With this said, as she climbed out of her car, Anjli wondered whether her bravado was just that; was Johnny Lucas a better man than he previously was? Or was this whole "going for Parliament" act nothing more than a replacement for the now-gone psyche of his missing "brother," Jackie?

'I know what you're saying, but I could stay here for your sake,' Cooper said, and Anjli finally realised what the PC was suggesting – after she'd come clean to Declan a year earlier about spying on him for the Twins, they'd worked together to provide misinformation until it was no longer needed, but this was a part of her career she wasn't proud of.

Cooper was giving her the opportunity to have a conversation that might involve this information with no other officers around.

'I've got no secrets from you, Esme,' she smiled. 'Well, none that matter, anyway.'

Crossing the road now, Anjli grinned as she looked at the front of the Globe Town Boxing Club. Traditionally an East End boxing gym, it was always low key in appearance, a long-time deliberate choice to draw attention away from it.

If you didn't know it was there, this red-brick building would pass right by you, while holding some of the darkest moments in East End criminal history inside. The Kray Twins were supposed to have boxed in there, and less than a year ago, a West-London crime boss was tortured and killed in there.

But not by Johnny Lucas.

His blamelessness in the latter situation had given him a chance to change his ambitions, looking to become an independently running political candidate for Bethnal Green and Bow in the following week's By-Election, and based around a campaign that had him going up against the establishment.

And so, the boxing club that for so many years had hidden in plain sight, was now shouting loudly about its existence, with a banner draped along the wall above the entrance.

JOHNNY LUCAS – FIGHTING FOR LONDON

Anjli glanced at Cooper and caught the half smile.

'When he does something, he doesn't do it by halves,' she said as she entered.

Even though the outside of the club gave the impression of a candidate's headquarters, the inside still looked a little different as well these days, as it had been renovated a few months earlier. The spit-and-sawdust look was now long gone, and instead had been replaced by state-of-the-art equipment, shiny weight and running machines that lined the walls, and equally new leather heavy bags surrounding the boxing ring itself, positioned in the centre of the gym space.

In the back were the offices of Johnny Lucas, and by the door was a recently created CrossFit corner, including chin-up poles and kettle bells.

'The more things change, the more they stay the same,' Anjli smiled, nodding over at Pete, one of the track-suited trainers of the club helping a large, young man attack a heavy bag. 'That boy? He's the nephew of Karl Monk. Used to be an enforcer for the Twins. Now, his son's likely learning the ropes.'

She went to say more, but paused as a man emerged from the back offices. In his sixties, his salt-and-pepper greying hair blow-dried back to give it volume, hiding the fact it was thinning a little now, he straightened his tie as he saw Anjli and grinned, walking over. He was suited, but no longer wore his trademark black or navy-blue shirts, for there was no need to. The Twins were, for all intents and purposes, gone. And so he wore a pale-blue shirt and burgundy tie, as he approached the two officers.

'Anjli Kapoor, and PC ... Cooper, isn't it?' he said pleasantly. 'What can we do for you today?'

'We've got some questions; something to do with your past, I'm afraid,' Anjli said, taking the offered hand and shaking it. 'But I know this is a bit public these days, and I don't want to cause any problems.'

'No, not at all, please, ask away,' Johnny's smile felt a little fixed on now, but the intent seemed genuine. 'The election's next week. And, if there're any problems coming at me, I'd like to know them now.'

He glanced at Cooper, flashing another smile.

'God knows, the last thing I want is a bloody newspaper telling the world something bad about me – allegedly, of course – and costing me the race. We're pretty much neck and neck.'

Anjli nodded at this, motioning for Johnny to at least walk with them to a corner of the room, so the conversation was a little more private than in the entranceway.

'Do you remember a copper named Arthur Snider?' she asked.

Johnny didn't react to the name, but he did nod his answer.

'Many people claimed Arthur Snider was a scumbag of the highest order,' he said calmly. 'And not because he was a copper, no offence. He was almost as bad as Derek Salmon when he was alive.'

He stopped, his eyes widening.

'He's not popped up again, has he?' he asked with genuine concern. 'I thought the old bastard was dead?'

'Well, that depends on how you want the answer phrased,' Anjli rubbed at the back of her neck as she tried to find a way to tactfully explain this. 'I mean, he has popped up again, but he's still dead. We found his body in Temple Church last night with a sign around it.'

'Masonic?' Johnny enquired, leaning in. 'That church is filled with Templar Knight history and all that Freemason stuff, like you read in the books—'

'No,' Anjli held up a hand to stop Johnny before his flight of fancy carried him too far away. 'His body, well, mainly a skeleton now, was dumped in a cell there.'

'Didn't realise there were cells there,' Johnny considered this, and Anjli watched the onetime gangster carefully.

'If we find someone else turning up there, we'll know it's you,' she said coldly.

Johnny smiled.

'I'm legit now,' he said. 'But that's weird, isn't it? They had to dig him up to do that.'

He laughed.

'You sure you want to ask me questions? According to the legends, which I can't of course confirm or deny the validity of, the people me and my brother buried never returned.'

'Listen to you. "I can't, of course, confirm or deny the validity." You're sounding less like a crime boss and more like a politician every day.'

'Why, thank you,' Johnny flashed another smile.

'It wasn't a compliment.'

Cooper pulled out her notebook now.

'Mister Lucas, what was DS Arthur Snider to you?'

'I like her, she calls me "Mister Lucas,"' Johnny said. 'Can I be interviewed by her instead?'

'No, because we like her, and we don't want you getting

your hooks into her,' Anjli held up a hand to stop Johnny from replying. 'I know, I know, you're a changed man, yada yada. Just answer the question.'

'He was an informant,' Johnny said, mouth shrugging as he did so. 'Like DS Kapoor was.'

Anjli bristled at the comment. It wasn't that Cooper had heard the words, she already knew what had happened. She was part of the team, had seen enough things. What bristled Anjli was the fact this small, offhand comment was true. Like Snider, she'd also made a deal with Johnny Lucas a few years earlier. Payments for private treatment for her mother's breast cancer, and in return she'd keep him up to date on certain people's interests in him, in particular, when he first arrived at the Last Chance Saloon, DI Declan Walsh. Working from notes written by his now dead father, Declan had Lucas as a suspect, until the *Red Reaper* case effectively exonerated him. And, in turn, this allowed Johnny to free Anjli from her obligations after she saved his own life later on.

But the thought she was once the same as Arthur Snider was not something she wanted to think too much about.

'It wasn't quite the same though, was it?' she retorted.

'No, I suppose not,' Johnny admitted, giving ground perhaps a little too easily. 'To be honest, he did it willingly and for a lot less than you or DCI Ford did it for. But mainly, all he did was give me a couple of heads up here and there, you know, drop me a line and tell me when things were about to happen.'

'What sort of things?'

'The usual. If there was an upcoming raid on a warehouse, or if somebody in my crew was arrested, he'd tip me the nod, keep me in the loop. Usually in the stands at a West Ham game.'

'You'd go to football matches with him?'

'God no. He was up in the cheap seats. We had a box in the Dr Martens Stand, pretty much above where the players came out.'

'We?' Anjli smiled. 'Wasn't this when you were playing pretend with Jackie?'

'I think it was around that time he became more real to me than ever,' Johnny shrugged. 'But we – Snider and I – were both supporters, and being seen at a match together wasn't some kind of clandestine meeting, if you get my gist.'

'So he worked for you?' Cooper was writing as she asked. 'He was loyal to you?'

'He was a loyal man to whoever gave him money,' Johnny shook his head.

Cooper nodded.

'Did he work with anyone else?

'In his time, I know he worked with the Simpsons, with the Seven Sisters, and with us,' Johnny looked across the gym, lost in his memories for a moment. 'I think if there was anybody there with a wad of cash and a criminal enterprise he wanted to help them for a fee. It's a shame he was stabbed, but at the same time, it wasn't long before he was about to be found out.'

He took a breath, let it out, and then sniffed.

'Arthur Snider was a nobody,' he finished. 'He would turn up and tell us stuff, we gave him money, and then told him to piss off. It's all been explained in the past, and it's not going to affect my chances in next week's election.'

There was a woman hovering near the door. She was

elderly, likely a local, and Johnny held a hand to Anjli to pause her.

'Are we done yet?' he breathed. 'I have surgery.'

'Like a doctor?' Cooper, misunderstanding, asked.

'No, like an MP's surgery,' Anjli smiled coldly. 'He's acting like he's already won the election.'

'Start as you mean to go on, Anjli. But I asked, are we done?'

'Chloe Mainsworth,' Anjli ignored the question. 'Do you remember her?'

If he was intending to walk away, all thoughts disappeared, as Johnny looked back from the elderly woman.

'She worked with Walsh senior, Derek Salmon, the Scot and his wife – or *not* wife, the one who scrubbed her entire identity rather than be married to him – we lose track,' he said. 'She's dead too, but she was cremated and her ashes scattered, so I'd be *stunned* if she came back.'

'It's not her, it's her daughter,' Cooper explained. 'She's been kidnapped. We believe by the same person who left the body, with a note on it saying they'd been found wanting and weighed.'

'Ah. "Weighed and found wanting,"' Johnny ominously intoned. 'You know where that comes from?'

'The bible, I believe,' Anjli replied. 'I haven't looked too closely recently.'

'You should,' Johnny looked up to the windows of the gym, searching his memory. 'Book of Daniel, chapter five. Nebuchadnezzar is no longer the king of Babylon, succeeded by his eldest son, Belshazzar. However, this wasn't an easy time, and armies now surrounded Babylon. Belshazzar didn't give a monkeys though, and held a feast for a thousand of his lords. He was foolish enough to not only lose all semblance of self-control at this party but also to openly mock God during the damned thing, by toasting and drinking from golden and silver vessels which his father Nebuchadnezzar had taken out of the temple in Jerusalem.'

He returned his gaze to Anjli.

'Sacrilege,' he continued. 'A sin few people are concerned with these days. But right there, fingers of a man's hand appeared, and wrote words of warning on the wall. This is where the phrase "writing on the wall" comes from, too.'

Cooper wrote this down.

'Never took you for a devout man,' Anjli was impressed.

'Sunday school, and a mental nun who made sure we remembered,' Johnny grinned. 'But this is the important part. Nobody understands the words until Daniel is called in. He takes one look at the words and knows instantly what they mean. Old Belshazzar hasn't been giving God his full attention. He's been taking the piss, in fact, stealing gold trinkets and goblets, and using them in ways they weren't created for – piss-ups rather than rituals, that sort of thing. And in return, God's got his number, and he fell way short of the mark. He's been weighed and found wanting, and his lands are about to be conquered and divided. That night, after giving Daniel his crown, Belshazzar is murdered and Babylon effectively falls.'

There was a moment of silence at this.

'I'm not a stupid man,' Johnny said. 'In all my years, I remembered that story. Because it's a cautionary tale never to take your eyes off the goal. "God has numbered your kingdom and brought it to an end," as Daniel said. And to me, if someone's placed this on Arthur Snider's body? Then it's not justice or revenge against one man. It's someone with righteous fury, that they believe he stole and squandered priceless items, and they're going to have a checklist.'

He sighed, shaking off the thought.

'Or it's the ghost of Paul Carmichael,' he said. 'I also remember the line because it's what he used to tell gamblers that couldn't pay their debts, who effectively stole from him while he covered the costs.'

Anjli looked up at this.

'I don't think I know Paul Carmichael.'

'Way before your time,' Johnny shrugged. 'Okay, I'm due at Bethnal Green in an hour, but I can make some phone calls afterwards, see what's being said. You should get your hacker boy looking into Chloe and her daughter.'

'She was corrupt, too?' Anjli asked.

'She wasn't no angel, especially at the end,' Johnny shivered. The conversation about being judged by God, or the memories of a man named Carmichael from years earlier, had obviously unsettled him somewhat. 'After the problems with Snider she stepped down from duty; stayed at home while her husband worked. But he ran off with somebody. I don't know the full story, but I know that a few years back, Chloe was on the scene again, offering her services—'

He held up a hand.

'I don't mean in an "oldest profession in the world" kind of way, I mean she was basically a form of hardcore bodyguard and bouncer. You know, muscle. We're talking 2010 here. There were a lot of women getting involved in criminal activities, and a lot of the men I was using, well, they were a little squeamish about hitting a woman.'

'Whereas Chloe was quite happy to hit a woman?'

'And other things, to be perfectly honest. But then that's what happens when you need money,' Johnny admitted ruefully. 'Anyway, I know she skirted close to the line. And there was definitely a case going against her daughter when she was a Mile End uniform – you should speak to DCI Ford about that, as she was the one dealing with it—'

He paused, smiling, the Johnny Lucas Anjli knew returning to the conversation.

'Oh wait. She's in prison, sent there by Walsh. Well, that's gonna be a fun conversation.'

'What do you mean by "the problems with Snider?"' Cooper asked.

Johnny raised an eyebrow.

'You don't know?'

'We're on the back foot a little right now,' Anjli interjected.

'Chloe and Snider had a thing going,' Johnny replied. 'They were both married, and she was seeing someone else on the side as well, so when it got out, it was messy.'

'Messy enough to kill Snider?'

Johnny grinned at this.

'Didn't you hear?' he replied. 'Arthur Snider died a hero's death, taking down a drug dealer. Although they did find a locket in his pocket, a gift, with the initials "CM" in it, which pretty much proved everything that people had been muttering about for months.'

And, this said, he looked back at the woman waiting before turning expectantly back to Anjli.

'Thanks,' Anjli placed her notebook back into her jacket pocket. 'We'll let you do your electioneering now.'

'One more thing,' Johnny added. 'If anybody knew Arthur Snider and Chloe Mainsworth? To be honest, it would be Danny Martin. He worked on my behalf on a lot of the times they sniffed about. He might be worth having a chat with.'

'Thank you. But there's one thing that reads wrong,' Anjli added. 'At the start, you said "Many people claimed" that he was a scumbag, but not that *you* did. So, I'm curious whether you had any issues with Snider as well?'

At this, Johnny grinned.

'Arthur and me? Nah, we were thick as thieves,' he said. 'Hammers' fans until the end. And he even helped with a pub purchase, in a roundabout way. So no, I never wanted him dead, although he was way more profitable to me dead than alive.'

And with that, after a simple nod, he turned to walk over to the elderly woman, still waiting.

Anjli watched him; his line about profit had been an odd thing to say. *How was Arthur Snider more profitable dead?*

'Hey, what are your chances?' Anjli shouted.

'Next week?' Johnny shrugged. 'We'll see, but it's looking good. I mean, the guy they've got going up against me is a dinosaur. He doesn't know the people like I do, either.'

He smiled.

'The Tories tried to parachute someone in to go against me, because the government's scared of me. They know that I've got a grassroots campaign working. And, in a week's time, I'll be leaving all this for good, and hopefully joining the hallowed ranks of Her Majesty's Government.'

'You know that's a terrifying thought, right?' Anjli mocked. 'They're bigger crooks than you can ever be.'

'Don't be a stranger,' Johnny ignored the jibe. 'You still have free membership here if you ever want to hit something.'

And, now with big smiles and handshakes, Johnny walked over to the elderly woman, shaking her hand warmly as he walked her to the back of the boxing club and his office.

'Well then,' Anjli sighed. 'Sounds like this whole thing has got a *lot* more fun.'

DECLAN HAD RECEIVED THE CALL FROM THE FRONT DESK THE moment he'd walked out of Monroe's office. With impeccable timing, Louise Straw, the woman who'd opened up Temple Church and waited outside while the mysterious police officer had entered, was downstairs, having arrived to give her statement. It made sense; she probably started at the church at noon, and this being a five-minute walk away made it far easier and less out of her way.

Usually, Declan would have allowed one of the uniforms to take it, but he was still shaken a little from the conversation with Luke Snider – there was something there, and he still didn't know *exactly* what it was. However, he knew he would eventually work it out.

Louise Straw was exactly how he envisioned her: around five feet tall, slim, with short grey hair and a pair of oversized glasses on a chain that connected each stem looped around her neck. She looked like a slightly pious librarian in her pink duffle coat, and Declan felt a real "Nana" vibe when he saw her.

'Mrs Straw?' he asked as he entered the reception area, nodding to the desk sergeant. 'I'm Detective Inspector Declan Walsh. Thanks for coming in.'

'Oh, my pleasure,' Louise stood. 'I felt so sorry for Lance, to see such a hideous thing. Why someone would do that ...'

'Absolutely,' Declan replied, opening the door to allow her through. 'We'll take your statement, and then I'll bring in an expert in composite sketches to speak to you. He'll work out what the man looked like—'

'What man?' Louise frowned now.

'I'm sorry, I thought they explained,' Declan stopped at the doorway. 'The police officer that spoke to you and asked you to stand outside? We can't place him, and there was no record written of a call-out to you, so we need an image—'

'Oh, you don't need an image, you can just speak to him,' Louise looked back into the reception area. 'He was just here.'

'He was?' Declan glanced at the desk sergeant, who shook his head. 'Are you sure?'

'No uniforms have gone in or out since you arrived, miss,' the desk sergeant explained.

'That's because he wasn't in his uniform,' Louise laughed now. 'You silly billies! He was in normal clothes! PC George Dixon, that was his name, told me so when he came by yesterday!'

An icy chill went down Declan's spine.

'Was he blond, centre parting, a scar on the eyebrow?'

'See? You *do* know him—' Louise Straw began, but jumped back with a yelp as Declan ran past her, hurtling through the reception and out into King's Bench Walk, stopping on the pavement outside the Unit.

Of course, Luke Snider was gone.

He'd had a good couple of minutes' head start. And suddenly, the thing that had been niggling at Declan's brain cleared its throat.

'This man you have, this skeleton connected with wires and bolts, that's not my father. That's some gruesome made up toy – someone's created a Meccano set with bone.'

There was no way from the photo that Luke Snider could have seen the skeleton was connected with wires and bolts.

Maybe wires, maybe he'd seen a skeleton on display before, but the bolts weren't common.

He wouldn't have known about them unless he saw them personally.

'Shit!' he screamed out in anger, spinning around in a slow circle, trying to guess which way Luke Snider had gone.

Of course he came to see us. He wanted to see how far we'd got, how much we knew.

No. He wanted to gloat.

'Dammit!' he shouted again, punching the side of one tree that lined the pavement, and instantly regretting it.

'Dad?'

Declan stopped, turning to face his seventeen-year-old daughter, Jessica. She was standing there with an Indian teenager, who Declan knew to be her girlfriend, Prisha.

Both were staring at him as if he was insane.

'Blond man!' he quickly shouted. 'Centre parting! Blue corduroy jacket! Did you see him?'

Jess shook her head, looking at Prisha, who did the same.

'Sorry, no,' she replied. 'You okay? I said we'd be coming by for lunch?'

Declan deflated, nodding.

'Change of plans,' he said, looking back at the building. 'How about a nice, exciting lunch in the office?'

Jess looked at Prisha, who reluctantly passed her a five-pound note.

'Told you,' Jess smiled, pulling a plastic carrier bag from behind her back. 'Don't worry, Dad, we brought you take out. So why don't you let us in, and we can discuss why you're chasing blond men over fish and chips?'

8

HUNT THE COPPER

As soon as they'd arrived back in the office, Declan had roused the troops, while Jess and Prisha watched on from his desk. They had tasked Billy with finding out everything he could about Luke Snider, while Monroe walked back into his office, shut the door behind him and swore loudly and constantly behind his window.

'Actually, I think I might have something,' Billy had explained as Declan was about to sit at his desk and start on his daughter-bought lunch. 'The evening Mainsworth was taken.'

A CCTV image appeared on the screen, and Jess rose from her chair, walking over to it. Declan glanced at Prisha, who, eating a chip from her hastily opened lunch, grinned.

'I'm fine with it,' she said. 'It's kind of sexy, in a Jessica Fletcher way.'

Declan pretended he hadn't heard this, as he tried to scrub the mental image out of his head, walking over to the computer monitors to stand behind Jess.

'Have you changed your hair colour again?' he asked,

suddenly realising her hair wasn't the usual short black, or even pillbox-red, but was instead her natural auburn.

'You're such a detective,' Jess smiled. 'I did it last week. It's so I don't stand out at Mum's wedding.'

Declan mentally groaned. He'd forgotten for the moment that tomorrow his ex-wife became someone *else's* wife. In particular, his old boss, DCI Farrow.

'Is that going okay?' he started, realising he hadn't asked either, but a subtle and loud cough from Billy brought him back to the screens.

'Christ, if we need to have Hallmark Channel time, can we do it away from my domain?' Billy was rubbing at his temples again, his hangover still there.

'You keep being a prick, your domain will be out on the street,' Declan smiled happily back. 'Jess is here. She can do your job in her sleep.'

'Not with my scintillating personality,' Billy forced a weak, embarrassed smile. 'I'll grab a coffee in a minute. Sorry, Jess.'

'It's okay,' Jess, knowing how Billy had been suffering over the last few weeks, placed a hand on his shoulder. 'You're doing better than I expected, if that means anything.'

Billy's smile faded, and he looked to the screen, avoiding making eye contact with both Declan and Jess.

'What do you have?' Declan decided it was time to stop this therapy session and get on with the job in hand.

'So there's no CCTV where we need it to be, which is bloody typical,' Billy muttered.

Monroe walked back out into the office.

'What name did he give?' he interrupted. 'I just read the Desk Sergeant's report, but it can't be right.'

'PC George Dixon,' Declan said. 'Why?'

Billy, who had been in the middle of his explanation, wisely kept quiet this time. Monroe considered the name, mulled it over, and then shouted another stream of expletives before walking into his office, slamming the door behind him.

'What were you saying?' Declan asked Billy.

'We have the image of PC Mainsworth talking to the copper here,' Billy showed the grainy image he'd shown before.

Declan leant in.

'That could be Snider,' he muttered. 'The cap hides the hair though. And there are no others?'

'No, but there are ANPR cameras at both ends of the road,' Billy tapped on his keyboard, and two other camera images came up.

'Dad, what's going on?' Jess asked. 'Who's the blond guy?'

'That's Billy,' a fresh voice spoke, and Declan looked around to see Anjli walk in, Cooper following her. 'You've met him before.'

'Not *this* blond man, the one Dad was chasing,' Jess sighed.

At this, Anjli looked quizzically at Declan.

'The officer who went into Temple Church yesterday morning, who possibly placed the body of Arthur Snider in the penitential cell? The woman who dealt with him positively identified him as Luke Snider,' he explained, with a hint of embarrassment.

'Who was just here?'

'Yeah,' Billy was scrolling through the footage. 'We just let him walk out.'

He turned to face Declan.

'Hindsight is a harsh mistress.'

'You know, I'm not too sure I like this new version of you,' Declan said, and paused as he saw Jess's pale face.

'Bodies in cells?' she whispered. 'You had bodies in a Templar Church cell, and you didn't call me in?'

Declan almost laughed at this. And, as he quickly explained what had occurred so far, he paused as the door to Monroe's office slammed open and the man himself walked out again.

'PC George Dixon!' he shouted. 'Otherwise known as "Dixon of Dock Green," a bloody television copper! Oh, hello, Jess, Prisha. You wee lassies doing okay?'

Declan had to turn away to hide his smile – Monroe had gone from full-on shouting to a pleasant Scottish gentleman in the wink of an eye.

'Billy thinks he has something,' he said as Monroe walked over.

'We can't see what happens down the road, but we can see what happens at the end through the ANPR cameras,' Billy explained as the two camera images scrolled along. 'There's no east or west travelling roads, just a couple of cul-de-sacs, so north and south are the only options. During the next half hour, only thirteen vehicles left the road through the north junction with the A40, none of which were police cars.'

'How do you know they didn't go south?'

'Because the protest was still being cleaned,' Billy replied, his eyes glued to the screen. 'If our abductor drove south, he risked driving right into another group of police officers, several of whom might ask why a uniformed officer was driving a civilian car, or ask where their own officer was. Driving north takes him away.'

'So we have to chase down thirteen vehicles?'

'No,' Billy grinned, an "I know something you don't know," smile that irritated Declan immensely. 'Because only twelve cars drove up the road from the south end in that time. You can even work out the average speed from the time they were picked up at the bottom of the road to the time they left at the top. All twelve didn't stop. Or, if they did, it was for seconds. This one, however, was parked up for ten minutes.'

On the screen, a blue Peugeot 5008 appeared. The A40 camera was a HD one, and although the face of the driver couldn't be seen, the colour could be.

'This car arrived ten minutes before Charlotte Mainsworth was taken and disappeared less than two minutes after she walked up the street with the yet unknown officer.'

'Dixon of bloody Dock Green,' Monroe muttered. 'I loved the show when I was a kid.'

He looked at Anjli, who'd kept quiet during his rant.

'Tell me you got something from the Twins – I mean the bloody *Twin*.'

Anjli told Monroe what Johnny Lucas had said, and he scowled.

'Aye, he's right,' he admitted. 'We need to speak to Danny Martin and DCI Ford. We're now looking at the son of the man who died, digging his own father's body up and kidnapping the daughter of a woman his father worked with.'

'I'll go see Danny Martin,' Declan said quickly. 'I really don't want to see DCI Ford, especially after last time.'

'Aye, we'll go after you have lunch with your daughter,' Monroe nodded. 'DS Kapoor, see if Detective Superintendent Bullman wants a trip out, and if so, go have a chat with Ford.'

'Guv?'

'You worked for her so you know her,' Monroe explained.

'But she was a DCI while you were a DS, so she might not feel pressured to explain herself. Bullman is a higher rank. She also never met the woman. So there's a chance we can come at her from two sides.'

'Guv, Johnny also said the phrase on the paper was something a gangster named Paul Carmichael used—'

'Aye, well, he died years ago, so unless someone dug him up too and got him writing messages, let's start looking at the living, yes?'

This decided, Monroe glanced at the screen, and then walked off without another word. It obviously wasn't that subtle, as Jess picked up on it, too.

'Am I missing something here?' she asked.

'Dead colleague brought back up, and there are issues with a past case,' Declan said, and then paused.

'Wait, actually you *can* help me. You have your laptop with you?'

Jess patted her pockets mockingly.

'Can you see one?'

Declan deflated a little.

Of course this wouldn't be that easy.

'What were you thinking through when you asked?' Jess asked. 'Maybe I can help in another way?'

Declan moved Jess away from the others, lowering his voice when he spoke. When he'd first moved into the house at Hurley, he'd started going through his dad's notes. He'd been under the belief that someone within them had murdered his dad, tampering with his brakes and causing him to crash – and in a way he was right, but not in the way he'd expected. At the same time, during these long research sessions, he'd had Jess help him, partly to re-bond with her after the split with Liz, but also because one day Jessica

Walsh would be a better copper than either he or his dad ever were. As he worked more analogue, she was working digitally, though, taking the notes Patrick Walsh hadn't yet digitised, and scanning them into some semblance of order.

Scanning them and organising them before anyone else got to them.

'Back when we were working through Granddad's notes,' he started, checking around to make sure he wasn't being observed, 'you were digitising them, scanning them?'

'I was, until we stopped,' Jess frowned. 'Once we caught the Red Reaper, we kinda gave up on them, as they weren't needed anymore. And by then you'd started turning the secret room into a bedroom. But you still have the originals, right?'

'You'd think,' Declan replied. 'But there's a month missing. Early 2005. It was around this time that Arthur Snider was on the scene, when he would work with my dad ... and Monroe.'

'Who you know had a look through Granddad's files back when you were working on the Angela Martin case,' Jess nodded now. 'You think he took the folders? Or maybe just one? I thought he came clean about his past?'

'He did, but he might have forgotten about this one,' Declan pursed his lips together as he thought this through. 'Or, he deliberately kept quiet about it, or maybe I might even be wrong. There might never have been a file there, as Dad wasn't always so diligent. But I just wondered ...'

He trailed off as Jess starting tapping on her phone, scrolling up her screen with her finger.

'I'm sorry, are we distracting you?' he asked irritably.

In response, Jess grinned.

'You're a dinosaur,' she said. 'I have all his notes on an

encrypted folder on the cloud. I always meant to look through them again, but the A Levels, and Prisha ...'

She shrugged.

'Time got away from me,' she said. 'So while you're talking, I'm working. Because I'm the future, Dad, while you're just a dinosaur, waiting for the meteor to hit.'

'You know, I'm not a fan of this analogy,' Declan growled. 'And I'm getting enough backtalk from my subordinates with Billy.'

'Well, lucky for you, I'm not a subordinate, I'm your little princess, the light of your life,' Jess grinned as she stopped scrolling. 'Yeah, there's a folder for that time. Look.'

She showed the phone screen to her father; on it was a folder icon, a single word under it.

CARMICHAEL

This is the only folder I saw back then, in the early 2005 section,' Jess said. 'But then Granddad did things by case rather than date, so if whatever this was took a couple of months, that'd explain it.'

'This wasn't in the folders I checked, though,' Declan looked back at Monroe's office. 'I'd remember the name. Can you open that?'

Jess shook her head apologetically.

'Not on my phone, but I can get Billy to—'

'No, not here,' Declan shook his head quickly. 'If it was Monroe, and he took it for a reason, he might take it off your phone, too.'

'It's not on my phone.'

'You know what I mean,' Declan ruffled Jess's hair. 'Do it when you get a chance. Don't go into it, just send it to me.

You've got enough on your plate with your mum's wedding tomorrow.'

'Are you coming?' Jess asked. 'Mum wasn't sure.'

'Of course,' Declan smiled, even though he didn't feel like it. It was one thing to attend your ex-boss's wedding. Another to attend your ex-wife's. But to attend them both, at the same time ...

'Oh, how did the double date go?' Jess suddenly asked excitedly. 'With Eden Storm and Dominique Lacroix?'

'How did you know about that?' Declan glanced over at Anjli, currently speaking to Bullman, before the two women marched out of the office, most likely already on their way to see ex-DCI Ford.

In response, Jess swiped on her phone and showed her father an image. It was of a box in the Royal Albert Hall, of Declan watching an opera, while sitting next to Eden Storm.

Declan swore under his breath. He knew there had been photographers there. Eden had even pointed out where his security was confiscating the telephoto lenses. And, for a brief second, he wondered whether Eden had lied, or had deliberately left a couple, just to make sure this hit the headlines.

'You're on the Daily Mail side bar of shame,' Jess smiled. 'How you were part of Eden's night out. There are photos of him and Lacroix at a party with The Rock, and the guy who played Superman.'

She leant closer.

'Were you at the party with The Rock and the guy who played Superman?' she whispered.

'Not so lucky, I'm afraid,' Declan replied. 'We got the call to go to Temple Church during the intermission.'

He looked down at the photo.

'Stunned they got my name right,' he smiled.

'Are you kidding? You're the copper who's saved the Prime Minister, like three times. And the Queen, well, before she passed away. You're famous, Dad. I mean, not famous like The Rock or the guy who played Superman, but like "I'm a Celebrity, Get Me Out of Here" famous.'

Declan forced another smile at this, even though the thought churned his stomach, but Jess grabbed his arm before he could move.

'Why did you go, Dad?' she asked. 'You had to know this was a play by Eden, right?'

Declan paused, looking back at his daughter.

'And don't make a crappy "no it was an opera" joke. You know he likes Anjli. He never hid it.'

'I know,' Declan sighed. 'Anjli agreed to it. She said a night out would be fun. And it was only when I got there I realised it was an ambush.'

'What kind of ambush?'

'He wanted to know my intentions with Anjli,' Declan's face darkened as he continued. 'Like if I'd get out of the way for him. And maybe I should.'

'Are you insane?' Jess shook her head. 'Anjli's the best thing that's happened to you since, well, for a long time!'

'He can fly her to Paris for breakfast, she'd never need to work again, she'd have everything she ever wanted,' Declan countered.

'And what if the thing she wants is you?' Jess glared at her father. 'Jesus, Dad. How are you so bad at this? You've got comfortable. So get *un*comfortable. Take your comfort zone and throw it out of the window before you lose her out of one.'

Declan nodded, embracing Jess.

'How did you get so clever?' he asked.

'By watching every stupid thing you ever did, and making sure I never did it,' Jess laughed. 'Come on, your fish and chips are getting cold.'

As she walked back to Prisha and her food, Declan glanced up at Monroe's office. It couldn't be a coincidence that the name of the file was the same name as a gangster Johnny Lucas had mentioned, who Monroe didn't want to talk about.

All he had to do now was work out what the hell it meant.

ANJLI HADN'T WANTED TO GO TO SEE DCI FORD. IT WASN'T because the journey to HM Prison Downview, the women's closed category prison she was an inmate of, was long, or even difficult – Downview was located on the outskirts of Banstead in Surrey, a good hour's drive from the Unit – but because Anjli had conflicting memories of the woman.

Before Declan had arrested her for murder, after Ford had tried to frame him for the same crime, Anjli had worked at the Mile End Crime Unit under her. She'd been harsh, and expected a lot from her team, but she had been a good detective.

The problem was, she was also a really terrible gambler, and had owed the Twins tens of thousands of pounds in debts by the time she was removed from her post.

Anjli had left the Unit after she'd punched out a domestic abuser with connections to the Twins and it had been Ford who tried to have her kicked out of the police, which had surprised Anjli – hurt and betrayed her, even – but after she learnt the full lengths the woman would go to save her own skin, she realised how misplaced that loyalty had been at the time.

Now, this would be the first time they met again since that fateful day, almost two years earlier.

Anjli hadn't wanted to go, because she didn't know how she'd react – whether she'd laugh, cry, or launch herself across the desk.

It was probably good that Bullman was with her.

And, arriving at the prison, Bullman led the way as they went through security, waiting in a bare, windowless room filled with plastic chairs welded to tables. The visitors' room was empty, deliberately so, as "having coppers in the room could agitate the inmates", according to one guard. That, and other inmates seeing Ford talking to police, could actively affect her prison experience.

In a small way, Anjli had *hoped* for that.

After about ten minutes of waiting, the door at the other end of the room opened, and two female guards brought in a woman, wearing a pale-grey sweatshirt and joggers, her grey hair cut in the same short style she'd worn while serving at Mile End.

The small scar on the cheek was new, though.

The woman paused as she saw the two officers waiting for her, and her face broke out into a grin as she recognised Anjli.

'Bloody hell, as I live and breathe, Anjli Kapoor,' ex-DCI Marie Ford said as she slumped herself down in the seat facing Bullman and Anjli. 'Things must be terrible if you've come to *me* for help.'

9

WE ARE DETECTIVES

ANJLI KEPT HER VOICE CALM AS SHE REPLIED.

'I'll admit, I never thought I'd see you again, Ford.'

'Nuh-uh,' Ford waggled a finger. '*DCI* Ford, please, *DS* Kapoor.'

'Didn't you lose that when they fired you?' Bullman enquired pleasantly. 'You know, when you were kicked out for murder, corruption, and half a dozen other things?'

'Who's your friend?' Ford's smile had faded now.

'Detective Superintendent Sophie Bullman.'

Ford leant back in the chair, as she observed the woman in front of her, taking in the short, white, spiked hair, and the stoney expression.

'I've heard of you,' she stated. 'You're the woman who has to deal with Monroe and his screw-ups on a daily basis, aren't you? My condolences. And you're here to see little ol' me? This'll be fun.'

She stretched back in the chair, straightening her arms if she did so.

'Don't get many visitors in here, and I don't get to play

with the other inmates that much,' she explained. 'Although that's not because I'm a copper, more because of what I've done in my past.'

Anjli resisted the urge to correct Ford one more time, by pointing out she was no longer a police officer, and waited for Ford to finish.

'Go on then, tell me why I'm here,' Ford stated. 'I'm guessing there's something important that you need from me?'

'We'd like some background information,' Anjli started. 'But it's purely routine—'

'Bullshit,' Ford waggled her finger again. 'You wouldn't have brought the big guns if that was the case.'

Bullman's knee knocked against Anjli's under the table, and she realised she'd clenched her fists, so forced herself to smile, releasing them and trying to make her anger flow out of her body.

'We understand that before you tried to steal millions in made-up money,' Bullman smiled, 'You—'

'Crypto currency,' Ford corrected.

'As I said, *made-up money*,' Bullman was unfazed by the interruption. 'And, before you were taken down by the guy that you tried to frame for the murder of Bernard Lau, that you worked in Mile End with PC Charlotte Mainsworth.'

'Ah, *that's* what this is about,' Ford nodded, as if realising what this was about now. 'I worked with both of them if you want the full reveal. I was under Chloe Mainsworth when I first started in the force, and with her daughter, Charlie, before she was transferred, at my request, to Slough.'

She leant in, hand to her mouth in a mock stage whisper to Anjli.

'So you know, both of them were absolute nightmares,

although I'm sure that's no wild shock to you. I understand you're getting married. Congratulations.'

Anjli started back at this.

'No, I think you've got—'

'Yeah, you're right, I'm sorry,' Ford raised her hands up now. 'It's his *ex*-wife that's getting married, isn't it? You two are just ... well, I don't know what to actually class you two as.'

Anjli smiled as she violently resisted the urge to lean across and punch Marie Ford in the mouth.

'Well, rather than get into that, can you tell us about Mainsworth senior and junior?'

'I can tell you that Mainsworth senior is dead,' Ford thought to herself for a moment. 'And therefore that means we're looking at junior. I'm stunned she still has a job. Or does she?'

Ford moved eagerly closer.

'Is that why you're here? Is she getting fired?'

'She's gone missing.'

'Right,' Ford sat back, disappointed now. 'She's probably on a bender. She used to do that when she worked for me.'

'I'm serious,' Anjli continued. 'We've got CCTV footage proving someone's taken her; someone with a connection to her mother, and Arthur Snider.'

'Arthur Snider is dead.'

'But his son, Luke, isn't,' Bullman took over now. 'We think he's got some kind of axe to grind and we can't wait around to work out what's going on, while a woman, a still-serving officer's *life* is on the line, whether or not she's a good copper.'

Ford nodded, understanding.

'I've got four years left in my stretch,' she explained. 'They couldn't get me on over half of the things they wanted to – I have an exemplary police record, and I had a superb lawyer. So, if you can get me down to two years, I can help you.'

'We can't promise anything,' Bullman shook her head. 'But if you do help, your help will be taken into consideration.'

She looked around the room, shuddering.

'This is a miserable bloody place, isn't it?' she muttered. 'Your first parole hearing is, I believe, in a month. If you help, we might be able to convince them to move you to an open conditions prison, where middle-class women hang out to play tennis and things like that.'

'Nah, that's not my scene,' Ford smiled, tapping the scar on her cheek. 'I like it here. I mean, being known as an ex-copper doesn't help, but being a copper who used to work for the Twins, and one who *allegedly* committed murder, well, it helps a lot when it comes to reputations.'

She leant closer, lowering her voice.

'I'd rather you did something that helped in here. A rival, perhaps, one that's causing me problems. You understand? You move her somewhere far away, and I'll help.'

Anjli looked at Bullman, who shrugged.

'Give us a name,' she offered. 'We'll see if we can get her moved. If not, I'm sure we can make her life a little more uncomfortable.'

Ford watched Bullman for a long moment.

'What do you need?' she eventually asked.

'Well, you worked Mile End for most of your career,' Bullman started. 'But you were a uniform under Monroe when he first arrived, and you knew his people.'

'I did,' Ford nodded. 'And I knew he was as corrupt as everybody else.'

'Yeah, we've had that story, that's long past, so no big whoopsies there,' Anjli leant in. 'You weren't around at the time, on account of being in here. But it was a really cool read. Prime Minister herself brought him back onto the team.'

'Yeah, I heard – interesting how she did that shortly before you removed her from her role,' Ford smiled now. 'Even so, the new Prime Minister is on your side as well, isn't he? Hey, could you get him to give me a pardon too? Does it work like that? You know, like Presidents?'

Anjli said nothing, relaxing back onto the quite uncomfortable plastic chair.

'So I was a uniform moving into CID when all the shit happened with Chloe,' Ford sighed, realising nobody was biting.

'What do you mean, "all the shit happened with Chloe?"'

Ford watched Anjli for a moment, as if trying to work out if she was being tested.

'You were at Mile End, you made your bed with the Twins, and you honestly didn't know about this?'

'If I did, I wouldn't be here, would I?'

Ford made a "whatever" shrug with her mouth, accepting the comment.

'Okay, sure. It's a fun story, I don't mind telling it.'

She settled into her chair.

'So you had your merry band of miscreants, led by Patrick Walsh, and when I came into the unit as a uniform, they were quite a tight-knit team. Then things fell apart.'

She counted on her fingers.

'Monroe's missus decided that she would rather change her entire identity and disappear than be married to him anymore; one day she was around, the next she was gone.

Your boyfriend's father got promoted up to D Supt, which obviously moved him out of the area, and which probably saved his career. Derek Salmon moved to Tottenham. Monroe was still around, but by then he was under the Twins' thumbs.'

She paused.

'Well done on that, by the way,' she said, and for a second, it sounded genuine. 'I heard how you sorted out Johnny Lucas once and for all, something nobody else could do. I'm genuinely impressed with you for that.'

She frowned.

'Actually, I trained you when you were under me, so I should be thanking myself.'

Anjli's lips thinned as her mouth tightened.

Bullman wisely kept out of this one.

'I heard what happened with you and Johnny Lucas,' Ford smiled. 'You're a chip off the old block. My protégé in every way—'

'Can we get back onto the subject at hand?'

'Sure,' Ford gave a small, triumphant smile. She knew she'd got under Anjli's skin, and Anjli could see with an element of extreme annoyance that it made her feel powerful. 'Anyway, the group had kind of fallen apart after the attacks on 7/7. Wintergreen left, and Special Branch wasn't really looking to do these undercover police units anymore, because they obviously didn't work – or the detectives in them weren't up to the grade. But, when you go undercover and take bribes and look the other way as part of your job, once that undercover life stops, and you've been playing the same part ...'

She trailed off, shrugging.

'People don't realise that you were undercover,' she

finished. 'People don't realise you lived by a distinct set of rules, and you're too far gone to explain why you're still doing it.'

'Is that what you say to yourself at night?' Anjli wanted to get away from this conversation as quickly as possible.

'I was working undercover to stop DC Sonya Hart from killing people and stealing cryptocurrency,' Ford said in response. 'Do you believe me? Of course not. But you can't *prove* I'm wrong. There's no paper trail because it got lost in a fire. Or the dog ate it. Something like that. Am I telling you the complete story? Who knows?'

'You can lie to yourself all you want—'

'I'm not lying to myself, Anjli, I'm lying to *you*,' Ford chuckled. 'Or am I? That's the problem. Look at Ellie Reckless. She was Mile End police, under Monroe too. And then she got kicked out because of rumours about her past. Luckily for him, Patrick Walsh had a stellar record up to this point. He hadn't been dipping his hand into the cookie jar as much as the others.'

She sniffed.

'Although, there were rumours during the Carmichael investigation, he did a little more than he should have.'

'And what's that supposed to mean?' Anjli was getting angry again.

DCI Ford paused, considered her words, and stared directly at Anjli as she spoke.

'Well, let's just say if Declan takes a really good look around, he might find some new brothers and sisters. Because I know for a fact that Patrick Walsh wasn't only having an affair at the time, but he was actively considering leaving his family.'

THE PLAN HAD BEEN TO DRIVE TO BELMARSH PRISON AND SPEAK to Danny Martin, but even the best plans change.

They were in Declan's Audi, Declan driving while Monroe stared moodily out of the window. They'd been like that for about twenty minutes, since leaving the Unit, and Declan couldn't work out if the morose bloody Scot was angry at the case, or with him.

'You do anything fun last night?' he asked, deciding that perhaps some small talk might help.

'And what the bloody hell's that supposed to mean?' Monroe snapped, but then waved a hand to apologise. 'Sorry, laddie. Knee jerk reaction. I went for a drink in Whitechapel with an old friend. But the pub was bloody noisy, and I called it a night. Knew we'd have an early start, too.'

'Doctor Marcos wasn't there?'

'Rosanna wasn't going to leave Snider's skeleton until it gave up all its secrets,' Monroe smiled weakly. 'I knew I wouldn't be seeing her until the sun came up.'

He peered wolfishly across at Declan.

'You're remarkably melancholy,' he said. 'I mean, even more than usual. Is this the wedding?'

'Liz and Farrow? I'm fine.'

'Aye, I can see that, especially as you still won't call him by his given name.'

Declan paused.

'He was my boss, always DCI Farrow,' he said. 'Feels weird calling him Henry, you know?'

'Aye, I get that,' Monroe nodded, as he absently tapped his phone.

'You expecting a call?' Declan couldn't help himself.

'Waiting on a text from a friend, the one I saw last night,' Monroe looked up.

'Case related?'

'Haven't you worked it out yet?' Monroe chuckled. 'Everything I do is work related.'

He looked up at the road.

'I had an interesting chat with Bullman the other day,' he said. 'About Anjli and Billy.'

'Oh aye ... I mean, oh yes?'

Monroe glowered at Declan as he side-eyed him, trying to work out if he was being mocked or not.

'They've not gone for promotion,' he said. 'It came up after De'Geer got his sergeant's stripes.'

'I've been thinking about that, too,' Declan said. 'Shaun Donnal mentioned that to me before Christmas.'

'It's bloody February,' Monroe raised an eyebrow. 'You still thinking? Or bothering to do anything?'

'You're DCI, it's your call.'

'You're DI, they're your subordinates.'

Declan watched the road for a moment, working out his next words.

'Boss, we both know I'm not getting DCI unless there's a miracle,' he said. 'And Anjli won't go for DI while I'm one, and Billy won't go for DS while she's one.'

'Why?'

Declan clicked his tongue for a moment.

'Because the Unit budget can't afford two DIs,' he said. 'One of us would have to transfer.'

'Oh,' Monroe said. 'Bugger. So what do you want to do?'

Declan glanced at Monroe as he turned left down a side street.

'Put them through anyway,' he said. 'They can be fast tracked. Bullman could—'

'Bullman could, and has already,' Monroe replied, settling back in the seat. 'Should get a response on whether she can do this soon, and the answer in a couple of weeks. I wanted to run it past you first, though. See what you think.'

'I think it's a good idea,' Declan said.

'I've also told her to push for your promotion to DCI,' Monroe held a hand up. 'Don't start with "budget" complaints, either. We can manage two DCIs, one would be senior. We just need to convince them you're worth promoting.'

'Good luck with that one,' Declan chuckled. 'Hey, can I ask a question?'

Monroe waved a hand to insinuate he was okay with this.

'What does the name "Carmichael" mean to you?' Declan asked.

At the name, Monroe straightened.

'Why would you be asking that, laddie?'

'I mentioned there was a missing folder earlier, one where Snider looked to be working with you,' Declan continued on, locked on course. 'I know it was named "Carmichael," so maybe named after someone, perhaps? Paul Carmichael? The man Johnny Lucas spoke to Anjli about?'

'And how would you know a name on a folder when the folder's missing?' Monroe growled, and it was a low, angry tone Declan had heard before, usually when someone was pushing the Scot in a direction he really didn't want to go in.

'Because Jess digitised it before someone took it,' he said, deciding to continue the deduction. 'Before *you* took it, Guv. And I'll know what it is later, when she checks the folder and sends me what she scanned, so how about you stop whatever this is, and get me on the same page here?'

Monroe didn't speak, simply looking out of the window, clicking his tongue against the roof of his mouth, in the way he did when he was considering something bad.

'This isn't a good start to your DCI promotion prospects,' he muttered, but Declan knew he was just grumbling, and would eventually give in. He went to speak again, but his phone, connected to the car's speakers, rang.

Declan tapped a button on his steering wheel, and Cooper's voice echoed through the speakers.

'Guv?' she asked. 'And Guv's Guv?'

'What is it, lassie?' Monroe smiled. 'Can it wait until we're back?'

'I think you might want to delay the prison visit,' Cooper's voice sounded nervous. 'There's been a call in from a pub in Millbank. Morpeth Arms.'

'And?' Monroe frowned. 'What do they want?'

'They have cells in the cellar,' Cooper explained. 'Apparently it used to be a prison and transfer facility for the old Millbank prison nearby and also housed prisoners about to be deported.'

Declan could already feel someone walking over his grave as he started typing the pub's name into the sat nav screen.

'What have they found?' he asked.

'Well, their security cameras were disconnected about four this morning, and off until six,' Cooper replied. 'And nobody checked it, because, well, it's just a cellar—'

'Come on, lassie, out with it,' Monroe barked.

'They went down at lunchtime to show a drinker the cells,' Cooper sounded as if she was reading from notes. 'But when down there, in the furthest cell, they found ... well, they found another body.'

Declan was already U-turning as Cooper spoke the words he'd expected.

'Doctor Marcos?'

'About to leave,' Cooper replied.

'And do we have a name for the victim, or is this another bloody skeleton?'

'No, boss, this is a recent death,' Cooper sounded nervous. 'A man named Harry Sullivan. We've already checked his file on HOLMES 2 and ... well ...'

'He used to be my informant,' Monroe was tight-lipped. 'Another connection. Good work, we're on our way.'

Monroe turned off the call, tapping the screen with more force than he needed to.

'So, do you want to tell me about Carmichael now?' Declan asked. 'And why you took a folder from my dad's notes over a year ago?'

'Not really,' Monroe sighed. 'But I suppose there's never a good time for the truth. Because the body we're now about to see? He's the man I saw last night.'

10

SHOW AND TELL

'Bullshit,' Anjli snapped. 'Stop with your bloody lies.'

'Oh, I don't need to lie about this,' Ford shrugged, leaning back on the chair as she watched Anjli with a small gloating triumph. 'It's way more fun to tell you the truth. '

'Go on then,' Bullman interjected, shaking her head at Anjli to stop her speaking. 'Tell us the truth.'

'Patrick Walsh was shagging Chloe Mainsworth,' Ford smiled. 'I was told it second-hand, but we knew it across the station. There had been problems in the Walsh bed, and your boyfriend was away with the army, so daddy dearest started a fling.'

'This isn't relevant to the question we asked,' Anjli fought to keep herself calm.

'Oh, but it is,' Ford shook her head. 'Context is key. You wanted to know what caused the death of Arthur Snider.'

'He was killed by a drug dealer.'

'Well, he was killed while *shaking down* a drug dealer,' Ford replied patronisingly. 'But whether he was killed *by* the dealer or not, nobody can really be sure.'

She leant closer, lowering her voice with mock fear.

'What is for sure, and I learned this from Danny Martin himself a few years later, is when Arthur Snider died, there was a hit out on him. And, to make it more fun, the word on the street was it had been placed by one of the officers in the Mile End unit.'

'Bullshit. The word on the street has always been just that. Words.'

'You're the ones here asking me for the truth,' Ford sniffed. 'I've got nothing to lose. But when I came on board, I was just a uniform. By the time I became a Detective Inspector in my own right, Monroe had gone to Vauxhall and he'd taken Reckless and the other miscreants with him, and I had an opportunity to carve my own path.'

She looked directly at Anjli as she continued.

'But I still had parts of the past niggling at me, nipping at my sleeves,' she carried on. 'The daughter of Chloe Mainsworth was one of these. She was a nightmare to manage. And I'll be honest when I say she'd bounced around the police for a good ten, fifteen years at that point.'

'If she was such a nightmare, how did she get in?' Bullman frowned.

'No idea. All I can say is that everything she did was rotten to the core. And, she had a rep from what happened during her teenage years that, if she had been over seventeen when it happened, would have killed all chances.'

Anjli understood what Ford was saying; although the age of criminal responsibility in England and Wales was ten years old, once you turned eighteen, the laws altered. If you were cautioned in your teens, the chances were it would be removed from the record by the time you legally became an adult. If Charlie Mainsworth had some kind of police-related "road to Damascus" revelation at eighteen, she could apply with effectively a clean licence. And at the time, Chloe was still a respected ex-officer. This would have given her daughter a definite leg up the ladder, regardless of what she did as a teenager.

And Anjli wanted now to know more than *anything* what that was.

'She only transferred to us recently,' Bullman was continuing the interview now. 'What was she doing under you that was so bad?'

'She screwed around. She didn't play by the rules,' Ford replied. 'She'd cut corners, take money to look the other way, all the things you'd expect from a Mainsworth.'

'This is rich, coming from you,' Anjli laughed. 'Sounds like she learned from the best.'

'I had no choice.'

'You had tens of thousands in gambling debts. You could have chosen not to make them.'

'That's not how addiction works.'

'You weren't an addict,' Anjli snapped. 'You were just a shit gambler with a chip on her shoulder from when the male coppers wouldn't take your orders.'

Ford ignored the insult, instead shifting in the seat to face Bullman fully.

'Anyway, eventually, one day she was gone,' she said, obviously blanking Anjli. 'Transferred to Slough, and the Thames Valley Police.'

'You did this?'

'Not my choice, actually. It was my boss who did that, then-DCI Schultz. He's retired now. Came in after Monroe left, had enough of Mainsworth's shit, decided she was the last guard of the Monroe era, and removed her. I may have helped steer his decision, though. Then he left; took an early retirement a year later.'

'Convenient for you.'

'Yes, it was,' Ford flashed a smile at Anjli. 'Thank you for noticing.'

'If you cared so little about her, why did you open a case into her?' Bullman looked up from the notes she was taking.

'I was looking into *her* because I was looking into her mum's death. Which, to be honest, even though the official cause of death was classed as cancer, I don't think it was.'

Ford thought about what she was about to say, weighing up her words, and Anjli gained the impression this was a weighty statement about to be made.

'I think Charlotte Mainsworth smothered her mum,' she stated. 'Possibly in a euthanasia setting, to save her pain. Possibly in anger because the woman had a temper. And I tell you now, as you both probably know, having met her, that woman is built like a brick shithouse, and a terrifying woman in a fight.'

'And this is why you were looking into her?' Anjli scoffed. 'Because she might have killed her mum? Come on, Ford. You didn't give a shit about that. What's the real reason?'

Ford stared at Anjli, a surprised look on her face.

And then, it slowly faded away as she smiled.

'Yeah, alright,' she replied. 'I also believed she was the only person out there who knew where the Carmichael money was.'

'You mentioned Carmichael before, as if we're supposed to know it,' Anjli replied. 'Pretend, for the moment, we don't have a bloody clue what you're talking about.'

'Monroe kept it to himself, then,' Ford nodded in understanding. 'And I'm guessing Declan's daddy never told you before he died?'

She stopped, sighing once more.

'I'm doing him a disservice,' she said. 'And I apologise. Patrick was the best of all of them. Well, that wasn't saying much, because it wasn't a high bar to beat when you're facing Alexander Monroe, Derek Salmon and half a dozen others, all of whom had their hands in a dozen different cookie jars … but he was a good man. He shouldn't have gone out like that.'

There was a long moment of silence, and Anjli actively wondered if Ford meant the words she was saying.

'I mean, of *course* I was going to turn out like them, I'm a product of my upbringing and mentorship. Patrick Walsh might have liked the ladies, and the money helped him in that respect – he might have liked the undercover life a bit too much as well, shall we say? But when the Carmichael case came up, he at least knew when to back away. In fact, the Carmichael case was pretty much one of the last things they did as a team.'

'So tell us about the Carmichael case,' Bullman closed her notebook, placing her hands on it as she watched Ford. 'Off the record. Nothing written.'

Anjli did the same, closing her own notebook.

'Paul Carmichael, gambler and casino owner, vicious little bastard who worked with The Turk in Soho,' Ford started. 'At the time we're talking like 2003, maybe 2004. It was before my time, and I think they'd just solved the Victoria Davis murder – well, they *thought* they had – and they were on a high.'

She leant back in the chair, staring off into space as she recounted.

'Paul Carmichael had his casino robbed at gunpoint and lost four million pounds. And we're talking almost twenty years ago, so a million was worth a lot more than it is now. Anyway, the Met went in with some uniforms, they searched around and eventually realised this was an inside job. The Turk wanted to remove Carmichael from the game, as he was getting a little too big for his boots. The culprit, some high-level manager was found drowned in the Regent's Canal and, even though they couldn't prove anything for certain, enough circumstantial evidence was found to stop all parties from retaliating, in a kind of "mutually assisted destruction" way. The Turk could kick off, but then it'd come out that he set it all up.'

'How did they get the money back?'

'At the start, nobody knew where the money went. The manager had friends, and they started popping off, or being hurt, like *really* hurt, all with Paul Carmichael's calling card on them.'

'Was it "Weighed and Found Wanting?" by chance?' Anjli asked.

Ford smiled.

'See? You do know the story. Anyway, the police came in looking for it, and it was a race, you see. Paul on one side, Patrick Walsh the other. The police won though, they found the money, but only half of it. Two million in total. Everyone claimed The Turk must have taken half, but he always claimed he never saw a penny. Paul Carmichael went to the grave convinced Johnny Lucas took it, and his son Peter Carmichael spent years arguing we'd stolen it from them, but the insurance covered the theft completely, so nobody was out of pocket.'

She placed her elbows on the table, propping her chin up on her fingers as she thought through the case.

'But a lot of the fingers pointed at Arthur Snider,' she finished. 'It was believed he, being the only one who had custody of the money at any point, managed to hide it, place it somewhere where no one could get to it. There was talk he'd turned it into a pile of gold bullion coins, and he had priors with this sort of thing after he tried to take evidence after a jewellery robbery.'

'The one Monroe punched his teeth out after?'

'Maybe, yeah,' Ford smiled. 'Serves the bugger right. But, as to the Carmichael money, Snider denied this, of course.'

'Sure,' Anjli shrugged. 'Not the sort of thing to broadcast to the world.'

'Problem was, you can be as careful as you like, but if you're constantly spending a lot more money than you're making, people work it out,' Ford continued 'Eventually, people followed the small additional amounts he was spending, and it came out that he was having an affair with Chloe Mainsworth.'

'You sure about that?' Bullman pursed her lips.

'People saw him leaving her house, even when they weren't working on cases together. He'd bought two season tickets to West Ham and never took his wife, although he was seen there with a woman. And about three months before his death, he showed some uniforms at Mile End a beautiful and very expensive golden necklace with "CM" written on it, saying it was a gift for a special person.'

'Real under the radar, Arthur,' Anjli muttered.

'Go figure,' Ford shrugged. 'But, when you occasionally work with a Chloe Mainsworth and you have a "CM" locket you're flashing around, eventually someone grasses to your wife. And they did. When it all came out, she was furious. His workmates were furious. Apparently he'd been telling her he was off to the office, while actually meeting up with Chloe at home matches. Chloe took time off work. Her daughter, Charlie, was a real troublemaker teen with a drinking problem around that time, and "officially", Chloe was sorting that out, hence the leave. But it meant Snider found himself friendless, and then a couple of months later he tried to shake down a dealer to gain some clout with the Twins, and got stabbed.'

Ford chuckled.

'Bloody fool. The dealer was done for manslaughter and a dozen other things, I think. He's still around. Or he's dead by now and I'm wrong. I've been in here for over a year, after all. Things happen fast in that area. He might even be released by now. Something we all dream of.'

She ended the comment with a visible wink.

'So when Snider died, if he *did* take the money, what happened to it?'

'That's the thing. Nobody ever found it,' Ford tapped at her nose. 'That's why I looked for it years later. I know that his son Luke, growing up, knowing his father stole all this money and gave nothing to the family – it changed him. Chloe might even have quit the force around that time. I can't remember. At the time I was going for my DC exam, so I wasn't really paying much attention.'

'And then, years later, Charlotte Mainsworth joins the police.'

'Yeah, but it was a few more years before she eventually turned up in Mile End. And by that point, I was a DI going for promotion, and I decided to keep an eye on her.'

'Because she could have inherited Snider's money, given

to her mum?' Anjli suggested. However, at this, Ford started laughing.

'God, no!' she exclaimed. 'The bloody daughter was as bad as the mum, always looking for a way to make money. If Chloe Mainsworth *had* the money, she kept it from Charlotte. But I suppose you're right in a way. I started my investigation because there was always the opportunity she might find the missing millions. And by that point, I was deep in Johnny's pocket.'

She spat to the side.

'I'd mentioned to him about it, suggesting we could team up and split the proceeds, and he told me to walk away, that the money was long gone, like he knew something. But then at the time he was becoming way more "Jackie" than Johnny, and he had his own problems.'

She trailed off, staring at the table, lost in her own world for a moment.

'You want someone with an axe to grind, though? Go look at the wife, Laura Snider, the grieving widow. She was convinced Monroe and his people were hiding something. Monroe would regularly apologise, offer her money – and she threw it back in his face. As far as she was concerned, *they* took the money, her husband was a scapegoat because of his affair with Mainsworth, and the truth of Snider's death was another of Alexander Monroe's many secrets.'

Anjli didn't want to look at Bullman – she didn't want to catch the eye of her superior. They'd both known of Monroe's prior indiscretions, but this was something new.

And it was something that was scarily plausible.

'Anything else you can think of that can help us find Charlotte Mainsworth before we leave?' Bullman eventually asked.

'Oh yeah. Absolutely. Look for a place that is really, really well hidden and sound-proofed,' Ford nodded. 'Because that bitch would scream her head off when she was furious. You wouldn't be able to hear anything else.'

Grabbing her notebook, Anjli rose from her chair.

'I'd say it's been a pleasure, but it hasn't,' Ford said up at her.

'I'll see if we can do something about your rival, if you give us her name,' Anjli offered stiffly.

'Nah, actually, don't worry about it,' Ford looked over to the door, where the guards walked across, aware the meeting was over. 'I don't want the inmates to know the police helped me, you know? I can fix it myself.'

She paused.

'Although I'd love to know how Sonya Hart's doing,' she added. 'If you ever get a chance, I'd like to chat to her. Maybe a phone call?'

'I'll do my best,' Anjli nodded. 'Thank you for your assistance, DCI Ford.'

At this, Ford smiled, a genuine, beaming smile.

'Thank you, Anjli, that means a lot,' she said, noting the usage of her now removed title as respect. 'I hope you find her. She was a nightmare, but she was a copper and we look out for each other.'

And, this said, Ford allowed the two guards to lead her out of the room.

'If she was your DCI before you left, now I understand why you prefer Monroe,' Bullman muttered as the door closed.

Anjli went to reply, but stopped, thinking about the woman who'd just left.

'She wasn't that bad when I worked there,' she replied.

'That's what working for The Simpson family, and the Twins, and half a dozen other gangland bosses does for you.'

She let out a long breath.

'Unfortunately, it sounds at the moment like she learned how to do it all from Patrick Walsh.'

'Do you want to tell Declan, or shall I?' Bullman asked as they walked to the door. 'Actually, don't answer that. You're doing it. What's the point of being the boss if I can't get rid of the really shitty jobs?'

Anjli chuckled, but as she left, she wondered about what DCI Ford had stated. If Arthur Snider had an affair with Chloe Mainsworth and stole two million, it made sense for her daughter to somehow inherit it.

Or, rather, for Luke Snider to come to the same decision.

'We need to pick this up,' she said. 'This isn't going to end well.'

11

HOLDING CELLS

DECLAN PULLED UP OUTSIDE THE MORPETH ARMS TO FIND armed police standing on duty outside the pub's side entrance in Ponsonby Place.

'Something I should know?' he asked Monroe, nodding over at the officer as he climbed out of the car.

Looking around, Monroe shrugged.

'We're a hundred yards from Thames House, so MI5 are probably twitchy, not to mention that the godawful looking building across the Thames is MI6. Also, the poor wee buggers probably wanted a break from guarding doors filled with spies.'

'And dead bodies are better?'

'Dead bodies are always better than spies.'

Nodding to the uniform guarding the cordon, showing their warrant cards and ducking under the tape, Monroe led Declan towards the door of the pub.

'I ought to tell you,' he whispered, so the guards at the door didn't hear him. 'About what happened when I saw Harry last night.'

'Before or after he was dead?'

Monroe flashed an angry glare at Declan, who held a hand up.

'Sorry, poor joke,' he said in defence. 'Go on then, why did you meet with Harry Sullivan? And was it here, by chance?'

'No,' Monroe shook his head sadly. 'I went to see him because of bloody Carmichael.'

Declan didn't reply to this. On the drive over Monroe had explained in detail about the Paul Carmichael affair almost twenty years ago, complete with the missing two million, believed to have been stolen by Arthur Snider, and the affair Snider had with Chloe Mainsworth.

'Is there anything else I need to know about that before we go in?' Declan eventually asked cautiously. 'I don't want to be on the back foot here.'

He wasn't sure, but he thought he sensed the briefest of hesitations before Monroe replied.

'No, laddie, you're up to date on everything.'

Declan stopped in the pub's entranceway.

'What aren't you telling me?'

'Laddie, I said—'

'Dammit, Alex, *stop trying to protect me!*' Declan snapped, the use of Monroe's first name making it more personal. 'If there's something out there about my dad, I need to be ahead of it.'

Monroe looked pained as he nodded.

'Your father,' he started slowly, unsure how to phrase what he wanted to say. 'There was an officer on the team. They got close.'

Declan mentally ran through the names he knew.

'My dad had an affair with Chloe Mainsworth?'

'I don't think it was an affair, but it was incredibly messy and convoluted,' Monroe shook his head sadly. 'I think he was just having a bad time, and she was a shoulder to, well, you know ...'

Declan stared at his superior for a long, uncomfortable minute.

'My dad would never have cheated on Mum,' he said, before adding 'Christ, *my dad cheated on Mum?*'

'I didn't know if he talked about it in the Carmichael notes, as the bloody fool wrote everything down, mostly to his own detriment,' Monroe explained. 'But they were just case notes. I burnt them in case anyone knew I had them. I never thought I'd be needing them, and I thought it was best you never found out. The case was long forgotten, even by Pete Carmichael, Paul's son. I didn't think anyone would ever dig it back up.'

'That's why you didn't mention the relevance between Paul's calling card and the note around the neck?'

'Actually, I'd forgotten that one,' Monroe scratched at the back of his neck. 'Or, rather, I wanted to forget. When Paul died, all that went away.'

'And this was why you met this Sullivan guy?' Declan walked to the bar now, where PC Cooper was standing.

'What are you doing here?' he asked, diverting his attention to her before Monroe could reply.

'Came with Doctor Marcos,' Cooper nodded behind the bar and, as Doctor Marcos wasn't to be seen, Declan assumed this meant the Doctor was in the vague direction of the nod. 'De'Geer was away from the office when the call came in. I gave her a lift.'

'As long as you don't want to be a forensic whatsit as well,' Monroe growled. 'Go on then, what do we have?'

'About three this morning, the motion alarms went off inside the pub,' Cooper read from her notes now. 'The manager of the pub lives up above, as does the chef, and the first time anyone knows about this is when the police are knocking on the door.'

'Probably bloody armed police too, from the looks of things,' Monroe glanced at the armed officer at the door. 'Then what?'

'The manager, his wife and the live-in chef were escorted outside, and the officer went inside to check.'

'This is sounding remarkably familiar,' Declan muttered. 'Description of the copper match the one we know?'

'Unsure,' Cooper admitted. 'The armed officers aren't thrilled with having uniforms from the City traipsing about, so they're being ... obstructive ... with uniforms asking questions.'

'I'll ask the manager,' Declan smiled. 'The armed police will have to back down for a detective.'

'Aye, let me know how that one goes,' Monroe grinned.

'One thing I do know is there were two this time,' Cooper said. 'Copper and a sergeant. But that's it.'

'He might have a friend,' Monroe pursed his lips. 'Okay. And then?'

'Then nothing,' Cooper replied. 'They had a quick look, saw nothing, came out after a couple of minutes and then everyone went back in once the alarm was reset.'

'Couple of minutes isn't long,' Monroe mused. 'When was the body found?'

'Just after lunch,' Cooper nodded at an elderly couple beside the window, the woman's hand shaking as she sipped at a brandy. 'The couple there asked to see the cellars, the cells, that is. They're a bit of a tourist trap here. And on quiet days, people can go down and have a look.'

'And there they found the body?'

'Yes, boss. Doctor Marcos can explain more.'

Monroe nodded.

'Good work,' he said, patting her on the shoulder as he walked past. 'Get yourself back to the unit, see if De'Geer or Billy need any help. I don't think we'll be that long here.'

Cooper nodded and left the bar, visibly ignoring the officers at the door. Monroe sniffed, and then started through the small bar entrance that led into the stairs at the back.

'Rosanna?' he called.

'Down here,' a voice called back up.

'I bloody hate underground tunnels,' Declan mused. 'Tunnels and caves. Banes of my bloody life.'

'Well, if we both wish real hard, maybe the ceiling won't collapse on us this time?' Monroe smiled sweetly as they walked down the staircase, entering the Morpeth Arm's cellars.

Built in 1845, the pub was originally established as a deportation facility; a tunnel system running beneath the city streets carried convicts from the old Millbank prison to a holding area beneath the pub, while they waited for transportation to whisk them away to Australia, or worse. The prison itself, which featured six wings attached to a central chapel like the petals of a flower in a 'Panopticon' design, closed in 1890, and was ultimately demolished, but the holding area stayed the same, as the pub above it had no intention of being demolished any time soon.

Declan had read that the cellars were supposed to be haunted, in particular by the ghost of a man who'd died trying to escape the prison through the cellars, but if it wasn't the ghosts, he could feel on the back of his neck, it was the weight of history pressing down on him.

The cellar was used for storage now, and the first of the several arched recesses that followed the right-hand wall was filled with wicker tables, while to his left, Declan could see the modern beer barrels of the twenty-first-century pub upstairs. Each recess was about eight feet in width, and six feet in depth, although the arch, taking the whole of the width and ending around six feet up, meant the space was tighter the further to each side you went, so most prisoners would have had to stay low to keep some semblance of personal space.

'They had hammocks, you know,' Monroe said, as they continued along. 'They'd lie in them while they waited to be banished forever.'

At the end of the corridor, and standing beside the final alcove, was Doctor Marcos in one of her custom-made grey PPE suits, her frizzy black hair free of the hood, and with no mask on.

'Gloves and boots,' she said as Monroe stopped, nodding, pulling out a pair of blue latex gloves and plastic booties to go around the soles of his shoes, nodding at Declan to do the same. 'It's not going to help much, but who knows?'

'What do we have?' Monroe, now garbed accordingly, stepped closer, looking into the cell. The body of a man was lying on the ground, a noose around his neck, a PPE-suited forensics officer examining his hand.

'Harry Sullivan, but you know that,' Doctor Marcos replied casually. 'Strangulation marks around the neck are fitting with a hanging, but he couldn't have been hanged here.'

She tapped the top of the arch.

'Not tall enough.'

'So the body had to be brought here,' Monroe's mouth was set tight as he spoke. 'Wee bloody fool. What were you doing here?'

'Has he told you?' Doctor Marcos asked Declan. 'That he saw him last night?'

Declan nodded.

'I told him to check around, see what he could find out about Carmichael,' Monroe was watching the body as he spoke. 'There aren't that many people left who know about the case, and Chloe, Derek, Patrick are all dead—'

'Emilia Wintergreen isn't,' Doctor Marcos growled. 'She was there, and she only works a hundred yards from here.'

'You think Sullivan met Wintergreen?' Declan looked from Doctor Marcos to Monroe. 'Would he know her?'

'With her, I don't know,' Monroe shuddered as the body was adjusted, the CSI checking pockets. 'Anything found on him?'

'No items, but there's skin under the nails, possibly a defensive wound,' Doctor Marcos suggested. 'We've sent it for DNA comparisons, as it could be from whoever killed him.'

'Luke Snider was scratching at his forearm when he was in your office,' Declan said ominously. 'Maybe it was a wound?'

'White shirt, but he could have had it bandaged,' Monroe nodded at this. 'Anything else?'

'Not yet, you only got here a few minutes after I did,' Doctor Marcos smiled. 'I'm good, but I'm not that good.'

She turned to speak to the other forensics woman, and Monroe pulled Declan to the side.

'I think we might need to have a chat with Emilia,' he

said. 'If she wasn't with him when he died, the fact he's here is either a message to her or me.'

'We should see if the pub manager has anything else for us,' Declan suggested, but Monroe was already staring back at the body.

'You go chat, laddie,' he breathed. 'I just want to pay my respects a little more.'

THE MANAGER OF THE MORPETH ARMS WASN'T AROUND, BUT Ed, the live-in chef, was standing beside the lamppost on the street, having a cigarette as Declan walked over.

'Mind if I ask a couple of quick questions?' he flashed his warrant card as he spoke.

'Sure, I've spoken to about a dozen people, but one more time? Why not,' the chef replied mockingly, before realising he was back-talking to a police officer. 'Sorry. Long day. Even before this.'

'You were woken up last night?'

The chef nodded, stretching his shoulders as he did so.

'About ten past three, it was,' he said. 'I know because I checked my phone when the banging started. Two coppers at the door, both in uniforms and the bright yellow jackets. Said they'd had an alarm show up on their system, one of the silent ones we have in the bar, and they needed to check it, turn the bastard off. Sammy, that's the relief manager—'

'Relief manager?'

'Yeah, the actual manager's on holiday. Wedding in Barbados or something, and he's best man. Sammy came in through the brewery, he's been here a few times over the years. Anyway, he made a joke that it was probably the ghost.'

'Ghost?'

'Oh yeah, we've got tons. Even used to have a camera in the cellar, so people in the bar could look for it, but that's been off for ages. Copper wasn't impressed with the joke though, asked us all to step out so they could "make the premises safe," whatever that meant. By the time we were out though, he was done resetting the silent alarm so it wasn't going off any more, and they sent us back inside. That was it, really. Just went back to sleep.'

Declan frowned. If this went the way Ed believed it had, there was no time for Luke to bring the body in, especially if Sullivan was no longer alive at this point.

'Do the cells, the tunnels – do they go anywhere?' he asked.

'They used to, but not for decades,' Ed replied. 'You trying to work out where the body came from? Yeah, we've been head scratching that too. It wasn't there at closing, as I helped Sammy with the barrels, but neither of us were down there this morning, so it could have been any time after that, I suppose.'

Declan forced a smile, even though his mind was racing through all probable outcomes. Maybe Luke used the alarm story to get in and disable it, thus allowing him entry later? It seemed the only workable option. And it also meant the murder and disposal of Harry Sullivan could have happened *after* three am.

'Did you see the officer?' he asked.

'Yeah, both of them,' Ed nodded. 'The one outside, who waited with us – he was a snotty little shit, pardon my language – was actively telling his boss what to do.'

'How do you mean?'

'I mean, he was a PC, right, because that's how he introduced himself. PC Dixon. But the woman, she was a Sergeant, Roberta something. Cryer? Maybe. Anyway, she was obviously twice his age, and he was acting like he was in charge. Dick.'

'Was he young, blond, scar on the eyebrow?'

'Yeah, that's the one. You know him? Tell him he needs to respect his elders,' Ed stubbed the cigarette out on the side of the lamppost, tossing it down the drain beside him.

'What was he saying?'

'Oh not much, just to secure the scene. They weren't here long. It was the tone, you know?'

'And the Sergeant?' Declan asked. 'What did she look like?'

'Fifties, maybe sixties, old for the rank, you know? Like a career uniform, I guess. Must have pissed someone off to have the graveyard shift. Short white hair, or like a pale-grey. Silver? Slim woman, too.'

Declan wrote this down. He knew someone who was slim, with short white hair.

Emilia Wintergreen.

Monroe walked out of the pub now, and, seeing a chance to escape the questions, Ed used the opportunity to escape.

'Need anything else, feel free to ask Sammy,' he smiled as he left.

'Anything?' Monroe looked annoyed as he walked past the escaping Ed.

'Body couldn't have been left here at three when the alarm went off,' Declan replied. 'There wasn't enough time. But I think they did all this to gain entry, and turn off the security so they could come in later.'

'Makes sense,' Monroe agreed. 'Rosanna thinks the death was around five in the morning. So they could have come here, unlocked the door, and then killed him elsewhere before bringing the body here.'

'Hard work. Why not kill him here? No need to drag a body?'

'First, that's an old friend you're talking about and second, he'd scream the place down.'

Declan reddened.

'Sorry, Guv. He also saw the Sergeant, said her name was something like Roberta Cryer, and she—' he stopped, watching Monroe as he chuckled. 'Something funny?'

'No, laddie, sorry, it's just Roberta is female for Robert, and Sergeant Bob Cryer ... well, he was the Sergeant in ITV's *The Bill*,' Monroe replied. 'Our suspects have a flair for the televisual, it seems.'

'Well, that's not all,' Declan said, showing Monroe the page of notes, in particular, that of Sergeant Cryer's appearance.

Monroe read it and nodded, his expression dark.

'Aye,' he said. 'We should chat with my ex-wife.'

'You think she could have done this?'

'She wiped her entire existence on a whim, and runs disavowed spies on black ops, so, aye, I think she could do whatever she bloody well wanted,' Monroe growled. 'Come on, let's get back to the Unit. Rosanna's bringing the body back in a van.'

CHARLOTTE MAINSWORTH DIDN'T KNOW HOW LONG SHE'D BEEN left alone; there were no windows, and definitely no clocks in the cell at the side of the wide crypt cellar, the other side of the wooden grilled door. But the young blond bastard had been gone a couple of hours at least, leaving her alone, in her piss-stained uniform, tied to a metal chair.

Which was his *mistake.*

She understood the logic of it, a wooden chair could be broken with enough force. She'd seen it in films. It would fall apart like matchsticks if she threw herself backwards. But instead she'd been tied to a metal one, an unbreakable one.

And, luckily for her, a jagged one.

She'd found the piece of jagged metal, nothing more than a bad weld on the back of the right-hand leg about half an hour into the wait, and had been rubbing the zip ties back and forth across it for the last hour. Her arm was numb with effort, and she could feel blood trickling down her wrist from where the jagged edge, or the ties had ripped into her skin but the jagged edge, although mainly blunt, had cut through most of the ties, and even the surrounding tape. And now, with a muffled scream of frustration and pain, Mainsworth could pull her hand free, the last zip-tie snapping under the pressure.

Thank God for being strong, she thought to herself.

She couldn't see anything she could use, but when she'd been tied up, he hadn't made a thorough job of frisking her, and she still had a safety rescue cutter on her police vest.

It had probably been overlooked because it didn't look like a knife; it was a thermoplastic hook, only five inches total, but the inside of the hook had a serrated steel blade along the edge. It was useless in a fight, but brilliant for cutting through any cord or webbing strap to provide a quick release or rescue.

And that was exactly what she needed now. The blade wasn't as sharp as a scalpel or penknife, but it was a damn sight better than a knocked-out piece of rusty metal.

Using the cutter, she hacked at her left hand's restraints and then, when this was free, moved down to her ankles. And, within a matter of minutes, she'd freed herself from the chair.

Standing up, she had to steady herself against the back of it; she hadn't stood up now for probably a whole day, and her legs were screaming out with pins and needles as the "dead legs" came back to life.

She didn't have time to shake the feeling out, and there was no time to find a weapon. She'd seen the door he'd entered and exited through, and to her delight, after staggering out of the cell through the wooden grille door, realising it didn't even have a real lock and was there pretty much for show, she found the main door out of the cellar was unlocked.

Opening it, she saw a half-lit wooden staircase leading up to a second door. There was light coming from the end, but she couldn't see where from. However, when she got to the top of the steps, she could see the light was from under the door, not quite flush against the frame, the daylight from outside illuminating the top of the stairs.

Praying the door was open, she ran to it, grabbing the handle and pulling at it – to her joy, it opened out into the fresh air—

And a terrified old woman.

'Where the hell did you come from?' the woman exclaimed, almost clutching at her heart at the sight of this dishevelled, tear-stained woman.

'I'm a police officer,' Mainsworth explained. 'I was taken. Where am I?'

The woman frowned.

'You don't know where you are? These are the Clerkenwell Catacombs. Well, technically it's the Hugh Myddelton School now, but the kids don't really know the history of the place. I walk my dog here. He's off in the bushes right now—'

'Do you have a phone?' Mainsworth grabbed at the woman. 'I need to call the police.'

'Oh, goodness, of course!' the woman started rummaging around in her pockets. 'Here I am, waffling on about my dog ... ah, here you go.'

Mainsworth reached for the offered phone, but realised just that little too late that not only was it not a phone, but it was sparking with electricity at the end, the sparks crackling around two vicious looking prongs.

And, as the old woman's face turned into one of hatred and anger, she rammed the shock taser into Mainsworth's chest, sending the larger woman stumbling backwards, her foot slipping over the edge of the top step and causing her to overbalance, tumbling badly down the stone steps, landing in a broken heap, blood oozing from a wound on her forehead, at the bottom.

The woman stared down dispassionately before placing the taser away and pulling out an actual phone this time. Then, brushing away a strand of short, white hair, she dialled a number, waiting for it to connect.

'It's me,' she said when the call was answered. 'You didn't search her, did you? You bloody idiot. It's a good job I was here.'

She looked back at the unconscious body.

'You're as useless as your father was,' she said. 'Get your arse here right now and help me do the job properly this time.'

12

COPPER DROPPER

ILLY WAS WAITING FOR THEM WHEN DECLAN AND MONROE entered the unit offices. It had been almost two hours since they'd left, and they *still* hadn't reached Danny Martin to ask questions, but that seemed a little more like a moot point at the moment. Monroe hadn't spoken the entire journey back, lost in old memories and guilt for potentially throwing Harry Sullivan to his own death, blaming himself for all that had happened.

Declan knew that look. He'd had the same one many times before.

But Billy, for a change, looked like his old self. He was bright-eyed, and more importantly, had the arrogant smile he often wore when he knew something other people didn't.

'Whatever you've got, laddie, it can wait,' Monroe growled as Billy went to talk, and Declan saw Billy's posture slump as the wind was taken out of his sails.

However, Monroe must have counted to ten in his head, because a moment later, he grinned and continued.

'Ah, I'm just playing with you. Go on then, amaze us with your insights.'

Billy nodded, the smile returning.

'I think I've found our man,' he said, returning to his monitor station. 'We started looking for his blue Peugeot 5008, right? When Mainsworth was taken, and we realised he was likely driving her?'

'Aye, and what of it?' Monroe walked to the side to watch as Billy worked on the computer.

'I followed the car, but I lost it here, near Farringdon,' Billy tapped on a map of London that was up on the left-hand screen as he grabbed his mug, drinking deeply from it. 'And today, after Declan realised Luke Snider was Dixon, I followed his car the same way. We were behind, never using live footage as we'd given him too much of a head start, but I was able to find him again. Until ...'

'Until he reached Farringdon,' Declan peered closer at the map. 'Camera down?'

'Yeah, and it's at a busy crossing area with five feasible routes away,' Billy tapped on his keyboard, and on the map seven red circles appeared, all in the vicinity of the crossing. 'For some reason, there was a relay feedback of some kind a couple of weeks back, and all the cameras here stopped recording.'

'Deliberate?'

'Probably not, to be honest. These things are more common than you'd expect.'

Billy took another drink, and Declan noticed it wasn't coffee.

'What are you drinking?' he asked suspiciously.

'Electrolytes,' Billy replied, a little too cautiously for Declan's taste.

'Can I try it?'

'No.'

Declan went to speak, but Monroe, realising what was going on placed a hand on Declan's shoulder.

'Did I ever tell you how I fell apart after Emilia left me?' he asked. 'It was bad. I started taking to keeping a wee flask of whisky on me at all times. Not to drink, but there just in case it got a little too much, aye?'

Declan said nothing, watching Monroe carefully before glancing over at Billy, seeing the young detective's face pale.

'The problem was, after a while, *everything* was a little too much,' Monroe continued. 'I'd drink now to keep myself from breaking. Just a wee dram, now and then. And then I needed a wee dram more, because the last one hadn't been enough. And then I was drinking straight from the hip flask. And then … well, why bother pouring into the hip flask when you can drink straight from the bottle?'

Billy didn't reply to this.

'I wasn't an alcoholic, I was a more heavy and constant drinker,' Monroe continued. 'And I still drink, as you both well know, but nowhere near the amount I did back then. And more importantly, I keep myself on the straight and narrow while at work.'

He now looked back at Billy.

'So, when I ask you what's really in the mug, laddie, know that it's from the place of a man who's been there?'

Billy swallowed.

'It really is electrolytes,' he said carefully. 'I have sachets.'

'And what do you mix it into?'

'It's called a Borg,' he explained. 'It stands for "BlackOut Rage Gallon." It's a new drink. Half water, half vodka, a caffeinated flavour sachet and a sprinkle of powdered electrolytes.'

He sighed, mournfully.

'Hangover free, apparently.'

Monroe watched Billy for a long moment.

'Jesus,' he moaned. 'You can't even be a police drunk properly.'

Billy forced a smile at this, pushing the mug away.

'It's not to get drunk,' he promised. 'It's just to … I dunno, lessen the background noise. In my head. It stops me from being who I need to be.'

'Och, you wee bampot, it's the noise in the background that *makes* you who you need to be.'

Mortified at being called out, Billy simply nodded dumbly.

'Sorry,' he said. 'I'll do better.'

'You always do, laddie. Now, how about you tell us how these things are common and you probably have a genius solution to it.'

Declan stepped back from the monitor station as he considered Monroe's words, noticing Billy's face breaking out into another smile.

'I want to ask who knows about this, but I'm sure from the smile on your face, you already know, and are simply dying to tell us,' he said.

Billy fully grinned now, all worries about the effective off-the-record bollocking he'd just had now removed.

'Copper Dropper,' he said in response.

Declan frowned at the two words.

'Am I supposed to know what that means?'

'It's a forum for corrupt cops,' Monroe grunted.

At this, though, Billy shook his head.

'Yes and no, boss,' he replied. 'I'd say officers more inclined to bend rules than corrupt. That's a very umbrella terminology.'

'I agree,' Declan smiled. 'To some people, watching the way we ignore police proceedings, we could be classed as corrupt by that definition.'

'Either way, it's not our finest on there,' Monroe growled. 'Salmon used to talk about it. He was on the bloody thing as well, so that's not exactly a glowing recommendation.'

'So for those of us who don't really know what this is, can we get an explanation?' Declan asked. 'Going with the belief it's a little more than a chat room for bent coppers?'

'It's a forum, but not a back and forth, as such,' Billy explained. 'It started off as a private chat room on a Geocities site back in the late nineties. It was created as a way for members to "drop" any information they found useful. Contact details for informants, places that opened out of hours, that sort of thing. It was originally a way for police to bypass red tape.'

'But I'm guessing that didn't last long?'

Billy nodded.

'You could only gain access if two people vouched for you. But as it continued, the quality level of coppers lowered.'

'Bent cops vouching for bent cops,' Monroe snarled. 'Diminishing returns. No honest buggers in the room.'

'The message board was anonymous to allow plausible deniability, and only the admins knew actual identities,' Billy continued. 'Each user took on a fictional police officer's name. People like Inspector Lestrade, Axel Foley ...'

'Dixon of Dock Green,' Declan finished.

'Yeah, I thought that, too,' Billy nodded. 'Copper Dropper

has been an open secret for years. I got onto it a year or so back.'

'Oh aye?' Monroe raised an eyebrow. 'They head-hunt you, laddie?'

'They wish,' Billy grinned. 'Remember DI White?'

'How could I forget?' Monroe growled, and Declan knew exactly how the old Scot felt. A year earlier, when Declan was accused of terrorism and Monroe had almost been killed by DI Frost, otherwise known as "the man with the rimless glasses", DI White had taken control of Temple Inn. At the time Declan had believed Billy had sided with White, following the rule of law rather than siding with his hunted colleague – only Anjli, using a secret code with Billy, knew the truth; that Billy was using his relationship with White to get in close, learn what he could, and then bring the entire house of cards tumbling down.

'What *about* White?' Declan asked.

'He was on the forum,' Billy explained. 'And, when I hacked his phone, I accidentally gained his login. And, well, let's just say that when DI White left the police —'

'When the traitorous wee bastard was kicked out.'

'— exactly, I continued to log in on his account,' Billy smiled. 'It's helped a couple of times, actually. But, as much as I try, I can't work out who's who in the forum.'

Billy tapped on the keyboard, and the computer lit up, with a forum browser appearing in the middle.

'The forum had a post appear a week back, pointing out the broken relay south of Clerkenwell, where the ANPR cameras were off,' Billy pointed at a post. The poster was the aptly named *DCI Burnside*, named after a rogue officer in *The Bill*, and the post was mainly suggesting the blackout area as a place the other members of the forum could use to "interrogate" people without fear of being picked up on camera.'

'Nice,' Monroe's eyes were tight as he read the post. 'Good to know our taxpayers' money is being spent on fine, upstanding *bastards*. So Luke saw this?'

Billy nodded, typing on the keyboard as the source code of the web page now scrolled up the screen.

'I can guarantee it,' he replied, pointing at a line of code. 'Because his dad created this.'

Monroe's eyebrows raised at the words.

'I knew he was an early adopter of the internet, but I didn't realise that,' he said, his voice almost impressed. 'However, I'd be remiss to point out, laddie, that he died two decades ago.'

'The Geocities site existed while he was alive, but it was too open to the public – well, public who could read source code. So, at the end of 1999, worried about the "Millennium Bug" exposing the site, they moved to a designated server,' Billy explained. 'I spoke to a friend in cyber, one of the OG—'

'OG?' Monroe asked.

'Original Gangster,' Declan explained. 'Slang for "old school," so I'm guessing this is a first wave police hacker?'

'Pretty much,' Billy leant back on his chair. 'Anyway, he said that it was known that Snider started it as a hobby, but some moderators he'd set up on the site to keep things "honest" were trying to get him out. This was when the forum wasn't completely for corrupt police, and his off-books jobs were becoming more known openly, aiming more attention at him and the site. So he took less and less of an active role in it, in the years before he died.'

Billy pointed at another line of source code, and Declan

wondered for a brief second whether he was simply pointing at random lines of code for dramatic intent.

'So, when I heard that, I started checking the code, moving into the packages—'

He sighed as Monroe yawned theatrically.

'Clever computer God do clever computer things,' Billy said, forcing back the urge to continue the sarcasm. 'And I found that before he was kicked off for good, Snider created a back-door account creator.'

'Yeah, but it's been twenty years,' Declan shook his head at this. 'Surely the site's been moved and re-written a dozen times by now.'

'It has,' Billy agreed. 'But the database has to be kept intact, so the archive stays linked, and that's where the code was. And about three months back, someone used this back-door to the forum to add two new accounts to the list. Can you guess what fictional coppers they used?'

'PC Dixon and Sergeant Cryer,' Declan didn't even need to guess the answer as he spoke the names. 'Okay, so we know Luke is now on the site. We know the blackout in Clerkenwell is on the site. How does he use this to his advantage?'

'That's the part I have an issue with,' Billy looked sheepish now. 'He knew if he went in the black spot, we wouldn't be able to follow him. The question now, however, is *where* he came out, or even *if* he did. I'm having to check every exit out of the black spot to see if the car appears.'

'That's almost impossible!' Monroe exclaimed. 'You'd have to spend days watching the screen! Can't you write some kind of clever computer code to ...'

He trailed off as he saw Billy's smug expression.

'Let me guess,' he growled. 'Clever computer God do clever computer things?'

'I should have something from the incredibly cool algorithm within a couple of hours,' Billy smiled.

'Good work,' Monroe nodded. 'But imagine how much further you'd be without your weird, bloody drink.'

Billy went to reply, but stopped as the doors to the office opened and both Anjli and Bullman stormed in.

'I'm glad you got that bitch arrested and kicked off the force,' Bullman said angrily at Declan. 'But I wish you hadn't.'

'Why?' Declan looked around the room at the others, confused whether he'd missed something.

'Because then I could have nailed the smug cow to the wall,' Bullman hissed. 'I need a shower, just to wash the stench of corruption from me.'

She looked at Monroe as she passed him.

'I'll never complain about you again,' she said as she continued into the office, closing the door behind her.

'Wait, she's been complaining about me?' Monroe was perplexed. 'Who's she been complaining about me to?'

Declan ignored this, turning to Anjli.

'What did you get?' he asked.

'I'd rather not say,' Anjli looked uncomfortable with the conversation.

'Why?' Declan worked through all the conversations they could have had about Mainsworth, her past …

'Ford talked about my dad,' he said as a statement, his voice flat and emotionless. 'About his affair with Chloe Mainsworth.'

Anjli was surprised at the revelation.

'You knew?' she asked. 'You knew, and you never told me?'

'In fairness, lassie, he only just found out,' Monroe admitted. 'I told him while we were checking into a new body.'

'Well, either way, we have updates,' Anjli replied to Monroe. 'I'm guessing with this new body announced in Millbank, you do too. Briefing room time? We still don't know where PC Mainsworth is, and we're heading towards twenty-four hours now ...'

She trailed off, as she realised everyone was looking behind her. Turning, she saw a white-haired woman standing in the doorway.

She was slim, attractive, and bore a faint resemblance to Helen Mirren.

It was Monroe who spoke first.

'Emilia,' was all he said.

And with that one word, everyone in the room knew this was Emilia Wintergreen, his ex-wife-turned-Spymaster, returned to the police force after almost fifteen years of not existing officially.

13

OLD LOVES AND OLDER PARTNERS

'Good evening, Alex,' Emilia Wintergreen replied guardedly. 'I understand you've been looking for me.'

'Well, I wouldn't say we've been looking for you,' Monroe forced a smile. 'I just shouted your name out loudly and knew one of your spy drones would hear it.'

'Are we really going to do that right now?' Wintergreen's voice was tight.

Monroe sighed at the question.

'No, it's fine,' he admitted. 'Thank you for coming, Emilia. We were looking to speak to you, as we have some questions.'

'I would have preferred to do it elsewhere,' Wintergreen clutched at her arm as she looked around, and Declan couldn't help but wonder if old memories were returning. 'My offices, perhaps?'

'I'm sorry, but that wouldn't be possible,' Monroe's voice was also tight and emotionless as he spoke. 'Would you come with us to the interview room, please?'

'You're interviewing me? Officially?'

Monroe clicked his tongue against the roof of his mouth, and Declan realised how hard this was for him.

'Yes,' Declan quickly interjected, mainly to help Monroe. 'You see, one of the problems we have is we now find ourselves with two dead bodies. One long dead one, and another that's recently dead.'

He took a deep breath. He'd dealt with Wintergreen before, and he knew how dangerous she could be, even when she was on the same side.

'And the other problem we find ourselves with is that we also have a witness description of *you,* seen at the scene last night, before the body was discovered.'

Wintergreen was silent for a moment, mulling the comment over.

'I can see that being a problem,' she nodded. 'Do you want to know my whereabouts?'

'Aye, it would help if we knew where you were last night,' Monroe agreed.

'That's classified.'

'Of course it is,' Monroe sighed. 'Okay, let's try this a different way. Where were you between the hours of three am and six am this morning?'

'That's classified.'

'You're not really helping yourself here, Emilia,' Monroe, tired of the game, snapped. 'You might be a big thing in Whitehall, but in here, you're just another suspect. An ex-copper who left her role.'

'I get that, and I also get why you aren't likely to trust anything I say,' Wintergreen softened a little as she replied. 'But I'm hoping the fact that Trix, and also Tom, speak highly of me—'

'Last I heard, you burnt Tom and kicked him out of MI5,

and Trix was on suspension,' Billy, unable to hold his tongue, interrupted.

Wintergreen watched him for a moment, as if the irritation at being interrupted had turned into amusement on who'd done it.

'That's due to their own actions and nothing to do with me,' she argued. 'But I'll answer your question. There was a drone strike in Ukraine this morning at oh-five hundred hours. I had agents on the ground, and I was in a meeting, making sure they were safe at the time.'

She shifted her stance, still defensive.

'I was nowhere near the Morpeth Arms at the times you mentioned.'

'And how would you know we were looking at the Morpeth Arms?'

'Because I'm not an idiot, Declan,' Wintergreen snapped, glancing back at him. 'You think someone of my clearance wouldn't hear about a murder literally next door, or see the police tape as my car drove past? I heard what happened. I know who Sullivan was, and about his connection to Monroe.'

She turned her attention back to Monroe now.

'I also know that you met with him last night in one of the most busy and well-known pubs in Whitechapel. I mean Jesus Christ, Alex, if you're going to meet with a confidential informant, meet them somewhere confidential! The clue's in the bloody word!'

'Wasn't my choice,' Monroe shrugged. 'Where was this secret meeting, then? I'm guessing it was Thames House? A place, as you just said, next door to where the body was found?'

'No, actually. It was across the Thames in MI6,' Wintergreen snapped. 'I can get a witness if you want. Someone who was also there, you might know, named Charles Baker.'

She went to argue more, but then sighed.

'Let's not fight, Alex,' she said. 'I know the next step here, I've been your side of the line. If it wasn't me helping these fake police, then you need to work out who else it could be.'

'If your people pick up anything, we'd appreciate a heads up,' Anjli spoke now. 'An officer's life is in the balance.'

'Thank you,' Monroe reluctantly added. 'And I appreciate you popping by for a wee visit to clear yourself from the list.'

Wintergreen raised an eyebrow, unsure if the Scot was mocking her or not.

Undeterred, Monroe continued.

'Before you leave, though, do you have any information about the Carmichael casino robbery? Anything you may have picked up at your, um, newer place of employment?'

If Wintergreen had expected this question, she did an amazing job of pretending she hadn't.

'Is that what this is all connected with?' she asked.

'It looks that way,' Monroe nodded.

'Well, I can tell you for a fact Arthur Snider was killed because of it.'

Now it was Monroe's turn to look surprised.

'We heard similar,' Anjli spoke now, looking at Monroe. 'That the dealer who was put away for it was a handy tool that just happened to be there at the time.'

'We monitored the drug dealer that was convicted of murdering him,' Wintergreen walked over to the desk now, placing her bag on it. 'A few years later, there was a believed terrorist in the prison they'd placed him in, and we thought he could be a good asset in getting information.'

'And was he?'

Wintergreen smiled, and Declan realised this was possibly the first time he'd ever seen her do that.

'No, he was useless,' she said. 'His name was Casey Smith, and they released him from prison about eight months ago. And here's the interesting part for you, as the moment he got out, he started telling people he *wasn't* the person who killed Arthur Snider. He claimed it was a reputation he'd kept in prison because it kept him safe.'

'Killing a copper gives you a bit of a reputation while behind bars,' Monroe nodded. 'Wise choice to make. Ballsy, though, if you're forced to act on it.'

'Lucky for Casey, he never needed to. But once he was out, it came out quickly that he had nothing to do with the attack. That while he was inside, he'd been approached by somebody who let him know, in no uncertain terms, that claiming the kill for a professional hit was not ... well, it *wasn't the done thing*. And all we know is that it was a woman who said it.'

'So Arthur Snider *was* hit?' Declan looked over at Monroe.

'Feels that way. I never looked into it,' Wintergreen replied. 'It was part of a life I'd walked away from, and to be brutally honest, I've been a little busy with affairs of the nation.'

'But you could have let us know, Emilia,' Monroe snapped. 'You could have let *me* know. Snider worked with us!'

'And you punched his teeth out, so don't get all noble about the corrupt bastard,' Wintergreen gave as good as she got in her response.

Monroe, realising he wouldn't win this, turned back to the others.

'Okay,' he started. 'We know he was having an affair before he died, and we know he was most likely hiding at least two million pounds' worth of Carmichael money somewhere, which isn't that bloody simple.'

'Money that was supposed to have gone to London crime lords,' Billy added, already pulling news reports up onto the screen. 'Money that they never got back.'

'Do you know who the hit was put on by?' Declan asked Wintergreen, who simply shrugged.

'I have my suspicions, but you probably have them as well,' she said noncommittally. 'I can tell you now, though, it wasn't any of the usual suspects. The hitman was found a few years later, up near York. He claimed to have killed Snider, but there was no proof, and we already had someone in prison for it. The case was done and moved on.'

'How come you know this and we don't?' Monroe was angering at Emilia Wintergreen's attitude.

'You never heard about it because the police didn't really care,' she sniffed in response. 'It wasn't an active case, and people didn't want to reopen it, in case they found ... well, in case they found things they didn't want to.'

'Actually, that fits with what Ford told us this afternoon,' Anjli flicked through her notes. 'She said she learned from Danny Martin there was a hit on Arthur Snider. And, in her own words, she said, "and, to make it more fun, the word on the street was it had been placed by one of the officers in the Mile End unit." We thought she was lying, but now, I'm not sure.'

'That makes it me, Emilia, Patrick, Chloe or Derek,' Monroe shook his head. 'I sure as hell didn't do it, I'm guessing Emilia here didn't, Derek didn't have the balls, and Patrick ...'

'Was having an affair with Chloe Mainsworth,' Declan said coldly. 'Maybe he did it to remove a rival?'

'Or maybe she did it?' Billy spoke from the monitors.

Everyone turned to look at Billy, and he shrugged.

'Cooper said Charlie Mainsworth wouldn't have gone off with Luke because he wasn't her type. She liked them older. What if that's *always* been the case?'

'You think Charlie Mainsworth was the one having the affair with Snider?' Monroe raised his eyebrows at this.

'We know she was off the rails, she was sixteen, maybe seventeen years old at the time, we know Snider was seen near the Mainsworth house but not with Chloe,' Billy was counting the points off on his fingers. 'What if the "CM" on the locket wasn't for Chloe Mainsworth, but instead for *Charlotte* Mainsworth?'

'That's just wrong,' Monroe muttered. 'But it is common, and Snider always had a weird relationship with the girl. She smoked, and he always lit her cigarettes on the roof. I assumed it was to get information on her mum.'

'And if Chloe found out Snider was seeing her daughter, even talking about leaving his wife for her, if she believed this was twisted, wrong, even for a man to pursue a girl half his age, she could have put a hit out on him,' Declan nodded. 'Maybe it was a beating, something to send him away, but then Casey stabbed him in the middle of it, and it escalated?'

'Leaving two million quid in limbo,' Monroe shook his head. 'Bloody marriage issues.'

'On the subject of marriages, Declan, I understand your ex-wife is getting married tomorrow,' Wintergreen said, changing the subject. 'Please send my congratulations. Is there anything else you need from me on this, Alex?'

'We're fine for the moment, but we know where you are, Emilia,' Monroe replied.

At this, however, Emilia Wintergreen smiled sadly.

'You've always known where I am, Alex. And I'm sorry that you felt this was a personal slight to you when I did what I did. But sometimes you have to follow your heart ... I'm glad you followed yours.'

With this last, heart-warming line spoken, Emilia Wintergreen took her bag and, with one simple nod to Declan, left the office.

Left alone once more, the team of the Last Chance Saloon looked at each other.

'Well, if the bairn here is correct, and Charlotte is the one who, twenty years ago was seeing Arthur Snider, then things make sense,' Monroe spoke eventually. 'Let's work through this. Arthur Snider is having an affair with Chloe Mainsworth's daughter. Chloe is angry at him.'

'You said they weren't seen as friends in the Unit, and that was probably a smokescreen for the affair, but now I'm wondering if this was genuine,' Declan said.

Monroe nodded.

'Aye, I reckon you're right, and this, if it's correct, is why they fell out. It wasn't because she was having an affair with two people. She was still having the affair with Patrick, but there was nobody else in the story.'

'Maybe Snider knew about Chloe's affair and threatened her to shut her up, or he'd run off with Charlotte and tell everyone about her and my dad?'

'Maybe Chloe was the one who told Snider's wife,' Anjli suggested. 'Maybe Mrs Snider and Chloe put the hit out together?'

Billy was typing on his keyboard, and an image, taken

from a Facebook page of an older woman, slim with white hair, appeared.

'This is the most recent shot I can find of Laura Snider,' he said. 'Arthur's widow. And, from the looks of it, I'd say she's a dead fit for the witness description too.'

'Luke said he didn't speak to his mother anymore,' Monroe frowned.

Declan, reaching into his pocket, pulled out his notebook.

'That's not quite true,' he said. 'When we spoke to Luke, he said *"when I went to university, I never looked back. I never returned, and never saw her socially again. It's all business with her, anyway."* He didn't say he didn't speak to her. Just that it was all business.'

'Christ ...' Monroe breathed. 'They're working together. They bloody hate each other and they're working together.'

'Working together to do what?' Anjli asked. 'Find the missing money? Why dig up the body after all this time? Why not do it last week, or last year, or even ten years ago?'

'Something happened that changed everything, and it happened recently,' Monroe stroked at his beard, deep in thought. 'Something that's forced her to work with her estranged son, to gain revenge on the woman who had an affair with her husband.'

Declan shuddered, shaking his head.

'We're still missing something,' he grumbled. 'There's still something just out of reach here.'

Monroe nodded.

'Billy? Check Luke Snider's credit cards for yesterday. I want to know if he was calling our bluff about being in a coffee shop. Anjli? I want you to write up what you found with DCI – sorry, *ex*-DCI Ford, and then get down to Luke Snider's apartment. Smash the door in if you need to, but I want you to go through everything there. Actually, belay that, I'll go with you, so I can smash the bloody door. Declan, speak to Doctor Marcos, and get the details of the undertaker that dealt with the Snider burial ...'

He stopped as a memory suddenly hit.

'Chloe Mainsworth didn't go to the funeral,' he whispered. 'The rest of us did. Even Patrick. But Chloe didn't. *Charlie* did.'

'Why would she go to Snider's funeral?'

'At the time we assumed she was there for her mum, but what if she was there because ...' Monroe shook his head. 'It was there all the time. Snider had an open casket funeral. I think it was Laura's way of proving to everyone he really was dead. Charlie was broken up, though. I remember her grabbing at the body, having to be pulled away ...'

He shook himself out of the memory.

'We need to find her first. Then we can work out the rest. Declan, speak to the undertaker. See if there's anything else they might recall. Billy, credit cards. I'll send Cooper and De'Geer over to pick Mrs Snider up. I think it's time we had a wee chat with her, too.'

14

HOME VISITS

AFTER ARTHUR SNIDER HAD DIED, HIS WIFE HAD NEVER LEFT the Clerkenwell house they owned, and for most of his life, Luke had been brought up there before moving away when he was eighteen. But still Laura Snider had stayed, mainly out of spite, Cooper assumed, as she walked up to the main door. Laura had been a victim of hate campaigns – her husband's criminal activities had been brought to light when he'd died while shaking down a drug dealer, and professional hit or not, her life hadn't been easy.

Ringing the doorbell, Cooper looked back at the squad car. De'Geer sat uncomfortably inside it, a sullen expression on his face, and glowering up at her. She'd pointed out that this could be a sensitive situation – although they had a good idea Laura Snider was involved somehow, possibly even with the death of Harry Sullivan – the fact that Winter-green had been a suspect showed that currently *anyone* with white hair was in the frame. With this in mind, and with her dead husband recently dug up, Cooper had suggested a woman's hand here. And besides, the sight of a seven-foot

Viking in a police uniform would probably scare her into next week.

And so it was Cooper, alone, who stood in the doorway when Laura Snider opened the door.

'Oh, God, what's he done?' were the first words she spoke.

'Can I come in?' Cooper asked politely. 'I'm PC Esme Cooper. I'm with the City of London police. I'm guessing you're Laura Snider?'

'You here to remind me, in case I've forgotten that my late husband's a crook?' Laura sniffed. 'It's what the coppers around here usually do.'

'No, but we are investigating a case connected to your late husband,' Cooper replied. 'Has your son spoken to you recently?'

'About what?' Laura stared suspiciously at Cooper.

'Your husband.'

'What about him? He's dead.'

Cooper realised with a slow dread there was a very strong chance here that Laura Snider didn't even know yet that her husband's body had been exhumed.

'I'm sorry, but I really think this needs to be something we should talk about inside,' she said, a little more forcefully this time. 'Can I?'

'Fine, whatever,' Laura Snider turned and walked off. 'Get what you need to do out of your system and then leave me alone.'

'Actually, I can't do that right now, as we may need you to come with us to the station,' Cooper said, entering the hall and closing the door as she continued through. 'I'm sorry to be the bearer of bad news, but we believe your son has dug his father's body up and placed it inside a City of London church.'

'And why the hell would he do that?' Laura asked, her back to Cooper.

'Actually, we were hoping he could tell us,' Cooper made light of the comment, her hackles rising. For someone who, a moment earlier, seemed oblivious to the news her husband had been exhumed, to the point Cooper had wondered if she even knew, Laura Snider hadn't seemed surprised about the news she'd just heard about it. 'Can I ask, have any other officers been here in the last couple of days?'

'No coppers come here anymore,' Laura walked into the kitchen now, turning the kettle on. Cooper paused at this, standing in the hallway. The house was narrow, a staircase rising to her left, and on her right were two doors into small, red-walled living spaces, the wall between them removed, making one hideously red room. Cooper wanted more than anything to nose around, but she needed to monitor the woman in front of her.

If nobody from the police had come by, then the only way she'd know about the body being exhumed before Cooper said anything was if her son told her. So, either this had happened, or she was colder than anyone had imagined.

'Is that Luke?' Cooper asked, noting a framed photo of a young blond boy in a school uniform.

'Year four,' Laura replied without looking back. Cooper wondered briefly how she could know what photo Cooper was looking at until she realised there were no other photos of Luke Snider on the wall.

'Don't recognise the uniform,' she said, peering at the school tie.

'It's a local one,' Laura said, still fussing around the sink but refusing to elaborate.

'Oh? Which one?'

'Look, are you here to discuss school admissions, or talk about my family's current situation?' Laura asked, and Cooper noted the woman's hands were now tightly clutching the sink's countertop, the knuckles white.

'Sorry, just making conversation,' Cooper apologised as she continued to look around.

'If I wanted conversation, I would call someone in for it,' Laura reached for the milk. 'Someone not connected to the bloody police.'

There was something automatic about the way she was working; as if she was going through the motions of looking like she was making a drink, while actually her mind was far away.

Something to the right of Cooper caught her eye; a small table in the hallway, probably once a place for a downstairs phone to go when such things were commonplace, was a couple of feet to her right and in front of her. There was a bowl, a glass one with keys in, but on the wood beside it, tucked out of the way as if to hide it in a hurry, possibly when a copper arrived on the front door, was a black leather wallet.

Cooper knew the style of wallet – she had one in her own pocket. It was where her warrant card was.

'There's something else,' Cooper said, her hand reaching slowly to the table, hoping Laura wouldn't turn and see this. 'There's a police officer missing. We think your son might be connected.'

'Why would you think that?' Laura spun to face Cooper now, and the officer froze, hand now resting on her hip.

'The officer abducted was Charlotte Mainsworth,' Cooper replied calmly, watching Laura Snider's face for any sign of emotion, or even empathy to the situation.

There wasn't any.

'If I'm supposed to feel sympathy for the crooked little bitch, you're sadly out of luck,' Laura turned back to the kettle, and Cooper quickly reached out for the wallet. 'I'm sure you know what happened between her family and mine.'

'Beyond my pay grade, ma'am,' Cooper grabbed and flipped the wallet open, and almost gasped as she saw the name on it.

PC CHARLOTTE MAINSWORTH

Cooper glanced up and saw Laura watching her from the kitchen.

'My husband was a nightmare,' she said calmly, ignoring the fact that PC Mainsworth's warrant card was now out in the open. 'He left me with a lot of problems. Why would I kill him? I'd rather he was in jail, because at least that way he could still pay alimony.'

'I never said you'd killed him,' Cooper went to reach for her Taser 7 device, but paused as Laura held up a vicious-looking kitchen knife.

'Yeah, but you probably thought it,' Laura growled. 'Just like they all thought he was the victim here. Nobody thinks of the widow when they don't see the scars.'

'Mrs Snider, I really think we've got off on the wrong foot here,' Cooper forced a smile. 'I'm guessing Luke was here, and he left the wallet, right?'

It was a "get out of jail" offer, to let Laura lower her guard for a moment, thinking Cooper was looking for Luke still, but it didn't work, probably because the moment she opened up the warrant card, she knew Laura was involved.

Who now squared off against Cooper, knife in her hand.

'She tried to break our family up,' she whispered. 'She took what was ours.'

'Your husband?'

'*I don't give a shite about Arthur!*' Laura Snider screamed, her eyes wide and desperate now. 'I mean the *money!*'

Cooper had a split second to weigh up the situation. By closing the door behind her, she'd blocked off an exit, and if she ran for it, she'd be stabbed before she could even pull the bloody thing open. She could run into the room beside her, but that was nothing more than a delay tactic.

Laura Snider had a foot in height on Esme Cooper, and a weapon in her hand. To go on the offensive was madness.

Cooper smiled.

She knew what De'Geer would do, though.

'*For Valhalla!*' she screamed as she charged.

'I'M SORRY WE CAN'T REALLY HELP YOU,' THE MAN FACING Declan sighed with what seemed to be genuine concern, but considering that he was a funeral director, and being sympathetic with clients was a large part of his day, Declan couldn't be sure how genuine this was.

'Look, you left the ticket on the suit, so you must have buried him,' he explained.   The man facing him, Julian Wrightman, was in what looked to be his seventies, and as this was *Wrightman and Sons, Funeral Directors,* Declan assumed he would have been involved in the funeral details.

He'd arrived ten minutes earlier, flashing his warrant card, and explaining how Arthur Snider's body had been found, in his funeral suit, in a church crypt. He hadn't mentioned the true location – a crypt was a far less concerning location than "cell" in his mind. Julian had at first misunderstood, and thought Declan was accusing him of something unspoken, but after one of his sons had appeared, and had learnt why Declan was really there, he'd gone off to hunt down the old records, pointing out they might take a while as "they only went digital in 2010."

Now, Declan was forced to stand still and smile at Julian as the older man wrung his hands together in worry.

'I hope they won't blame us,' he moaned. 'We don't bury the bodies, you see. The church has people who do that. We just get the bodies to the hole. If the hole isn't to specifications, there's no way you can—'

'Nobody's blaming you,' Declan forced yet another smile, secretly wishing for the son to hurry the hell up. 'It's purely information gathering.'

Julian nodded gratefully at this, and then his face brightened as his son returned, waving an old piece of carbon paper.

'Knew we had a copy somewhere,' the son said.

'Darryl knows where everything is,' Julian smiled.

The now-named Darryl passed it to Declan.

'It was a simple deal,' he explained. 'Usually the family will provide a suit for the demised to wear. Often they'll want certain things left with them. A favourite ring, or a watch. If they wore glasses in life, we'd pop them in the outside jacket pocket. Just in case.'

'Just in case of what?' Declan looked up from the sheet.

'I dunno,' Darryl shrugged. 'We just say it to give them peace of mind.'

He pointed at the note now.

'As you can see here, they buried him in a *Duffers of St George* suit, black, a *Van Heusen* white shirt – they were very trendy at the time – and black tie. We provided the tie as they didn't have one. They also gave us socks and shoes. We provided enhancements for the face—'

At Declan's gaze, he nodded.

'I mean makeup,' he explained. 'You know, to make the body less ... well, unsightly. They wanted an open casket, and it'd been a few days. Anyway, he wore his watch, he had a police warrant card in his left-inside jacket pocket, held in a black leather wallet, and on the other side he had a Zippo lighter, with some kind of playing card symbol on the front, in brass. We made sure to fill it up; never know if you need a light, you know, up there.'

He looked at the ceiling as he spoke, and Declan resisted the urge to correct him, and point out the only direction Arthur Snider went was *downwards*.

Placing the paper on the table, he pulled out his phone, snapping a shot of the sheet of carbon.

'Could you not do that,' Julian moaned again.

Declan paused, placing his phone away.

'What's the problem?' he asked. 'I assumed that would be easier than asking you to photocopy it?'

In response, Julian pointed back at the table.

'That's Mrs Merryweather,' he said simply.

Declan looked back at the table and realised it wasn't a table – it was in fact a mahogany wood coffin he'd used as a placeholder for the sheet.

'Oh, God, I'm so sorry,' he apologised, mortified, as he passed the sheet back to Darryl. 'Thank you so much for your help, I'll see myself out.'

Turning and hurrying out of the funeral directors, Declan stopped and took a deep breath as he reached the fresh air, forcing himself not to laugh at the absurdity of the situation.

Eventually, after gathering his composure, he looked around the street, but his mind was far away.

There hadn't been a watch on the skeleton, and no warrant card, and no lighter, either. Monroe had mentioned Snider never smoked when Luke had accused him of taking it.

Was the lighter important, somehow? And if so, how? He used to light Charlie Mainsworth's cigarettes with it – was that all it was?

Declan started towards his Audi, parked down the street. The one thing he was sure of, however, was that Luke was fixated on something here – maybe even to the point of digging up his father's corpse. And, if Declan found the now missing lighter and the warrant card, he might understand things a little more.

Declan shook his head. When this was all over, he'd pay his respects at his own father's grave in Hurley.

As long as some maniac didn't dig him up.

———

CHARLIE MAINSWORTH'S HEAD WAS SPINNING WHEN THE COLD water hit her face.

It was a bucket's worth, thrown from a distance of about four feet, and as she awoke spluttering, her vision focused on the image of not-a-real-PC Dixon.

This time, bucket beside him, he was sitting calmly on a chair, facing her, the wooden grille of the fake cell door behind him.

'You were very silly earlier,' he said. 'You could have fallen badly and hurt yourself.'

'Piss off.'

'My name's not really Dixon,' he said, observing her.

'No shit,' Mainsworth growled, shaking her wet hair to stop it from dripping down her nose.

'My name's actually Snider,' not-Dixon continued. 'Luke Snider.'

Mainsworth's blood turned to ice at the mention of the name.

'You're his son?'

Luke Snider nodded now.

'Yeah,' he said. 'I was a toddler when you were sixteen. That was how old you were when you tried to take Dad from us, right?'

Mainsworth shook her head.

'I never tried to take anyone from anyone,' she insisted. 'I was a kid then. I had issues. I wanted to hurt my mum, and shagging – I mean, *see*ing your dad did that. But he made the first move. I swear on my mum's life.'

'Your mum's dead,' Luke hissed. 'Just like my dad.'

Mainsworth struggled against her bonds and realised this time there were more zip ties securing her. A *lot* more. She looked around the room, the same one she'd been in before.

'Where's the old woman?' she asked. 'The one that sucker punched me?'

'You mean my mum?' Luke smiled. 'I had to send her home. The things she wanted to do to you ...'

He let the sentence trail off, the possibilities of what might happen far worse than if he'd actually named them.

'She blames you too,' he said. 'If you hadn't turned up, played with Dad's mind, made him think he was better than he really was, he wouldn't have been killed. Your mum wouldn't have arranged a hitman—'

'Bullshit,' Mainsworth snapped back. 'My mum didn't send a hitman after him. *Your* mum did, the mad bitch.'

'Actually, in a way, you're right,' Luke shrugged with his mouth. 'They had a long chat together about my dad. Then, they had a chat with Paul Carmichael's son. And then one day, boom! Gone.'

He leant closer on the chair.

'Even I don't know which one of them actually paid for the job, but I know they both arranged it. A Mainsworth and a Snider working together. Who would have thought it?'

'Maybe we could work together, then?' seeing a way out here, Mainsworth smiled weakly. 'You want something from me, and I want to give whatever it takes to get out of here.'

Snider thought about this for a moment.

'Where's the lighter, Charlie?' he asked.

Mainsworth frowned.

'What lighter—'

'*I said where's the bloody lighter!*' Luke burst upwards from his chair so fast that it clattered to the floor behind him. 'The one you stole from his dead body!'

Mainsworth's eyes filled with tears of fear.

'I-I don't remember—' she started, but she didn't continue any more, as Luke had pulled out the same shock weapon his mother had used on her and, using her wet skin as a base, he jabbed the sparking ends into her collarbone.

As she bucked and screamed in agony, Luke watched dispassionately, only stopping when she passed out.

Then, walking to the fallen chair, he placed it back up, carefully positioning the taser on the seat.

Taking a deep breath, he picked up a second bucket of ice-cold water and, with a sigh, he hurled it into Charlie Mainsworth's face for a second time. And, as she awoke spluttering again, he took the taser once more, calmly sitting back down to face his now weeping prisoner.

'Now, let's try that again, shall we?' he cooed. 'Where's the lighter? Did you give it to Alex Monroe, maybe? Is that why he allowed you to join his Unit when Mile End wanted you gone?'

But Charlie Mainsworth didn't answer him.

Because all Charlie Mainsworth could do was whimper and sob through the pain.

15

CHANGE THE FLINT

'Aye, it's a shitehole, all right.'

Monroe stared around Luke Snider's apartment. He'd found the door to the apartment block easy to enter through, but the door to the apartment itself was another issue. There was no unit supervisor who could pass them the keys, but before Anjli could pull out her personal lock pick set and start on the door, knowing that waiting for official channels to gain entry would take too long, he'd circumvented this by simply knocking on a neighbour's door and asking if they had a spare key.

The neighbour, of course, now stood on the walkway, watching as they opened the door, staring down at the pile of discarded letters on the floor.

It looked like Luke Snider hadn't been there for a while.

'And when did you last see him?' Monroe turned back to the neighbour, a bulky woman in her fifties named Janine. In response, she considered the question while having a good root around the inside of her left nostril with her pinkie finger.

'About two days ago, I reckon,' she said. 'Yeah. Tuesday or Wednesday.'

'And you're sure about that?' Monroe looked back at the letters on the hallway floor. There was no way that many had amassed in a matter of days.

'Are you calling me a liar?' Janine growled, finger now out of the nostril and being examined.

'Of course not,' Monroe gave a winning smile. 'I just found it odd that he would leave his mail so.'

'Everything about him was odd,' Janine muttered. 'If you're here to nick him, better for it. And he went even bloody worse after the drug dealer started looking for him.'

'Drug dealer?'

Janine shifted on her feet.

'Well, he looked like one. Skinny bastard, ginger hair. Grovelling little shit, he was. Early forties, maybe. Came here two, three times to speak to Luke, then never came back.'

'You know why he came here?' Anjli asked, noticing Monroe pull out his phone.

'Not really, these walls are thin but not for clarity. He kept saying he was sorry, and it wasn't his fault, if that helps.'

'Is this him?' Monroe turned the phone to face Janine, and she stared down at the image on the screen.

She then coughed up a phlegm of mucus and spat it over the railing.

'Yeah, that's the prick.'

Monroe wanted to ask if she'd seen the man after this, but after she finished speaking, Janine walked off, slamming her own apartment door behind her.

'Lovely neighbourhood,' Monroe muttered. 'Remind me to look into a place here.'

'Who was the image of?'

'Billy sent it. Casey Smith, the dealer who was supposed to have killed Snider.'

'Who was released a few months ago,' Anjli, checking the mail, her latex gloves already on, replied. 'And obviously filled with guilt.'

She looked back down at the letters.

'Well, if Luke Snider is coming in and out, he's ignoring these,' she said. 'Janine's right. I've got footprints, more like boot marks on them, as if he's walked over them and the mud from his shoes has wiped on the envelopes.'

'Bag a couple,' Monroe suggested. 'Maybe Rosanna can do something amazing with the mud traces.'

'I'm sure she'll be thrilled to do that,' Anjli grinned, pulling out a clear baggie from her jacket as Monroe continued into the apartment.

It was minimal. Painfully so. There were no pictures on the white-painted walls, the furniture was sparse and from IKEA, the television resting on a box by the wall. If he didn't know better, he'd believe Luke Snider had just moved in, rather than live here for a year or two.

'Could you live like this?' he asked, more rhetorically as he walked around the living room. A side table had remains of a Chinese takeaway on it. Checking the bag, he saw it'd been delivered three days earlier.

'This matches Janine's statement,' he waved the receipt. 'Last time I saw a place like this, it was Declan's new place, after he split from Liz.'

He reddened.

'Sorry,' he said. 'I didn't mean to mention—'

'No, it's fine,' Anjli smiled. 'The wedding's tomorrow afternoon and Declan's been a bit off. Eden Storm last night didn't help, either.'

She looked around.

'But you're right,' she said. 'This is what I call a transitional space. Someone in the process of moving in, or moving out.'

'Aye, but where to?' Monroe stroked his goatee. 'He's a mature student doing a Law degree. There should be bottles of beer everywhere and lewd posters on the wall.'

'That's your student days, not everyone else's,' Anjli shook her head as she walked into the bedroom. 'There's no bed.'

Monroe walked into the bedroom behind Anjli, to find her investigation skills still on point. There was no furniture in the bedroom, just a wall to wall wardrobe unit.

'Och, the bed's here, but it's hidden,' he smiled. 'It's a Murphy Bed. You pull it down.'

To emphasise the point, Monroe reached up and pulled at the top of the middle area, stepping back as he pulled a Murphy double bed down from the wall. The duvet and pillows, although dishevelled by the vertical storage, were still on the bed.

'And I never went to University,' he grinned, but as Monroe locked the bed down with a triumphant smile, he noticed Anjli wasn't paying attention.

Instead, she was staring at the now exposed wall.

A wall covered in photos and newspaper clippings.

'Oh Christ,' he muttered. 'It's worse than Declan's bloody crime wall.'

Anjli was clambering onto the bed now, pushing aside the pillows as she moved closer to the wall.

'It's clippings about his dad, about the team, there are pieces here on Mainsworth ... on Peter Carmichael and his daughter Jennifer ...'

She looked back in horror.

'He's got photos of you and Declan,' she said. 'Taken candidly.'

'Well, that's not creepy in any way,' Monroe mocked. 'I wonder where he's going with this?'

'There are photos of a lighter, too,' Anjli pointed. 'Look. It's Snider, showing it off.'

She pulled aside some photos, finding more notes attached to the wall.

'"Find the lighter,"' she read aloud. '"The clue is with the lighter." It's a treasure hunt.'

'Well, that explains the digging up,' Monroe nodded. 'If I recall, it was buried with him.'

'Then Luke has it,' Anjli clambered back off the bed. 'If he dug his dad up, then he'll have everything.'

'No, he asked if I had it, when he came to see us,' Monroe shook his head. 'If he had it, and it was important, there's no way he would have brought notice to it.'

'Fair point,' Anjli pulled aside some more papers, checking the additional sheets behind it.

'Who's the bairn?' Monroe pointed at a photo on the side of the makeshift crime board. It was a newspaper clipping of a young woman with dyed-black hair, the photo taken at night, as she was walking out of a bar.

'She's on the phone, so it's not that old,' Anjli peered closely. 'Girlfriend, perhaps? No name on the cutting, just the image.'

'She seems familiar,' Monroe frowned, pulling out his phone and taking a photo of the woman, sending it to Billy. 'Might be nothing, of course.'

'Of course,' Anjli looked around. The bed coming down had also revealed a pull out drawer, likely some kind of makeshift side table. Pulling it out, she whistled.

'Okay, he definitely dug up dad,' she said, picking up and showing Monroe an old black wallet. 'This is the warrant card for Arthur Snider. And the watch is old, analogue, and the battery's died.'

'Any sign of the lighter?'

'No, that's all he's left here,' Anjli bagged the two items. 'Doesn't mean he never found the lighter though. Although, you're probably right, and it wasn't there. Maybe one of the funeral people nicked it? I mean, who'd know?'

She moved back to the drawer, pulling out sheets of paper.

'It's possibly a ton of junk mail,' she said, flicking through it, 'but there are notes, handwritten ones, with Casey Smith's details on. And old file pages, on carbon, of his father's murder.'

'Where did he get those from?' Monroe grabbed one page, looking at it. 'I know Patrick made copies, but not of this. He must have someone in the police archives who could help him.'

'Copper Dropper,' Anjli mused. 'Maybe he found someone there who could assist? Or maybe he got them from Ford before she was removed?'

'Aye, maybe,' Monroe started looking through the wardrobe now, pushing the clothes aside and tapping the back as if he was looking for a way into Narnia. As he ruffled his hand along the top shelf, however, he stepped back as a shower of old video cassette cases landed on him.

'You okay, boss?' Anjli, alarmed by the sudden yelp by her boss, looked over.

'Aye, just surprised, that's all,' Monroe grumbled as he crouched down. 'So, what do we have here? *The Bill, The Sweeney, Juliet Bravo?* Aye, I remember that one. I had a crush on the other girl, though, the one that replaced this lassie in the later series ...'

His voice trailed off as he looked from the back of the videocassette to the wall of photos and cuttings.

'The lassie who found the body,' he breathed. 'The one with Lance whatshisname. Did you get her name?'

Anjli pulled out her notebook, flipping back through the pages.

'Here we go, Jean Darblay,' she said, looking up.

'"*Enjoy the second series of BBC One's Juliet Bravo, starring Stephanie Turner as Inspector Jean Darblay,*"' Monroe read from the back of the tape. 'Jean sodding Darblay. Another bloody TV copper.'

Furious, he hurled the video cassette across the room, where it smashed against the bare wall.

'*I am sick of these bloody games!*' he yelled. 'Get hold of Billy. See if he can send a uniform to Temple Church. I want to know if that woman up there is the same one the Verger was talking to when he found the body.'

'She did ask to see in the cell,' Anjli read. 'That's a little damning already.'

'We thought it was just Luke working alone,' Monroe muttered. 'And now it looks like there's a bloody ton of them!'

DE'GEER HEARD THE SCREAM, AND THE CRASH OF GLASS FROM within the house, and within a matter of seconds was sprinting up the path, shoulder-barging the door, the lock splintering apart as he continued through into Laura Snider's hallway.

'Esme!' he shouted, spinning in a slow circle as he called out. 'Where are you?'

'In the kitchen,' the slightly exerted, tired voice of PC Cooper echoed out from the end of the hall. 'I could do with some help.'

The tone didn't express any kind of urgency to the situation, but nevertheless De'Geer ran at full speed into the kitchen, where he found Cooper sitting on the back of Laura Snider, her hand holding Snider's wrist in a vicious lock, pulling it upwards.

'I dropped my handcuffs when she attacked me with a knife,' Cooper explained matter-of-factly. 'Could you be a dear and cuff her with yours before I give in to my base desires and tear this bitch's arm off?'

De'Geer leant in, pulling his cuffs out and obliging Cooper's request. Pulling Laura Snider to her feet, he sat her down on one of the kitchen chairs.

'I know we came here to bring her in, but I thought you were supposed to be the non-scary cop?' he joked.

Cooper, meanwhile, was looking around, her lips thinned.

'She didn't want to talk about the school,' she said. 'Why?'

'You know I wasn't here when you had this conversation,' De'Geer smiled. 'I can only give supportive grunts and nods to that.'

'What's the importance of the school?' Cooper asked the woman. 'It was twenty years ago. Was it when his father died? Was he there then?'

'Go to hell,' Laura spat. 'You bastards killed my husband, made him the man he was in the end.'

'From what I hear, you set him up for a hit with the help

of Chloe Mainsworth,' De'Geer replied. 'So I'm not sure we're the ones you should be blaming for Arthur Snider's death.'

'Can you hold her here?' Cooper looked upstairs. 'I just want to check something.'

De'Geer nodded, and, grabbing her Taser 7 out of her side pocket, Cooper started upstairs.

She didn't know why she wanted to check out the upper floor, just that she'd felt during the scuffle with Laura Snider that it was some kind of diversion, a way to throw the attention onto herself, rather than allow Cooper to examine more of the house.

'If there's anyone here, you should know I'm armed,' she exclaimed, forcing her voice not to crack. 'It's a conducted energy device, or a *CED*, a bloody painful electric shock gun that'll have you twitching and crying for your mother. Who we've just arrested, by the way.'

It was a shot in the dark, a thrown out line, but as she said this, Cooper heard movement from the back bedroom.

Someone was definitely in there.

Steadying her arm, she took a deep breath, moved into the room—

To find it empty, with the window open.

Running over, she stared out of the window into the house's back garden. A few feet beneath her was the roof of a small conservatory, and there, sprinting across the grass, most likely having used the roof to soften his jump was Luke Snider, glancing back and staring furiously up at her as he vaulted the back fence.

Cooper wanted to scream – there was no point calling De'Geer now, as by the time he got to the fence, Snider would be long gone. He grew up here; he knew every nook and cranny around the estate.

He grew up here.

Running herself now, Cooper hammered down the stairs, sprinting into the kitchen and facing Laura, currently glowering up at her.

'He's local, isn't he?' she smiled. 'His car would have been nearby, and I'd have seen it. A royal-blue Peugeot 5008 is a big car. Easy to pick out. He was upstairs—' she ignored De'Geer's shocked expression '—and he ran somewhere on foot. So, where did your son hang out when he wasn't here, Mrs Snider? Where is he running to?'

With Laura not replying, Cooper nodded to herself.

'Morten, you're the superior here, do you want to give the order?' she asked.

Stone-faced, De'Geer nodded, pulling out his phone and dialling.

'It's Sergeant De'Geer,' he said. 'I want uniforms and forensics at the Snider house. We're taking it apart.'

Disconnecting, he looked over at Cooper.

'Can you take her in alone?' he asked. 'I mean, I know you can, you're completely capable and all that, but would you mind going solo? I think I should start the search while I'm here, being Doctor Marcos's go-to guy and all that.'

Cooper nodded and, walking over to Laura, pulled her sharply to her feet, the older woman wincing as the handcuffs pulled her arms backwards.

'It'd be my pleasure,' she smiled, as she started dragging the protesting woman out of the building. 'Sorry about the door. Maybe you could get your son over to fix it ...'

16

OLD SCHOOL TIES

MONROE WALKED INTO THE BRIEFING ROOM LIKE A MAN possessed.

'Right, we're so close I can feel it,' he said, looking around the room. Apart from De'Geer and Doctor Marcos, currently examining the Snider house for any clues, everyone else was there: Cooper sat beside Billy, in his usual spot, laptop open, the DC strangely more alert as the evening began, Bullman was by the door, and Declan and Anjli sat to the side. 'Let's get on the same page here.'

He looked at Billy.

'Got the car?'

'No, Guv, which means it's still in the dead zone,' Billy explained. 'I'm now working out likely places he might hide a screaming, pissed-off copper.'

'That's if she's screaming,' Cooper muttered, but then reddened. 'I meant she could be gagged, not ... well, worse.'

Monroe nodded.

'We get you, lassie,' he said. 'Declan. Go.'

'Funeral director gave me a list of items on Snider when

he was buried, three of which weren't with him when we found the body. A watch, a warrant card and a lighter.'

'We have the warrant card and the watch,' Anjli spoke now. 'They were hidden in Luke Snider's apartment.'

'So this now seems to be revenge, and a treasure hunt,' Monroe added. 'Tell us about the revenge.'

'Snider wasn't shacking up with Chloe Mainsworth, he was seeing the daughter,' Bullman said from the door. 'At some point the mum found this out, and from what it looks like, told the wife. Then the two of them told Paul Carmichael, probably getting him to put out the contract.'

'Any news on the drug dealer?' Declan asked. 'The one who was sentenced?'

'Casey Smith,' Bullman replied. 'He moved up to Manchester after his release. My old stomping grounds, so I've put the word out for someone to see if he's still there—'

'He was in London recently.'

'True, but someone might know *why* he came to London. I want to know exactly what he knows.'

'And what he told Luke Snider when he repeatedly went to his apartment to apologise,' Monroe added, pacing as he thought. 'Alright, let's look at what we've got here. Arthur Snider passed away twenty years ago, killed while shaking down a drug dealer. At least that's the official story. He's buried, it's very sad, and we all move on.'

'Then his son, Luke, decides to start looking into his father's death a few months back,' Anjli read from her notes. 'In particular, the attack by Casey Smith, the drug dealer who allegedly stabbed and killed him.'

'He's doing this because Casey goes to Luke, tells him he's very sorry for what happened,' Monroe still paced as he spoke. 'But at the same time, he tells him that contrary to what the laddie's been told, he didn't give the killing blow. And, that he had heard in prison that it was a hit, placed on Arthur by Chloe Mainsworth.'

'Chloe Mainsworth, who Arthur was supposed to have been having an affair with,' Declan added.

'But Luke learns, as we have, that Chloe and Arthur weren't having the affair, it was actually Arthur and her daughter Charlotte,' Monroe nodded to Billy, who clicked a button and threw up an image of PC Charlie Mainsworth. 'Who at the time was sixteen years old, and madly in love with Snider.'

'If it was just Charlie running away with Snider, I don't think it would have been a hitman-level situation,' Declan said now. 'However, you add the two million pounds of hidden money from the Carmichael robbery ...'

'Four million taken away from Paul Carmichael's London casino – no matter what the name was on the frontage, we all knew it was a front for The Turk,' Monroe replied. 'And only two million recovered. Nobody could prove it was Arthur, although we all knew.'

He paused, staring off through the glass walls of the briefing room.

'The attack on him, the murder – it could have been money orientated. I know Paul Carmichael was still convinced it was him. And his son spent years after dad died saying it was. But at that time, nobody was sure whether or not Arthur had the money. Mainly because he wasn't living the lifestyle of someone who *had* two million pounds to burn.'

'Maybe he planned to leave his wife and son, move in with this teenage girlfriend, and start a new life somewhere?' Billy spoke up now.

'Well, he'd been looking into travelling abroad, maybe living in America,' Monroe nodded. 'We assumed it was because of the side-eyes he got from other officers, but none of the moving plans happened before he was stabbed.'

'So, what's the deal with the lighter?' It was Bullman who asked now. 'He didn't smoke, so why the attachment?'

'I'm not sure, but he always had one,' Monroe almost smiled at the memory. 'In the late nineties, everyone was using Zippo lighters. People did tricks with them, where they'd flick their fingers and the lid would click back, or they'd pull it quickly across the thigh, opening it up and spinning the flint in one motion.'

He frowned.

'Tried that once. Almost set fire to my jeans. Anyway, Arthur picked one up at some point. Had the "Dead Man's Hand", aces and eights on it. He wasn't a gambler, but maybe it struck a chord, I don't know. He never smoked, but he was always there to light someone's cigarette, usually attractive women, often Charlie when she came to visit her mum, though we never put two and two together. Maybe he enjoyed having smoke breaks when they stopped us lighting up in the office.'

He laughed.

'The problem was that half the time the lighter didn't bloody work.'

'When he was found in Temple Inn, the watch, warrant card, and lighter were gone,' Anjli said. 'The lighter is the only thing unspoken for.'

'And we know Luke doesn't have the lighter yet, because he asked for it when he was here,' Declan flicked through his notes. 'So, we know the lighter, for some reason, is important to Luke. But that said, if he was buried with it, and the body *was* dug up by Luke, he would have found it – unless the lighter was removed before the body was buried.'

'The funeral directors?'

'I don't think so, they seemed quite clueless to everything,' Declan shrugged. 'What do we know about the funeral?'

'It was a normal funeral. I was there,' Monroe rubbed at the back of his neck as he cast his memory back. 'Regardless of what we thought of him, we all turned up to it. He was a serving police officer, killed in the line of duty. To not attend would have sent major alarm bells, and the last thing we wanted to do was point out we had a corrupt cop in the Unit when ... well ...'

'When you had other people doing the same?' Billy asked.

Monroe glared at him, and Billy shrugged, still very much in his "zero shits given" mentality.

'Just saying.'

'You know, I thought you'd come out of this prissy sulking phase,' Monroe muttered. 'But aye, you're right. Only one missing though was Chloe. She wouldn't come, and we assumed it was because of the affair, with her knowing that his wife would be there.'

'Because at the time you thought she was the other woman.'

'Aye. But Charlotte turned up. She was distraught, and we just thought at the time that he'd been good to her while seeing her mum, and there'd been rumours she had a crush on him. But at one point she went to the body.'

'Body?' Cooper asked.

'It was an open casket funeral,' Monroe explained. 'We

got to say our goodbyes to him, and at one point she threw herself across his body, crying as she was pulled away.'

He looked back at Declan.

'There's every chance she could have taken the lighter at that point, maybe as a keepsake,' he said slowly, realising the importance of the statement. 'She was light with her fingers back then. She would have seen him with it, too. Hell, she was a smoker, and he lit her cigarettes with it. Maybe that was how the bloody thing started.'

'Maybe she gave it to him?' Bullman suggested. 'It's the kind of gift a teenager could get, cheap, and doesn't look suspicious.'

'So, if we go with that scenario, then Charlie Mainsworth has the lighter,' Anjli was mapping this out on her notepad as she spoke. 'The lighter that Luke is looking for. Why is Luke looking for it? Maybe the lighter gives clues to where the missing two million is.'

'That'd make sense,' Declan nodded. 'And it would explain why nobody's found the money in the two decades since his death. If its location is in a lighter that nobody knows about, a lighter everyone believes is buried, nobody *would* find the money.'

'Arthur Snider's murdered and buried,' Billy said now, his voice strangely dispassionate. 'Eighteen years later, more or less, Casey Smith comes out of prison, hunts down Luke to apologise for what happened, and in the conversation points out it was actually a hit. Maybe even says who did it. Now, with this new information, Luke digs into it, asks around, and decides Daddy has the location of the money on him, literally taken to the grave.'

'It's a bit Edgar Allan Poe,' Declan muttered.

'But not unfeasible,' Billy argued. 'So he's dug up his

father to find this, and he finds the lighter he knew was buried, the one people might even have talked about, isn't there anymore.'

'Which makes it a bigger thing, as it's not in its expected place,' Cooper added, joining in now. 'So now he needs to work out who has the lighter.'

'He thinks back to the people who were with his father,' Billy stood now, looking like he wanted to pace, before pausing, and sitting back down. 'And Derek Salmon's dead, Chloe Mainsworth is dead, Patrick Walsh is dead ...'

'And then there's me,' Monroe clicked his tongue against his teeth as he considered this. 'This is why he was aiming things at me at the start. And he took Charlie Mainsworth as leverage, but then maybe ...'

He hammered his fist against the table.

'Shite!' he swore. 'I told Harry Charlie was more connected than anyone thought. I didn't mean the lighter, but if Luke questioned Harry before killing him, now he could think *she's* got the lighter.'

He looked at Cooper.

'Has your "boyfriend" and my fiancée found anything at the house?'

'No, but there's something that's been niggling at me,' Cooper admitted, ignoring the comment from Monroe – she'd been taking things slowly with De'Geer, and they were in the early days of their relationship, but as much as she wanted to throw a line back, Monroe was still her superior. 'There was a picture of Luke in a primary school uniform. I asked about it, and Laura Snider got really angry. In fact, I almost think she attacked me because I was pressing her on it.'

'Luke Snider went to Hugh Myddelton Primary School,

down the road from where he lived,' Billy was reading his laptop now. 'But it's been around over a hundred years, I can't see how ...'

He stopped. And then he smiled.

'Well, damn,' he said, clicking on the keyboard as an image of a brick tunnel appeared on the screen. 'The Clerkenwell House of Detention, north-east of Clerkenwell Green, has a long and turbulent history stretching back to 1617, including its destruction by fire in the 1780 Gordon Riots. The prison was demolished in 1893 to make way for Hugh Myddelton School.'

He looked over at Monroe.

'It was a prison, and it says here that beneath the school's playground are significant remnants of the older buildings. Catacombs and tunnels. Perfect for hiding a screaming woman in, especially during half term, and close to where Luke's mum lives.'

'Get the address to De'Geer!' Monroe shouted, suddenly bursting into action. 'All hands, right now! Get any uniforms at the house over there immediately! Smash down whatever doors you have to!'

By the time Monroe had spoken the word "address", the entire room, knowing exactly what Monroe was thinking, was already on their feet, pushing past Bullman and grabbing their jackets.

'Anjli, Monroe, with me!' Declan shouted. 'Billy, go with Cooper!'

'Bollocks to that, they can come with me,' Bullman replied, already pulling on her coat. 'I'm not letting you get all the action here! Come on!'

De'Geer was the first person to arrive at the wall.

Billy had sent him a website URL, one of those "urban tunnellers" sites, where people broke into underground tunnels and caves, taking photos so the world could see these mysterious, secret places. When he clicked on it, he'd been shown countless pictures of the tunnels, taken during one of the many visits down there, as well as the doorway that gave entry to the catacombs. It was along a southern wall, with white brickwork around it, and the words "SCHOOL-KEEPER" carved into the stone above it.

When he found it, the door didn't stay in one piece – past the second hammer of De'Geer's boot against it.

Now through and continuing on at speed, De'Geer ran down the steps and along a small, external pathway, and was about to kick the second door, a narrow, blue one with a simple lock on it, when a voice stopped him.

'For God's sake, Morten, allow CSI something to check for prints,' Doctor Marcos wheezed as she caught up. 'You're slamming dirty boot prints everywhere.'

'Noted,' De'Geer said, instead slamming his shoulder into the doorframe, feeling the door's wood give under his mass and force. There was also an uncomfortable twinge there, probably because this was the second door in as many hours he'd used his shoulder to enter through.

As the door gave way, De'Geer had to pull himself back before he tumbled down another set of stairs.

'PC Mainsworth!' he shouted. 'Are you down here?'

'De'Geer?' a weak voice sounded out from down the tunnels, and De'Geer turned on his torch to see if he could spy the speaker. 'I'm down here! On the right, in a cell.'

Doctor Marcos was already running down the middle of

the room, a wide, arched brick ceiling above her, and with cells on either side, wooden cell bar doors blocking them.

'These are fake,' she said as she pulled the door blocking her from Charlie Mainsworth, now weeping openly on her chair. 'Probably from a film or something ... Jesus wept. What did they do to you?'

PC Charlotte Mainsworth sniffled as she held her head up. She was bruised, soaked and bloody, a distinct uriney smell emanating from her. And as Doctor Marcos pulled out a scalpel and started cutting away the bonds holding her, she wailed, a screaming banshee cry to the Gods.

'Was it Luke Snider?' De'Geer asked to a now silent nod.

'And his bitch mum,' Mainsworth replied. 'Wanted to punish me for ... for things I did ...'

'We know about your fling with Arthur Snider,' Doctor Marcos finished cutting the bonds around Mainsworth's feet. 'Can you stand? Can you walk?'

'I'll bloody well walk out of here,' Mainsworth sniffled, pushing past the two officers, and staggering towards the steps and the light of outside. Already, sirens could be heard as other officers were arriving.

'Was that a line from *Highlander*?' De'Geer asked, watching Mainsworth walk off.

'Not the time, Sergeant,' Doctor Marcos scolded. 'But in answer to your question, yes.'

17

QUESTION TIME

LAURA SNIDER SAT SULLENLY ACROSS THE TABLE FROM MONROE and Declan, glaring at them both, her arms folded. Beside her was an older gentleman, his thinning grey hair neatly parted over a white shirt and burgundy tie, a pair of gold, wire-framed glasses on the end of his nose.

'My client isn't happy with the way she was brought in,' he said, pushing them back up.

'Mister Willoughby,' Monroe smiled, leaning across the table to reach for the recorder. 'In all the years I've known you, your clients have *never* been happy about how they've been brought in. You really need a better opening gambit.'

'Or, you need to stop bringing them in the way you do,' Mister Willoughby retorted.

Monroe shrugged, nodded, and then clicked on the recorder.

'Laura Snider interview, DCI Monroe and DI Walsh attending, Laura Snider's solicitor, Hugh Willoughby present.'

He leant back.

'Was it your idea?' he asked, watching Laura. 'To kidnap her? Or was it your son's?'

'My client won't answer leading questions like that,' Willoughby shook his head.

'Your client attacked my officer with a kitchen knife,' Monroe growled. 'So she can bloody well answer any question I have.'

'I was defending myself,' Laura said. 'I've had you police trying to get rid of me for years. I was in fear for my life.'

'Oh, you were?' Monroe mocked a concerned expression. 'I'm so sorry for you.'

'Your attitude is being noted,' Willoughby sniffed.

'Aye, it'd better bloody be,' Monroe snapped back. 'Otherwise I'm wasting my time.'

Declan leant forward now.

'When were you made aware of the affair your husband was having with the teenage Charlotte Mainsworth?'

Laura had been expecting the question – it would have been impossible for her not to, but still she paused momentarily as she looked over at him.

'I was told,' she admitted. 'I had my suspicions, and I knew he'd had ... well, he'd had relationships with a couple of others, but I didn't know who it was until someone told me. They'd seen him at a home game at Upton Park, cuddling up like lovers when they looked like father and daughter.'

'You were told by Chloe Mainsworth, her mother.'

'I can't remember,' Laura shrugged. 'It was a long time back.'

'And I'm guessing you can't remember which of you got Paul Carmichael to book a hitman?' Monroe smiled winningly at her.

Laura Snider turned her attention to Monroe once more and silently glared at him.

'I don't know what you mean,' she said.

'Did you help dig up your husband, or was it all Luke's idea?' It was Declan who spoke again, diverting Laura away from Monroe.

'As I said—'

'Yeah, whatever,' Declan interrupted. 'But before we dance this again, let's point out the following. We know your son left your dead husband's body in Temple Inn church.'

Laura smiled.

'I don't know what you mean, but surely if he did do this, his father may have left wishes to do this, which isn't against the law, and from the sounds of things, all he's guilty of is littering.'

'You're seriously likening the body being left in a cell to littering?' Monroe was appalled.

Laura Snider, however, just shrugged.

'If the police-size shoe fits,' she smiled.

'Littering aside, we also know your son abducted PC Charlotte Mainsworth,' Declan continued on.

'That's just your word,' Laura smiled. 'Charlotte is probably on some kind of piss up.'

'That'd be impressive, considering she's at the hospital being checked over,' Monroe commented casually, before looking up, a look of surprise on his face. 'Oh, didn't we mention we'd found her?'

He looked at Declan.

'Did we mention how we pulled her out of Clerkenwell Tunnels?'

'I don't think we did,' Declan shook his head sadly. 'I also don't think we mentioned she accurately identified

Luke, and also told us how the suspect here also attacked her.'

Laura Snider didn't speak in response, her face darkening as she considered the words.

'Whoopsies,' Monroe smiled.

'She's a lying bitch,' Laura spat, her voice no more than a low growl. 'She always had it in for me. Of course she'd lie about being shocked.'

'Did I mention any shocking?' Monroe smiled. 'No, I don't think I *did* mention that she claimed you jabbed a shock stick into her.'

'I meant shocked as in surprised,' Laura replied without missing a beat.

'Of course you did,' Monroe nodded sympathetically. 'Never doubted it for a moment.'

'When did you learn about the lighter?' Declan changed tack.

'What lighter?' Laura asked innocently.

'Was it you who dealt with Wrightman and Sons for the funeral details?' Monroe asked, changing the subject again.

'What? Yes,' Laura frowned. 'Why?'

'Because you gave them a brass-coloured Zippo lighter to bury with the body,' Monroe said.

'*That's* the lighter,' Declan smiled. 'Or was the funeral director we spoke to a liar too? I lose count of all these dishonest people.'

Laura went to snap back some kind of response, but then calmed herself, sitting back on the chair, looking at Willoughby.

'Do your job,' she commanded.

'Gentlemen, my client is within her rights to be released,' he said, with a hint of smugness. 'You have nothing on her. A witness who not only had an affair with her husband before his death, who led him astray at West Ham matches, knowing that his wife, who abhorred football was unlikely to attend and witness this, but also is known to have fraternised with wrongdoers—'

'Fraternised with wrongdoers?' Monroe exploded. 'I'll give you bloody fraternised with wrongdoers!'

'Is he wrong?' Laura asked with a smile, and Declan realised with a shiver down his spine that unless they found something on her, there was every chance they'd eventually have to let her go.

She could easily claim a history of police harassment to explain why she attacked Cooper – in fact, Cooper's own report talked about how she screamed a Viking battle cry as she charged the armed woman.

Esme's spending too much time with De'Geer, he thought to himself.

But at the same time, it was circumstantial and easily dismissed. And she wasn't wrong about Charlie Mainsworth, either, as an excellent solicitor could prove bias easily.

Yes, Luke had been in her house, but they hadn't been seen together, and she could claim he'd broken in. Even the witnesses who saw her as a police officer outside the Morpeth Arms wouldn't be able to do anything bar identify.

Everything was on Doctor Marcos to find DNA or finger-prints to change this to a more solid accusation.

Which might never happen.

Declan went to speak, but his phone buzzed. He'd put it on silent for the interview, but this could be Billy with news or something from Anjli.

Nodding apologetically at Monroe, he opened up the message that had just arrived.

FROM: HENRY FARROW

Hey Declan

Declan frowned. It was an odd message, and way more casual than Farrow's usual messages to him.

Quickly, he typed back.

Henry?

Monroe was looking quizzical, and Declan went to place his phone away, but the buzz of a new message stopped him.

No.

Declan didn't know why this one word affected him so much, but he suddenly felt a moment of panic building as the phone buzzed a third time.

Henry can't talk right now. Have you been back home yet?

Declan showed the message to Monroe.

Reading it silently, Monroe nodded, and then leant closer to the recorder.

'Interview paused,' he said, turning it off.

'Oh no, is there a problem?' Laura asked with a smile. 'I do hope everything's okay.'

Declan went to reply, but then his screen lit up again.

It wasn't a message this time, but a simple photo. A picture, taken during the day, of an empty grave.

His father's grave.

'You *bastard!*' he screamed at the phone, dialling Henry

Farrow's number. He ignored Laura Snider, who looked with mock concern at her solicitor.

After three rings, it was answered.

'You have my mother,' the voice of Luke Snider echoed through the speaker as Declan turned it on. 'So I now have your father. I think that's fair.'

'Where's Henry Farrow?' Declan hissed in impotent fury. 'If you've hurt him—'

'He was easy to get to,' Luke replied. 'All I needed was his address. And Alex Monroe gave me that.'

'And how did I do that, then?' Monroe snapped.

'Have you checked your overcoat recently?' Luke's voice was arrogant, mocking, even. 'When I placed my jacket over yours, I took your keys from it. Eventually, after a lot of searching, I found your address book.'

There was a pause, as if Luke was letting the realisation set in before continuing.

'I apologise, I might have trashed your place while looking,' he said. 'But I then visited DCI Farrow and his lovely fiancée—'

Declan rose, the chair clattering across the floor. However, all he could hear through the phone's speaker was the sound of Luke laughing.

'That's what I love about you, Declan,' he said. 'I know that was you, rising. Always quick to action.'

'What do you want, Luke?' Monroe spoke now, forcing his voice to be calm. 'Let's see if we can sort something out here.'

'I want the lighter,' Luke said simply. 'By midnight tonight. Do this and I'll give you back your father's body, and your copper friend.'

Declan looked at Monroe for a moment.

'What about your mum?' he asked.

'What about her?' Luke replied. 'She's nothing to do with me. She's innocent. You have nothing on her, and you'll have to let her go, eventually.'

Declan turned to Laura Snider, to see her smiling triumphantly at him. And what was worse was he knew she and Luke were right. They had no concrete evidence, especially if Luke was taking this all on himself.

'You're destroying your life for a potential two million pay-out, laddie,' Monroe growled.

'No, Monroe, I'm doing it for two million, and revenge against the people who caused my Dad's death,' Luke explained down the line. ' So, what will it be?'

'Give me a moment,' Declan said, placing the call on mute and looking imploringly at Monroe, hoping he had an idea.

Luckily, it looked like the Scot did.

Rising from his chair, he beckoned for Declan to follow him across the room, away from the others.

'We need to tell him about Mainsworth,' he said in a whisper, one loud enough for Declan to hear easily. Declan was a little confused at this, as usually something like this would be discussed outside the room, and he was about to say this, when he noted Monroe flicker his eyes across the room to Laura Snider, leaning forward eagerly as she tried to hear their conversation, while trying to look as unconcerned as possible.

Declan nodded. He now understood where Monroe was going with this.

'If you do that, he'll kill Farrow for sure,' he improvised, unsure exactly if he was going the right direction, but confident if he was, then his boss could pull him back onto whatever track he was now travelling.

'Aye, but the moment the bastard learns she died of her injuries in St Thomas's Hospital, he'll know we don't have the lighter,' Monroe replied, and Declan noticed a slight twitch of interest in Laura. 'Get the uniforms to give up on searching her apartment and get everyone on to this. We won't get the lighter, so we hunt Snider.'

'But what about the lighter?' Declan was warming to this. 'We know it's in her apartment somewhere.'

'We don't have the time, laddie,' Monroe replied sadly. 'We'll tell him we have it, and we'll swap it tonight. And then we'll work out how to trap him at wherever he arranges to meet us. Everyone gets there early, say eleven, and we'll nail the bastard once and for all.'

Declan nodded, and the two of them walked back to the table, Declan noting with amusement that Laura Snider had leant back nonchalantly on the chair. As Monroe tapped out a message on his own phone, Declan leant over the table, turning his phone off mute.

'Okay,' he said. 'We want to stop any bloodshed.'

'Good man.'

'We may know where the lighter is, but it'll take us time to arrange the meeting, so where do you want to meet?'

'Bunhill Fields at midnight,' Luke replied. 'You bring the lighter, I'll bring DCI Farrow.'

'And my dad.'

'Oh, yeah. Definitely,' Luke was almost enjoying the teasing here. 'But if you screw me over ...'

'No, we're playing it by the book,' Monroe said, placing his phone away. 'We'll bring you the lighter. You just be there.'

'Only you two, no others,' Luke's voice said coldly.

'Of course,' Monroe nodded, while looking at Declan.

'We won't risk anything,' Declan finished. 'But if Farrow is hurt in any way, I'll throw the bloody thing into the Thames and you'll never see a penny.'

And, this done, Declan turned the phone off, leaning back in his chair, glaring at Laura Snider.

'Your boy's a real sweetheart,' he growled.

Laura smiled.

'You don't know the half of it,' she replied.

It was Willoughby who spoke next, looking at his client, nodding slightly.

'I think this interview is over,' he said, turning to Monroe. 'And it sounds like you have a busy evening ahead. I'll just be leaving?'

He rose, gathering his items. Monroe rose with him.

'I'll escort you out,' he said with a smile, glancing at Declan. 'Can you wait here with Mrs Snider until the uniforms take her back to a holding cell?'

Declan nodded, still tight-lipped, as Monroe waved a hand for Willoughby to pass him, following the solicitor out of the room.

There was an uncomfortable silence in the room now, as Laura smiled smugly at Declan.

'Your man there's going to call Luke, isn't he?' Declan asked matter-of-factly. 'He's going to tell him everything you overheard, and he's not going to be at the meeting, is he?'

Laura didn't reply, instead shrugging, the irritating smile still on her face.

'You won't be getting your phone call until tomorrow morning,' Declan said.

'That's fine, I don't need one,' Laura said, too relaxed for the conversation.

'Because Willoughby's going to be the one to tell Luke everything?'

Again, Laura replied with a smile.

And now, leaning closer, Declan joined her.

'She's not dead, you know,' he whispered. 'I know you both heard us. I know Luke will be told this. But she's not dead. She's made of sturdy stuff, that woman. And she's getting better.'

Laura's eyes widened as she realised the implications of what Declan was saying.

'I know what you're thinking,' Declan rose from his chair now. 'You're thinking, "if they lied about that, what else did they lie about?" And the answer to that is *everything*. We know your son won't be at Bunhill Fields. But now he knows we will be, though, he'll be going to Mainsworth's place and hunting for the lighter.'

He paused, letting this sink in.

'And we'll all be waiting,' he said with a smile. 'And the best part of this is you'll be the one that gives him to us, through Willoughby. Right now? He's probably proving to our tech guy he didn't record any of the meeting on his phone. And while he does this, a simple, one minute examination, we'll be cloning the details. And when he calls Luke? We'll know.'

'You bastard!' Laura rose from her own chair in anger, but paused herself. There was no way she was winning a fight here, especially with a man with vengeance in his eyes.

'Don't worry, we'll let him know we played him,' Declan turned and walked to the door, opening it and standing in the doorway to the interview room, looking back. 'In fact, we'll even let him know it was you that told Willoughby to call. Goodbye, Mrs Snider.'

The interview rooms were soundproofed, so people outside couldn't hear what was happening within – mainly so informants couldn't be exposed – and, as Declan stood in the corridor closing the door behind him, the furious screams of Laura Snider morphed into muffled noise.

Taking a deep breath, Declan centred himself. He should have felt smug, or even victorious; after all, they'd possibly set Luke up to be captured, but he felt empty. Violated, even. His father's grave had been brutalised, his ex-boss was in danger …

And now he had to call his ex-wife to tell her the news the day before her wedding.

Declan sighed as he started back to the office, pulling out his phone as he did so.

This was going to *suck*.

18

ZIPPO CIRCUS

'HAS HE CALLED YET?' MONROE WAS STARING AT THE SCREEN AS he spoke.

Billy, sitting at the monitor station, looked up at him in confusion.

'You're literally standing next to me,' he said. 'Why would you think I'd see it without you noticing?'

Monroe shrugged.

'Just curious.'

Declan was sitting at his desk, working through Luke Snider's social media profiles, checking images with young women – one of them had to be the mysterious Jean Darblay. And, from the description Lance had provided when re-contacted about this, Declan had a pretty narrowed-down criteria.

'We should be out there looking for Farrow,' he muttered, not for the first time that day.

'Aye, and we said that while looking for Mainsworth, and look where that got us,' Monroe replied. 'Look, we know Luke has him, and at some point, in the next couple of hours, he'll reckon the police have left Charlotte Mainsworth's house, pop inside and have a look for the lighter, thinking we're all the way across London. Meanwhile, this mysterious woman is the only other person we have in Luke's circle, apart from his mum upstairs, so we'll find her, and there we'll find Henry.'

'What if it's the other way around?' Cooper, currently sitting at Anjli's desk and writing out reports, asked as she turned to face the two men. 'What if this isn't Luke's game, and it's this Jean woman pulling the strings? What if she's the one who goes to look for the lighter, and Luke stays with Farrow?'

Monroe's face darkened.

'Let's hope that doesn't happen, eh, lassie,' he grumbled. 'Because currently we're rolling the dice and they're already in the air.'

He looked at Declan.

'Anything?'

'Not yet,' Declan replied gloomily. 'I could really do with a CCTV image or something, though.'

His phone rang; answering it, he prepared himself mentally for the conversation. He knew who this was going to be.

'DI Walsh,' he said.

'What the hell's going on?' the concerned voice of Liz Walsh came through his phone speaker. 'You left a message to call urgently, and Henry's not answering his phone.'

Quietly and succinctly, Declan explained the events of the last hour to his ex-wife. And, once he'd finished, he found himself listening to silence on the other end.

'Liz?' he asked.

'I should have guessed,' Liz's voice was harsh and unrelenting. 'If you're not getting Jess into danger, it's going to be Henry. So, let me guess, you're "doing everything you can" and all that?'

'We are,' Declan nodded, even though Liz wouldn't be able to see it. 'I'll bring Henry back safe and sound.'

'There's the man I divorced,' Liz spat down the phone. 'The one making promises he can't keep. Get my husband-to-be back here safe, Declan. Or never come here again.'

The phone line disconnected, and Declan leant back in his chair. Liz had every right to be furious with him; after the Red Reaper case, he'd almost lost his rights to see Jess after placing her, accidentally, in danger.

Now, he'd done the same thing again, as there was no way DCI Henry Farrow would have been taken if Declan hadn't been on the case.

'Bugger,' he muttered, shaking his head at Monroe's quizzical expression, really not wanting that conversation right now.

Luckily for him, the room was distracted by Cooper, who frowned at the screen. She'd been using HOLMES 2 to confirm some facts, and it had beeped at her.

'That can't be right,' she said in confusion. 'Charlie Mainsworth's ID has just buzzed into the building.'

'She's been cleared by the doctors,' Monroe shrugged. 'She's probably back to get her personals. You know, her house keys, coat ...'

As he started listing items, Cooper rose, her face paling.

'She doesn't smoke on duty,' she said.

'And?'

'She never has a cigarette in uniform, but she smokes,' Cooper was already across the room. 'Which means she never carries her lighter with her. Back in a minute, sir!'

Monroe watched Cooper leave the office, running down the stairs at speed.

'If we find that bloody lighter is in her locker downstairs, I'm retiring,' he muttered.

CHARLIE MAINSWORTH WAS BRUISED AND BATTERED, BUT SHE'D had worse in a cup game playing rugby.

Well, maybe not worse, but she'd definitely been through the wars almost as much as this time.

Opening her locker with a five-button combination, she stared at the purple padded puffer jacket and Radley bag that faced her with an expression of almost-dread, as the image of Luke Snider, taser in hand slammed into her mind like a freight train.

'*I said, where's the bloody lighter! The one you stole from his dead body!*'

Mainsworth looked around, making sure she was alone before reaching in to the locker, her hand entering the outside jacket, rummaging around before pulling out an item from within.

A brass Zippo lighter, with a card hand emblazoned on the front.

Arthur Snider's Zippo lighter—

No.

Her lighter.

She stared at it, turning the brass case around in her hand. She'd held this, used this, almost every day for the last two decades, and in her mind there was no way there was any kind of link to the money Arthur had taken.

Could there be?

Slowly, and with more care than she'd used on the lighter over the last twenty years, she examined the inside of the cap, angling it to the light, trying to see if there was anything written there—

'Are you okay, Charlie?'

Mainsworth almost yelped in fear as she spun to face PC Esme Cooper, watching her from the door.

'Yeah, sorry, I'm okay,' she forced herself to give a little smile in response. 'They said I was fine, just some burns and bruises, and I should go home. But my keys are in the bag in here.'

'That's not the only thing in there, is it?' Cooper replied, walking into the room now. 'You've got the lighter, haven't you?'

'What lighter?'

It was a knee-jerk response, a normal "fake it until you make it" comment, one of many Mainsworth had made over the years, lies to get her out of problems, or into worse ones.

This time, unfortunately, she was still tired and aching, and her mouth acted before her body, and her fingers could.

'That lighter,' Cooper said, pointing at the brass case in Mainsworth's hand. 'You've had it since the funeral, haven't you?'

'I had it before the funeral,' Mainsworth snapped back quickly. 'Arthur borrowed it, but never gave it back. He wanted something real of mine, something he could hold and look at and remember me, while everyone else didn't realise.'

'I get that,' Cooper nodded. 'He needed something normal, didn't he?'

'He loved me,' Mainsworth looked down at the lighter. 'I

gave him this. I'd had it a couple of years by then. And, when he died, I took it back.'

'Because it reminded you of him?'

'No, because it was mine, and they were about to stick it in the ground,' Mainsworth's eyes were glistening with tears of anger now. 'They never once asked me if I wanted it back. I was nothing but an inconvenience.'

She smiled; a bitter, dark, thin-lipped one.

'But who's the inconvenience now?' she growled. 'I've had the clue all this time and nobody knew. Even me.'

'You need to tell the Guv,' Cooper said.

'Monroe?' Mainsworth barked out a laugh. 'Give him this, and potentially two million quid? What's he done for me that's worth that?'

'He saved your life.'

Cooper's comment was calm and balanced and filled with the truth. And, as she listened to the words, Mainsworth's confrontational posture softened, and she slumped a little as she leant against the locker.

'You can't ask me to do that,' she whispered.

'Luke's taken another police officer,' Cooper continued. 'A DCI this time. And if he doesn't get that by midnight, then he dies. The Guv has an idea, but it's filled with what ifs and holes. If he knew they had the lighter, it might ... well, it might help.'

'Give Luke the money after all. No thanks.'

'You seriously think Snider would stay out of prison for long the moment he takes it?'

Mainsworth grumbled to herself as she looked at the lighter. On one hand, she wanted to keep it, purely for herself. She deserved the money. But, there was the fact that even though the mum was caught, Luke was still out there. And if giving this up meant they could end him ...

'Okay, let's go speak to the Scot,' she muttered. 'Before I change my mind.'

Cooper grinned, already turning to the door, but Mainsworth paused before following.

She hadn't only returned for the lighter; there were more personal reasons for being here. And to be brutally honest, they were worth way more than simple money, which gave her the slightest of unpleasant tastes in her mouth. But she didn't mind that. It'd be gone soon, replaced by a fresh taste.

Because revenge was always sweeter.

MONROE LOOKED UP AS COOPER RETURNED WITH Mainsworth.

'Charlotte,' he said, frowning. 'You should be home in bed.'

'Not while another copper is being held by that bastard,' Mainsworth replied. 'I'll go to bed later, sir.'

'Charlie has something to show you,' Cooper nodded at her to open her hand up. And, when Mainsworth did, the Zippo lighter was visible in the palm.

'I understand people have been looking for this,' she said.

At the revelation of the lighter, Monroe looked at Declan before returning to Mainsworth.

'You know what that is?' he asked.

'Yeah, a lighter,' Mainsworth replied. 'And I'm not being flippant, I promise. It's just that all my life this has lighted my fags, and I've never seen it as anything else.'

'Then why take it from the body?' Declan rose now, walking over to her, holding his hand out. 'May I?'

Mainsworth passed the lighter across.

'I got this in a small shop in Chinatown,' she said. 'I was what, fifteen maybe? I could have been younger. I don't remember. I started smoking at fourteen, so it might have been then. Back then, loads of shops sold these, in little spinning glass cases. I was in a tourist shop with a mate and I saw it, and instantly fell in love with it.'

'And they sold it to you?' Billy asked. 'A fourteen-year-old?'

'They would have, they had no care about who bought their stuff back then,' Mainsworth looked embarrassed as she spoke. 'But I didn't buy it, I took the five-finger discount. I wasn't in with a good crowd back then, you see.'

'So you nicked the lighter,' Declan was examining it. 'How did Arthur get it?'

'I lent it to him,' Mainsworth was watching the lighter in Declan's hands like a hawk. 'I used it all the time, and then one day he was sharing a fag with me—'

'I didn't think he smoked?'

'He didn't, only with me,' Mainsworth's lips turned in a slight, nostalgic smile. 'He wanted something of mine, something he could have which wouldn't raise suspicions. I was sixteen, and I'd been around the block by then. I knew he was too old for me, and I knew he was married. But I didn't care. He was a man, while all I'd been with before that were boys.'

'You knew it wouldn't last?'

Mainsworth shrugged.

'At the start I did it to piss off Mum, but after a while, well, I hoped it would,' she said. 'I knew he always said he wanted to leave his wife, that it was a mistake to marry. But then over the years I've seen a lot of men say similar to get their way.'

She stared at the lighter some more.

'I kept asking for the lighter back, but he kept convincing me to let him keep it a little longer,' she explained. 'Almost like he was scared if I got it back, I wouldn't need to see him anymore. But I was completely in for the ride, you know? I loved him.'

'You were a child,' Monroe chided.

'I was old enough to know the truth of my feelings!' Mainsworth snapped, spinning to face him. 'At sixteen I could marry! Have a child! Join the army! Leave school! If I was classed as an adult for all those, then let me have this, yeah?'

Monroe nodded, backing down.

'So what happened?' Declan interrupted.

'I don't know,' Mainsworth shrugged. 'I was hanging out with the wrong people still and trying to get away, so me and Arthur could have a life. Arthur bought me a pendant, but his wife found out, and told my mum. Christ, she really kicked off. I thought she was gonna go out and kill him.'

Her face darkened.

'I knew this kid, Casey,' she continued. 'Little prick, really. Drug dealer on the Caledonian Road. He'd been trying to screw me for a while, and I'd led him on a little. I'm not proud of that, but he'd give me sweeties for free, and I like a deal. Anyway, one day he pressures me, tells me if I don't sleep with him, he'll grass me up to the police. I mentioned this to Arthur – I was worried, thought I'd get into trouble, and it'd land on him too – and he went to have a word.'

'Wait,' Monroe held a hand up. 'So Arthur Snider *wasn't* shaking Casey Smith down?'

'Christ no,' Mainsworth shook her head. 'The bloody fool was being all gallant on my behalf. And it got him killed.'

'Because of your mum and Laura Snider.'

'They didn't put the hit out on him,' Mainsworth shook her head. 'There was no way they knew the sort of people that could do that. But I know Mum spoke to Paul Carmichael about it, saying she believed Arthur stole her dad's money.'

'You ever speak to Paul about it?'

'Hell no. I kept away from the Carmichaels. All three of them were mental.'

'Three?'

'Paul, his son Pete, and his granddaughter Jennifer,' Mainsworth explained. 'She lives somewhere north of Crewe, but she's been around recently. I hear things.'

'You think Paul Carmichael set up the hit?'

'I know it,' Mainsworth nodded bitterly. 'Arthur went to fight for my honour, and they stabbed him to death in an alley.'

'So why take the lighter?' Billy asked.

'It was mine,' Mainsworth looked back at him. 'I wanted it back. And I wanted something to remember him by. I never got the locket.'

'Did you know the lighter was a clue to any missing money?'

'No,' Mainsworth shook her head. 'I never even believed he had the money. He never acted like he was rich, never had money to flash around. I liked him because of that. He was more grounded. Anyway, Mum refused to go to the funeral, and I'd been banned from going, but I snuck out and went.'

'I remember,' Monroe smiled. 'They had to pull you from the body.'

'That's because I was taking the lighter,' Mainsworth smiled faintly in response. 'I knew his bitch of a wife would never let me take it back. I'd called the funeral directors up, pretending to be someone from the family, confirming the itinerary of things being buried with him, and the locations of each one. As I grabbed the lighter, I knew exactly which pocket it was in. And, as it was being buried, I knew nobody would ever know. Perfect crime and all that. And nobody was hurt in the process.'

The smile faded as she looked away.

'Apart from me,' she finished.

There was a long moment of silence after this.

'I'm sorry for your loss,' Monroe said eventually. 'But all this, you could have told me it at any point. You didn't have to go through it alone.'

'You all hated him, so don't go playing the white knight now,' Mainsworth spat back. 'I knew all you gave a shit about was the money.'

'That's not true!' Monroe protested. 'Aye, it was a conundrum, but more of a "I wonder who hid it" kind of thing.'

'There's nothing here,' Declan had pulled the lighter's middle part out, and was examining the inside of the case. 'This needs someone with better eyes than me.'

'Doctor Marcos has microscopes and all that,' Billy suggested. 'Maybe it's in UV ink or something?'

Declan looked at Mainsworth.

'You mind if we send it downstairs?' he asked.

'Why ask me?' Mainsworth frowned. 'It's in your hands now.'

'Yeah, but it's your property, and always has been,' Declan replied. 'As far as I'm concerned, if Arthur hid the location in your lighter, the chances were he was always going to give it back to you. He wanted you to have the money if he wasn't there.'

Mainsworth was surprised at the gesture.

'What, you mean I can keep the money too?' she smiled.

'Aye, let's not get too carried away,' Monroe replied.

'Hold on!' Billy waved his hands as, on the screen, a line of code flashed up. 'Willoughby's calling a number.'

'Willoughby?' Mainsworth asked.

'Laura Snider's solicitor,' Monroe explained, watching the screen. 'We may have led him down a path that leads to him calling Luke Snider's number on behalf of Luke's mother. We didn't have the lighter, and we were looking to drag things out until we did.'

'Could be any number, though,' Declan suggested. 'Can we hear the conversation?'

'Not legally,' Billy was already typing on the keyboard. 'We're sailing really close to the wind here as it is. But we *can* hear Willoughby's side.'

'How?'

'Using AI,' Billy was opening up another window. 'A chat transcription program that takes the sounds and frequencies and reconstitutes them into words. That way, we're not listening to the conversation, we're reading something generated by frequency modulations. And that's not something we can use in a court of law, but ...'

There was a beep – Mainsworth's phone was ringing.

'Sorry, it's my cousin,' she said, checking it. 'I'll take it over here.'

As Mainsworth answered the phone, walking off, Declan looked back at the screen.

'As someone's life is on the line, I'll take whatever we can get,' Monroe smiled. 'We can argue the semantics after DCI Farrow has been saved.'

On the screen, the text appeared.

Speaker 1
I've been told to contact you on the half odd your mother

'What the hell is "on the half odd?"' Declan asked.

'It's working out words as it goes through,' Billy replied, watching the screen. 'I think it's probably misheard "on behalf of" or something similar."

'As long as it doesn't confuse the address and everything.'

The peace e you had is dead

'That's PC,' Billy translated. 'Likely talking about Charlotte Mainsworth.'

'I'm not dead, though,' Mainsworth frowned, finishing her call.

'Aye, we might have embellished a little,' Monroe kept his eyes on the screen.

She was in Sent Thomas Hospital, so check there first. They're removing everyone from mains worths flat right now so once you have confirmation on death go there

'Aye, we get the message,' Monroe smiled as Billy went to translate again.

'The call ended after that,' Billy leant back in the chair.

'Well, the lure has been cast,' Monroe mused. 'Get Anjli on the line and let her know she's likely to have company.'

'They could call,' Declan suggested, but Monroe shook his head.

'They'll want a personal touch,' he said. 'I'm sure of it.'

'So your entire plan is to convince him I'm dead, and then go to my apartment while you wait for him?' Mainsworth was mildly appalled by this. 'That's a terrible plan.'

'Aye, but it'll do until we decipher the lighter,' Monroe smiled. 'And as for terrible plans, welcome to the Last Chance Saloon, lassie. They're what we do best.'

19

IN MEMORIAM

'Excuse me, can you help?'

The woman in the Barbour coat stood on the other side of the receptionist's desk, smiling in that "I'm not threatening, I just want to be your friend" way that door-to-door sales agents were known for.

'What do you need?' The receptionist looked up from her phone, obviously annoyed at being distracted.

'A friend of mine was brought in here to St Thomas,' the woman explained. 'My name is Jean Darblay. I was hoping you could tell me how she is?'

'Are you family?' the receptionist sat back, phone still in hand, watching Jean suspiciously. 'You could be press or something.'

'Why would I be press?'

'You're telling me your "friend" isn't the one that came in with a whole load of nervous looking police?'

The receptionist returned to her phone, tapping out a message, ignoring the woman. Jean swallowed, forcing the smile to stay on her face.

'I am asking about PC Charlie Mainsworth, but because I'm a fellow officer,' she said, quickly flipping a warrant card. 'See?'

The flip was only a second in length, and her thumb obscured the image of the white-haired woman in the image, but it was enough to catch the receptionist's attention again.

'I don't want to see her, or even know where she is,' Jean continued. 'I heard on the radio she passed, and I wanted to confirm before I went to see her parents.'

At this, the receptionist sighed, placing the phone on the table.

'This is the copper brought in from the caves, right?'

'Tunnels, yes.'

The receptionist tapped on the keys, checking the screen. Jean couldn't see what was on it, but the receptionist's expression as she read the notes showed everything she needed to see.

'I'm sorry,' the receptionist said, reading the screen. 'But it looks like your friend died of internal injuries on arrival. I can get a doctor down to explain more—'

She looked up to see that Jean Darblay had already walked off, heading at speed for the main doors.

Rising from her chair, the receptionist pulled on her suit jacket, dialling a number as she followed her out of the hospital entrance.

'It's me,' Anjli said into the phone when it was answered. 'Declan was right. The woman came to check if Mainsworth was dead. I took a photo, sent it to you to do your computer wizardry with. And now I'm following. I'll keep you updated.'

And, as the call finished, Anjli Kapoor slowed down to keep a distance between her and the woman she was following as they walked down into the car park.

BILLY WAS ALREADY MOVING THROUGH A SELECTION OF IMAGES as Declan looked up from his desk. It had been fifteen minutes since the call from Willoughby had been made, and the room had been tense ever since.

'Anjli has the woman in sight, and sent me some photos,' Billy said, showing the images Anjli had snapped and sent while holding the phone against her. They weren't the best of images, but they showed a woman with dyed-black, asymmetrical hair and a Barbour coat on the other side of the counter. 'It'll take me a while to work out who it is, but I think we have a good chance here.'

There was another beep, and Billy opened up another email.

'Oh,' he said. 'Now that's interesting.'

'What?' Declan asked from his chair. Billy opened a CCTV image of a coffee shop.

'This is CCTV from the counter the moment "Luke Snider" bought a coffee with his credit card, contactless,' he said, pointing at the black-haired woman at the counter. 'Same woman.'

Declan rose from his chair and stretched. It was getting late into the evening now, and the clock was ticking. Cooper and Mainsworth had gone down to see Doctor Marcos, and Monroe had returned to his office.

'Need anything?' he asked.

'I'm good,' Billy replied, eyes glued to the screen. 'We'll work it out before the deadline, Guv. We always do.'

Declan tried to smile, but found he couldn't.

'Let's hope so,' he said, before turning to the main doors. 'I'm going to check downstairs.'

Before Billy could reply, likely to say there was no point, and that Doctor Marcos would let them know the moment something happened, Declan was already out of the office and down the stairs.

He needed to get out, to do something; the waiting around was killing him. He knew Farrow being taken was directly because of him, and he couldn't help but wonder whether, if he'd simply stayed away, if he hadn't put the two clues together and gone after Luke in the process, Henry Farrow would be safe right now.

But that wasn't how policing worked.

His phone went again; he checked the number. It started with 01628, which was Maidenhead, and also Hurley's dialling code.

'DI Walsh?' he answered.

'Is that, um, Declan?' An elderly voice spoke. 'It's Devlin Whimsall, I'm—'

'I know who you are, Devlin,' Declan stopped on the stairs. 'My dad spoke about you often. I'm guessing this is about his grave?'

There was a long, awkward pause at the other end of the line.

'You've heard already?'

'It's a small village,' Declan forced himself to stay light. 'I'm already looking into it. What can you tell me about the people who did this?'

'Marjorie's distraught,' Devlin continued. 'They had paperwork. Two men, with a digger, and a woman leading the way. Explained there was an issue with the internment, and they needed to move both bodies to a new location. They had sheets of signed forms and numbered lists, they bamboozled her with papers. By the time she'd got hold of the council to see what was going on, they'd taken up your father's coffin and, well, they made off with it.'

'Did they touch Mum's?'

'No,' Devlin was apologetic as he spoke. 'They just dug up Patrick and left before we could stop them.'

'Don't worry,' Declan reassured. 'We're on this already, and we'll get him back. I'm guessing we can rebury the moment we do?'

'We'll have to consecrate the ground again, I think, but yes.'

Declan drew in a deep breath, trying to fight the urge to scream.

'The men and the woman,' he said. 'Did you get descriptions?'

'Oh yes, the men were contracted,' Devlin replied. 'We got them through the number on the digger. It seems they were as confused as we were, the woman hired them, showed them paperwork and ID from the council, paid them handsomely and when they got the coffin out she had it placed in a van and drove off.'

'And the woman?'

'A Jean—'

'Darblay.' Declan finished.

'Yes!' Devlin seemed almost happy at the name. 'You know her? Oh, good. I hope this means you can fix whatever confusion this was.'

'Oh, I'll be doing more than that,' Declan replied. 'I'll speak to you soon.'

Disconnecting the call, he carried on down the stairs, walking without knocking into the forensic offices of Doctor Rosanna Marcos.

'Got anything?' he asked.

Doctor Marcos was examining the case of the lighter with a UV light, Mainsworth and Cooper beside her.

'I think we have numbers,' she said. 'Tiny, etched with some kind of UV paint. The inside of the lighter is lopsided, there's more metal on the left side than the right. It feels like a plate, but I don't want to use anything to loosen the glue until I can confirm it won't remove the numbers.'

She showed him the lighter. Where she was looking at was the cavity where the cotton wick and the felt, the material the lighter fluid soaked to keep the lighter going, was packed in. Although right now, the cotton was removed.

'Wouldn't the lighter fluid have loosened the glue over the years?'

Doctor Marcos shrugged.

'Depends on what was used,' she said. 'I'm checking everything else first, and then I'll look into the removal.'

'Can't you check that first?' Declan frowned. 'It's just that we're on—'

'If you tell me we're on a deadline, I swear to God I'm going to stab you with a scalpel,' Doctor Marcos snapped back in reply. 'I know Henry Farrow as well as you do, Declan. If you think for one moment I'm not trying to save him ...'

'Sorry,' Declan held his hands up. 'Of course you are.'

'This room is way too crowded,' Doctor Marcos decided. 'All of you out.'

'But it's my lighter—' started Mainsworth.

'I said *everyone out!*' Doctor Marcos shouted.

Declan quickly stepped backwards, out of the office and back into the corridor outside, as Cooper and Mainsworth followed, the door slamming shut behind them.

'I just ...' Declan trailed off.

'I know, Guv,' Cooper said as she started upstairs. 'Come on, let's go help DC Fitzwarren, eh?'

Declan looked at Mainsworth.

'Well done, you idiot,' she growled as she stormed upstairs after Cooper.

Usually Declan would have pulled her up on this, but right now, she was right.

Sighing, he followed her back into the office.

Anjli had been lucky as she followed Jean Darblay out of the door, as not only had the woman not noticed her, but she'd also walked into the car park, heading for a royal-blue Peugeot 5008 at the end of the underground car park.

Anjli had noted the number plate, realising pretty quickly that the plates had been changed from the one they'd followed on ANPR cameras from the previous night. She'd tapped in the new plate number, sending it to Billy as Jean, now in the car, drove off out of the car park, not noticing the woman by the pillar.

A moment later a motorbike pulled up. It was a Triumph, non-police issue, and the large rider wore a black motorcycle jacket and helmet.

'Here,' De'Geer said, passing Anjli her own helmet as she climbed on behind him. 'Let's see where she goes.'

And, with the helmet on, and her hands holding onto the bar at the back of the seat, Anjli and De'Geer rode off after the Peugeot and Jean Darblay.

'Anjli got us a photo,' Billy said to the new arrivals, as Declan followed the others into the main office. 'I'm putting it through an image search right now. It also matches CCTV footage of the woman using Luke's card in a coffee shop, so they definitely know each other.'

Cooper looked at the woman on the screen.

'This is Jean Darblay?' she asked. 'Or at least the woman who claims that name?'

'According to Anjli,' Billy nodded. 'Asked about Mainsworth, hinted she knew she'd died as well, said she was police, but hid the image on the card ...'

Declan leant closer, examining the image.

'Description matches what the woman at the church said,' he said, but something to his left stopped him. Straightening, he glanced across at Mainsworth.

Who was now trembling.

'Charlie?' he asked softly, realising this could be a triggering moment. 'Are you okay? Was she one of the people who hurt you?'

'No,' Mainsworth shook her head. 'It was Luke and his mum. But I know her.'

Monroe, standing beside Billy, now turned around.

'You do?' he raised his eyebrows as he spoke. 'Well, don't leave us both in the dark, lassie! Who is it?'

'It's Jennifer Carmichael,' Mainsworth almost whispered. 'The daughter of Pete Carmichael. I told you, she's been around here recently. I think she's been looking for the money.'

Monroe looked at Billy, who was already typing into the system.

'No arrests or convictions, nothing that raises her profile,' he said as he scrolled down a file. 'Official channels only seem to have a ton of information requests about her grandfather's death. She started about a year back.'

'I have something,' Billy tapped on the screen at a line of text and a scan of a signature. 'She visited Casey Smith a few months before he was released.'

Declan opened his notebook, flicking through the pages.

'Wintergreen mentioned something,' he said, flipping back through them, back to the visit earlier. 'She said while he was inside, he'd been approached by somebody who let him know that claiming the kill for a professional hit *wasn't the done thing*. And she said it was a woman.'

'Jennifer Carmichael primed Casey,' Monroe mused. 'She saw Casey, she would have known the truth if her granddad did the hit – she would have gone to warn him. And then a month or two later, after he was released, he went to visit Arthur Snider.'

'Maybe he was the go-to for them at the start?' Declan suggested, closing the notebook. 'Wait, could this all be because of her, and not Snider?'

'She bought a glazed donut,' Billy muttered, typing rapidly on the keyboard. 'I'm looking at the coffee shop sales receipts. She bought a coffee with Luke's card, probably to give an alibi, and then she bought a treat for herself on her Apple Watch.'

'So?' Monroe frowned. 'Why do we care about her eating habits?'

'Because I can check the same number for other sales,' Billy was already going through the HOLMES 2 network. 'Bullman said Casey went to Manchester, right?'

'Aye.'

'I can see three purchases made in Manchester pubs and coffee shops over the last six months. She was definitely there.'

'That doesn't mean she was with Casey,' Declan said as he stared up at the image of Jennifer Carmichael.

'She was the one who took my father's coffin,' he growled.

'I'll speak with Laura Snider again,' Monroe suggested. 'Maybe we can—'

Declan glanced at the clock on the wall – it was now just past ten pm.

'We've got less than two hours,' he said. 'There has to be something we can do with the lighter, something that brings everything together.'

His phone buzzed; he didn't recognise the number on the screen.

'Hello?' he asked as he answered. 'This is DI Walsh. Who's this?'

'Um, is that Declan Walsh?' a male voice spoke. 'This is Ben Marrs. I'm the duty manager for security at Phoenix Wharf in Wapping.'

Declan held a hand over his phone, nodding to gain Billy's attention.

'Phoenix Wharf, Wapping,' he said, before returning to the call. 'And what can I do for you?'

'Um, I was told to call you,' Ben's voice was a little confused. 'We have ... well, we've got a bit of an incident. What looks to be a body?'

'In Phoenix Wharf?'

'No, to the side,' Ben replied. 'We look after a couple of plots on Wapping High Street, you see. And a few minutes back, a young man came to us, white as a sheet. Said he saw a body hanging on Executioner's Dock.'

Declan froze.

'What?'

'Oh, it's what the place used to be called, it's the steps

down from King Henry's Stairs,' Ben continued. 'Said he'd gone to look at the Thames, which was bloody weird, because it's the middle of the night, probably wanted to get stoned at high tide or something, saw the body and ran. We went down there with a torch, and there's something down there, but we ain't touching it. And the note to call you was on the gate as you entered.'

Billy had pulled up a map now and was reading a page about the area.

'Execution Dock was a wooden embankment beside the River Thames at Wapping that was used for over four hundred years to execute pirates, smugglers and mutineers who had been sentenced to death by Admiralty courts,' he said. 'The "dock" comprised a scaffold for hanging. Its last executions were in 1830.'

'Looks like someone restarted the trend,' Monroe growled.

'Captain Kidd, who had been convicted of piracy and murder, was hanged there in 1701,' Billy continued. 'But there's literally nothing there now. Just a rickety ladder to the sand.'

'Well, there's something there now,' Declan returned to the call. 'Wait there, Ben. I'll send a car and some uniforms to check it. Okay?'

He disconnected, grabbing his jacket.

'And where do you think you're off to?' Monroe asked, surprised.

'The note was for me, and my dad was taken earlier today,' Declan replied as he pulled the coat on. 'Now, a body is found at an old execution site. It's a message. Of what, I don't know.'

'You're not going alone,' Monroe shook his head. 'I'll come with you. And we'll grab Rosanna on the way.'

'Doctor Marcos is busy, and I don't need to know the time of death,' Declan nodded to Cooper. 'If she finds anything on the lighter, let me know.'

'Billy can do that,' Monroe was already walking to his office to gather his things. 'Cooper, get down to Mainsworth's house. I want to make sure Luke isn't arriving early.'

'I'll go with her,' Mainsworth nodded, but Monroe shook his head.

'Stay here with the laddie,' he ordered. 'As far as Luke Snider and Jennifer Carmichael are concerned, you're dead. If they see you at your apartment, they'll know it's a scam.'

Reluctantly, Charlie Mainsworth nodded.

And, with Cooper already leaving to go to the apartment, and Monroe grabbing his jacket, Declan left the offices, almost at a run.

He may have had his issues with his father over the years, but this was beyond anything he'd ever expected.

And planned capture or not, now he intended to find Luke Snider and end this on *his* terms.

20

EXECUTION DOCK

THEY'D GONE IN DECLAN'S POLICE-ISSUE AUDI, BLUE LIGHTS flashing and sirens blaring as they headed to Wapping from Temple Inn.

'You know the area at all?' Declan asked as he ran a red light, Monroe gripping the upper handle of the door for dear life.

'Only in passing,' he said, wincing as Declan streaked past a lorry. 'It's near where the power station was, where Anjli, De'Geer and Cooper took down Lee Mellor.'

'You know, I could handle this on my own, Guv,' Declan gritted his teeth as he sped up. It was a twenty-minute drive, according to the sat nav, but Declan intended to do it in half the time. Monroe had also called ahead to the Metropolitan Police Marine Policing Unit; although they were purely Thames based, the MPU were also the closest to the scene, less than half a mile away, while the other closest Units would be Bethnal Green or even Bow Road, a fair journey away.

'I know, laddie,' Monroe smiled faintly. 'But Patrick was my friend, as well as your father. And if this is him, you'll need a friend with you.'

'If this is him?'

'Something feels off,' Monroe shrugged, then winced as they sped across a roundabout painted on the ground. 'The location feels iffy, and I can't explain why.'

Declan nodded at this, completely understanding. The last three locations – Temple Church, The Morpeth Arms, even the Clerkenwell Tunnels, had all been cells of one kind or another, while this was nothing more than a onetime execution spot.

This was personal.

He was on Wapping High Street now, a road that was as far from the stereotypical "High Street" as you could get. Instead of shops and restaurants, fast-food places and small supermarkets, Wapping High Street was a road of four-storey wharfs and shipping companies, brown-brick warehouses now turned into expensive apartments, the old metal balconies now painted bright blues and reds as they looked into well designed living spaces, with red-painted walkways crossing above him as he passed quickly under them, heading eastwards. Occasionally, a small open area of grass and trees would appear on the left, but it was only for an instant, and the lack of street lighting made them seem more sinister than they properly were.

Eventually, a few steps beyond the *Captain Kidd* pub, green-painted walls on either side of a green-gated mews entrance, now filled with drinkers wondering why the police had turned up outside, was a police cordon that stretched across the old, bricked street. Pulling up next to it, Declan was already out of the car and crossing under the tape before Monroe could unclip his seatbelt.

'Where is he?' he shouted, waving his warrant card at the confused officers. 'The body?'

'Down there,' the officer pointed along an alley leading to the Thames. 'None of us have touched it, or even gone near it. I understand Doctor Marcos is coming.'

'You know Marcos?' Monroe asked as he followed Declan.

At this, the officer laughed.

'Everyone knows Rosanna Marcos, and we all know not to piss her off,' he said. 'So the body has been left exactly as found, hanging at the bottom of the steps.'

Declan glanced momentarily at Monroe before heading down the alley. He wasn't intending to affect the crime scene either, but he needed to know for sure.

———

CHECKING HER WATCH TO SEE THE TIME, MAINSWORTH SIGHED as she leant back against the chair.

'I'm bored,' she said. 'Did Doctor Marcos find out anything before she left?'

Billy nodded.

'The plate was stamped with two words,' he said. 'Nothing else, just "Anne Boleyn", like that was supposed to explain everything.'

'Just that?' Mainsworth's eyes glittered. 'You think it'll give you the location of the money?'

'Currently, I have no idea,' Billy returned to the screen as Mainsworth, muttering to herself, leant back once more.

'If you're that bored, how about you make me a coffee?'

Billy grumbled. Although he was glad Mainsworth was safe now, she was starting to really annoy him.

'Sure,' she said with a smile. 'I'll go do that now.'

Rising from the chair, she walked to the back door, leading to both the stairs to the cells, and the break room on the upper level.

'White, no sugar?' she asked, before smiling. 'Actually, forget that. I don't care.'

Mainsworth left the office before Billy could answer, but she didn't walk up the stairs to the break room and the expensive coffee machine they had up there; instead, she headed quickly down the rear stairs to the minimal amount of holding cells the Unit now had.

Arriving at the only closed door, Mainsworth took a deep breath, and fully committed now to her cause, she opened it.

Laura Snider stared up at her from the bench at the back of the cell.

'I heard you were dead,' she spat.

'I know,' Mainsworth smiled darkly. 'I am dead. I'm here to take you to Hell.'

She pulled out a pair of handcuffs, tossing them across the cell.

'Put them on behind your back,' she ordered. 'I don't have any zip ties, I'm afraid.'

'And if I don't?' Laura picked up the cuffs, staring down at them.

'Then I do to you what you did to me,' Mainsworth reached into her back pocket and pulled out her police Taser 7 device. 'I'm a strong girl. I can drag your arse out of here easily.'

Reluctantly, and with great unease, Laura Snider placed

the handcuffs on, struggling to secure the second one while behind her back, but succeeding on the second try.

'Now what?'

Mainsworth walked over, roughly spinning Laura around so her back was facing frontwards, and squeezed the handcuffs tightly, tightening them so they bit into the skin, forcing Laura to wince in pain.

'Now we go for a little trip,' she smiled. 'If anyone asks, I'm taking you, on Monroe's orders, to a secret location.'

'There were no orders, were there?' Laura hissed. 'You're off book.'

'You're catching on,' Mainsworth pulled down on the cuffs, elongating the arms, and making Laura yelp. 'But you're still coming with me.'

'No, she's not,' a voice spoke behind her, and Mainsworth spun to face Billy, standing in the cell's doorway.

'You shouldn't have come, Fitzwarren,' Mainsworth sighed. 'You should have waited for your drink.'

'Looks like I'd have been waiting a wh—' Billy didn't finish, as he suddenly arched back in pain, the tines from Mainsworth's Taser 7, fired into his chest at close range, forcing fifty thousand watts of electricity through his system.

As he collapsed to the floor, Mainsworth tossed the taser to the ground.

'Sorry,' she said to the unconscious figure. 'Should have stayed upstairs.'

She turned back to Laura, now staring in horror at the scene in front of her.

'Don't worry, I may have wasted one weapon, but I still have another,' she said, pulling a scalpel out of another pocket. 'Got this from the Doctor's office while she was examining something. We'll be popping by there before we leave, as she has something of mine.'

'And if I don't?' Laura raised her chin defiantly.

'Then I use this to slit your throat,' Mainsworth replied, bringing the tip of the scalpel up to Laura's neck. 'Because currently, you're the main suspect in the murder of the man I loved, and I have a definite score to settle with you for what you did to me.'

She nodded at Billy's prone form.

'And between us? I think I just quit the police force, so I've got nothing to lose.'

DECLAN STARED OUT ACROSS THE THAMES; IT WAS LOW TIDE, and the moon's light gave a mysterious, shadowed and other-worldly state to the pebbled beach at the base of the steps.

The steps didn't really exist, though, as the concrete stairs halted a good fifteen feet above the sand, the only way down now a metal ladder that rocked when Declan grabbed at it, still not connected to the base.

But, to get down to the body, Declan had to climb down it.

Grimacing, Declan climbed onto the ladder, shutting his eyes as it rocked, expecting it to collapse to the ground at any moment, but surprisingly it held as Declan quickly made his way; not in haste to get to the body, but more a case of fear of what would happen if he stayed too long on it.

Now with his feet on the cold, wet sand, Declan pulled his torch out, shining it up at the hanging figure.

And, as he stared up, his stomach flip-flopped.

The body was in a funeral suit, the shoes almost falling off the hanging feet. The noose, a short roped one, was around the neck, and as Declan shone the light onto the face, he saw what he'd expected.

A *mannequin's* face.

Declan almost gave out a sob of relief, but this was followed immediately by a feeling of immense anger.

He'd been played.

There was a note on the body, tucked into the front jacket pocket. He pulled it out, staring down at it, his torch lighting it up.

> She says she's sorry
> She says she needed
> you to look

Declan looked up at the night sky as he pondered the message.

Was this Jennifer Carmichael? Had she arranged to get Declan and Monroe out of the office?

'Is it him?' Monroe shouted from the top of the steps.

'No,' Declan growled as he turned back to the rickety ladder. 'We got played, but I'm not sure who by.'

———

THE DOOR TO DOCTOR MARCOS'S OFFICE WAS LOCKED, BUT Mainsworth had expected this. Quickly, she took Billy's ID card and rubbed it against the RFID sensor, hearing the door click open. She knew her own ID wouldn't have done this, but Billy was one of the elite, the inner circle. Of course his ID would open all doors.

Pushing Laura into the room, scalpel still at her neck,

Mainsworth walked to the desk, where, on the surface and in two parts, was her Zippo lighter.

'Is that what I think it is?' Laura asked as Mainsworth placed both parts together, sliding it into her pocket.

'Yeah,' she said. 'And now we're going to have a chat. All three of us. Well, once we get out of here, that is.'

Laura was watching the lighter carefully as Mainsworth placed into her pocket.

'You know where the money is?'

'Yes,' Mainsworth motioned for Laura Snider to follow her out of the room once more. 'But it won't take long for them to work it out, too.'

Walking down the corridor, Laura in front, Mainsworth leant in close.

'As we go out, you might consider escaping,' she whispered. 'But know I hold the cuffs, and the moment you try that, I'm nicking an artery with this very sharp scalpel, yeah? You'll bleed out in seconds.'

Buzzing through the main entrance, Mainsworth groaned inwardly as she saw the desk sergeant. Mastakin wasn't her biggest fan, but he was still a serving police officer, and knew when and where to rock the boat – or, rather, not rock it.

'PC?' he asked, seeing Laura in cuffs.

'Message from Monroe,' Mainsworth shrugged. 'Said to bring her to my apartment, something about her son.'

'I was more surprised about seeing you working,' Mastakin replied.

'Stepped in when DI Walsh's dad appeared in Wapping,' she smiled. 'Short staffed, and I can always do with the suits owing me.'

'I get that one,' Mastakin smiled. 'Got a car?'

'DC Fitzwarren gave me his,' Mainsworth jangled a set of keys. 'Said a squad car is too visible for the sting operation.'

Before Mastakin could continue, though, Charlie Mainsworth dragged Laura Snider through the main door and out into the night air. Clicking the remote, she smiled when she saw a car lights flash, frowning when she realised it was a Mini Cooper.

'Thought he'd have something a little more flash,' she grumbled.

'You're going to kill me when this is all over, aren't you?' Laura asked, nervously.

Mainsworth grinned.

'Oh, you can be damned sure about that,' she said. 'Your actions until then, however, decide if you join Arthur quickly, or piece by bloody piece.'

BILLY'S PHONE WAS RINGING INCESSANTLY, AND BULLMAN POKED her head out of the office.

'Are you getting that?' she said, but paused as she saw the office was surprisingly empty. Walking over to the phone, she answered it.

'Bullman,' she said.

'Where's Billy?' Declan's voice came down the line.

'How should I know?' Bullman frowned. 'Probably in the toilet, letting his butler talc his bum.'

She paused, remembering why Declan wasn't in the office.

'Is it him?' she asked carefully.

'No,' Declan replied, and Bullman could tell the tone was clipped, tight; he was holding back some serious anger here.

'We got played. Someone dragged us out of the office for this.'

'Why would someone ...' Bullman trailed off.

Billy's phone was on the desk.

'Declan, when you go to the loo, do you take your phone?'

'Ma'am, I'm not sure if this is the time to ask—'

'Humour me.'

'Well, if I'm spending time there, then yes.'

'Billy didn't take his, and he's been a while,' Bullman replied. 'And Mainsworth's not up here, too.'

'Ah, bollocks,' Declan muttered. 'Sorry, boss, I think I just worked out what the message meant. Is Charlie Mainsworth still in the building?'

'I haven't checked yet, Deckers,' Bullman replied, using the nickname he detested, probably deliberately. 'Should I round them up like a mother hen?'

'Yes, please,' Declan said urgently. 'And I'd start with Laura Snider's cell, because if I'm right, and she's left the building, then Charlie Mainsworth's gone to get revenge for what happened to her. Or, worse, she's gone for the Zippo lighter, and two million pounds' worth of long-lost, stolen money.'

ON THE OTHER END OF THE LINE, DECLAN CURSED WILDLY ONCE the call ended.

'Problem?' Monroe asked.

'Charlie Mainsworth is missing, as is Billy,' Declan replied, placing the phone away. 'Bullman's gone to check if Laura Snider's still alive.'

'You think she might not be?'

Declan shrugged.

'Hopefully? I'm wrong. But if my gut's right, then your latest addition to the team just sent us on a wild goose chase, just so she could get her hands on the very things we needed hidden. And, if she took them, there's every chance the midnight meeting, and the saving of Henry Farrow, are off the table for good.'

21

UP TOWN PARK

DE'GEER AND ANJLI PAUSED THE MOTORCYCLE ON THE CORNER of a suburban housing estate somewhere between Islington and Dalston. Although the hospital had been south of the Thames, the Peugeot they'd followed had travelled back over at London Bridge, moving upwards, unaware, or at least giving the impression of someone who was unaware, they were being followed.

The car had eventually stopped in the middle of a tree-lined street of houses, the most innocuous location around, and the black-haired woman in the Barbour coat had climbed out, while talking on the phone, walking into a blue-doored house at the side.

'How do you want to play this?' Anjli asked, looking around. 'Usually it's a disused warehouse or some kind of underground tunnel network. I don't think we've ever had a simple house as a location for a kidnapping.'

'First time for everything,' De'Geer pulled off his helmet, placing it on the bike's handlebars as he rummaged in his jacket for his phone. 'We should call it in.'

'Not until we know for sure Farrow's in there,' Anjli shook her head. 'For all we know, she could be the messenger and nothing more.'

At this, her phone buzzed. She'd turned it on to silence mode while pretending to be the receptionist, but hadn't checked it since climbing onto the bike. Reading the messages, she whistled.

'She's Jennifer Carmichael,' she said. 'Recognised by Mainsworth, apparently. Granddaughter of Paul Carmichael, the man who lost two million. Well, I mean he lost four million, but he got two million from the police when they found it, and the rest back from insurance, but technically? Paul Carmichael lost two million.'

'The granddaughter of the man who had the money stolen is working with the son and wife of the man who stole it?' De'Geer questioned. 'That has to make strange bedfellows.'

'Possibly not,' Anjli rubbed at her head, the hair still tight from the helmet. 'None of them were there at the scene – even Laura was left in the dark. They could have joined forces to get the money back. Or Jennifer there could be controlling everything?'

De'Geer was reading the same message on his own phone.

'It says here she saw Casey in prison and possibly in Manchester, before Casey went to see Luke, so maybe he was a middleman between the two of them,' he suggested. 'Either way, I don't get "subordinate" vibes from her. If she has Farrow, it's because she needs Luke to do something else.'

Anjli nodded, reading the rest of the message.

'Ah, shit,' she said. 'Charlotte Mainsworth's gone—'

'Rogue? Yeah, I saw,' De'Geer growled. 'Did you get the text from Bullman or from Billy himself?'

'Bullman, after she found him tasered in a cell,' Anjli got off the bike, clenching and unclenching her fingers as she stared at the house. 'Mainsworth has Laura Snider and the Zippo. Makes sense she'll go for the money and get revenge on Laura, for the death of Arthur—'

'Or, she'll trade the lighter and the mum for her freedom,' De'Geer suggested. 'Currently, we don't know who's leading this, but if Mainsworth recognised her, there's every chance they've met before, maybe even know each other. Hell, Charlie Mainsworth might even work for her.'

'Whatever this was, it was planned,' now with De'Geer beside her, Anjli started towards the house. 'The last message said she called her cousin while in the office, but Declan believes she called someone else, maybe a friend or someone who owed her a favour, and she convinced them to put a mannequin on a noose down at Execution Dock in Wapping, purely to get the police there.'

'Hell of a friend.'

'She doesn't exactly hang around with angels,' Anjli smiled. 'And many of them probably jumped at the chance to piss off some coppers.'

'Billy dropped the ball there,' De'Geer thought for a moment. 'Luke wouldn't have placed Patrick Walsh's body there, anyway.'

'How can you be so sure?'

De'Geer grinned.

'Because it was a place of execution, not a cell,' he said. 'The others? All places of incarceration. Even where they held Charlie. But Wapping Steps and all those pirate hanging spots? No cells.'

'Well, when we get back from whatever insanity this is, feel free to give Declan and Billy an "I told you so," as I'm sure they'll feel much better for it,' Anjli mocked.

'Nah, I'm fine,' De'Geer said as he banged on the door.

The house was terraced, with no side entrance into it. Anjli knew there'd be a back garden somewhere, but without knowledge of the area, she'd be in the same situation Cooper had been in earlier.

'Police!' she shouted. 'Open the door!'

There was a noise on the other side of the door, as if someone was dragging something heavy, and Anjli nodded at De'Geer.

'If you will, Sergeant,' she said. And, with a resigned expression, De'Geer stepped back and slammed his boot against the door's lock, splintering it as the door swung into the house.

'I'm sick of smashing in doors,' he muttered.

The hallway was narrow, with stairs in front, the hallway passage snaking to the right and around them. The nearest room jutted out more than the back room, and the passage led to a kitchen at the far end, with a back door on the right, now open, leading to a paved pathway that eventually opened out into a garden. Anjli didn't need to check if she was correct; she'd been in enough of these sorts of houses over the years. And, with a nod to De'Geer, she stepped back to allow him space to move.

'Sic'um, boy,' she said as the Viking police officer charged through the door and into the back garden. Anjli, meanwhile, pulled out her extendable baton and moved into the side room—

To find it empty, apart from a wooden, mud-stained coffin on the floor.

It looked untouched, and Anjli wasn't going to open it any time soon. What it wasn't was a DCI by the name of Farrow, and so Anjli took the investigation upstairs. Annoyingly, there was nobody there, either, until Anjli, on a hunch, pulled open a door in a built-in wardrobe, but didn't get any further as the door beside her, a mirror stuck onto it shattered with the impact of a small metal blade, thrown hard from across the room. Ignoring the blood now streaming from a small slash of flying glass, Anjli dived for cover, as Jennifer Carmichael threw something small and metal this time.

'Will you quit it!' she yelled. 'I'm police!'

Jennifer threw another blade, what looked to be a fold out butterfly knife, the tip smacking into the bed frame.

'You're an intruder, and I'm defending myself!' Jennifer cried out. 'I'm aiming to wound, not kill. You broke into my house, and I'm protecting my property!'

'Does that include the body in your living room?' Anjli yelled back.

At this, Jennifer paused, lowering the blade in confusion.

'Body?' she said. 'I—'

She didn't get any further as Anjli launched across the room, using the bed to gain height on the other woman, swinging down hard with the baton, viciously connecting with Carmichael's wrist, hearing bones crack as the other woman screamed in pain, dropping the next blade in her seemingly unlimited list of knives.

Anjli didn't stop, quickly whipping up with the baton and catching Carmichael square on the jaw, smacking her head backwards, sending her into the door. And, by the time Jennifer Carmichael was in any kind of state to continue, Anjli was on top of her, turning her onto her front and twisting the good arm behind her back, while she pulled the phone from Carmichael's pocket.

'Who did you call?' she cried out. 'Was it Luke? Was it someone else?'

'I didn't call anyone!'

Forcing Carmichael to look at the phone and, therefore, unlock it, Anjli started scrolling through the recent calls. There were three numbers recently connected with, two of which were from a number unknown to her. The first one was a call she'd had, while the second one was called moments earlier.

'This is Luke, isn't it?' Anjli said, showing Carmichael the number. 'This is him calling you to tell you to check out St Thomas, see if his mum was right about Charlie Mainsworth, and this is you telling him she's dead.'

She leant closer.

'What was his plan?'

'I'm not saying a thing,' Carmichael replied bitterly. 'I don't know what you're talking about. And I'm not saying anything that will entrap me down the line.'

'You literally just spoke to me at the hospital.'

'I don't know anything about a hospital.' It was obviously a lie, but now caught, Carmichael wasn't going so easily.

'Fine then, you can talk about it at the station,' Anjli finished.

At this, Jennifer Carmichael stopped struggling, as if accepting her fate.

'You've pissed a lot of people off,' Anjli said through gritted teeth. 'You threw a knife at me, which really annoys me. And you stole a dead man from his place of rest.'

'I didn't steal him!' Carmichael growled. 'You know nothing, bitch!'

'DS Kapoor,' De'Geer panted as he got to the top of the stairs. 'It's not Declan's dad. It's Luke's dad.'

Anjli looked back at Carmichael.

'The coffin in your living room is the one used for Arthur Snider?'

'Of course! Who did you think it was?' Carmichael struggled.

'You dug up Patrick Walsh earlier today,' Anjli wasn't moving, still straddling Jennifer's back. 'Late Chief Superintendent Patrick Walsh, to be more accurate. That alone is going to give you a bad day, but kidnapping a DCI, as well as the PC officer you left in a cave and tasered ...'

'I didn't taser anyone. That was probably mummy dearest.'

Anjli leant close.

'She's not dead, by the way,' she growled. 'We wanted you to find out she was. I'm guessing you told Luke the news?'

Carmichael didn't answer.

'So, what was it, a way to get your money back? You scratch Luke's back, he gets a lighter back off his dad's body for your dad?'

'You don't have anything on me!' Carmichael struggled again.

'You're not your grandfather,' Anjli smiled. 'From what I hear, he wouldn't have got caught up this way. Well, maybe he would – he let his manager steal from him.'

She sighed.

'But, we're short on time and you could be of use. So, tell us where DCI Farrow is, as well as Patrick Walsh's body, and I might swing something. Because of your help here, of course.'

Carmichael stopped struggling.

'I don't know where the copper is,' she said. 'I thought he would be here, but they've gone.'

'And who would that be?'

Carmichael struggled to rise again, and this time Anjli let her, now sitting on the bed, watching Jennifer Carmichael carefully as she rubbed at what was believed at the beginning to be a broken wrist, but now seemed to be a severely bruised one.

'Luke was here with the DCI, but when I arrived, the back door was open and he was gone,' she muttered. 'He must have known you were coming, and he left me to you.'

She laughed.

'And there I was, about to betray him instead. Should have listened to Smith. He had his number.'

'Casey Smith?' Anjli frowned. 'As in the drug dealer, who did time for Arthur's murder?'

Carmichael nodded.

'I visited him twice when I heard he was mouthing off, trying to get a rep,' she said. 'I mean, he'd been doing it for years, but now he was about to come out, and there were people pissed at him. Dangerous people. So, I had a chat, made him an offer.'

'What sort of offer?'

'Stop being a prick, wait until release and then work for me in Manchester.'

Carmichael made it sound so simple, and Anjli wondered exactly how involved the woman had actually been.

'You seem to have quite a few fingers in this pie,' she said.

'My family's money is out there,' Carmichael growled. 'Look. I know I'm screwed here, so I might as well be honest. The plan was to use the Sniders and grab the lighter, find the missing money. I didn't realise they were gonna use real people as bait. I thought we were only playing with the dead ones.'

'So you had no knowledge of what happened to PC Mainsworth?'

'No, just that something had happened, and Luke asked me to look into it,' Carmichael looked up from her hand. 'Can I get a medic to look at this? It's hurting like hell.'

Sighing, Anjli rose, using Carmichael's good hand to pull her to her feet.

'We'll get someone to look at it, I promise,' she said. 'But, as we're short on time, to start with, you're coming to the station with us.'

'Do I get a phone call?' Carmichael asked.

'Eventually,' Anjli replied. 'Why? Are you in a rush to call someone?'

'My dad,' Jennifer snarled as they followed De'Geer down the stairs. 'Wanted to let him know Luke betrayed me.'

'Yeah, that ain't happening for a while,' Anjli smiled.

DECLAN ARRIVED BACK IN THE OFFICE TO SEE BILLY SITTING AT his desk, gingerly sipping at a mug of hot tea, Bullman mothering him as he shivered.

'Tasered,' she said. 'Mainsworth. She took the lighter as well.'

'Do we know where she took Laura Snider?' Monroe, entering behind Declan, asked.

'Well, she's going to have revenge in her mind, so I'm thinking it's not good,' Bullman replied. 'Kapoor and De'Geer are on their way back, too. They've got Jennifer Carmichael in tow.'

Monroe raised his eyebrows at this. 'Did they find Farrow?'

'No, but they found his jacket, so they know he was there, and Arthur Snider's coffin,' Billy replied. 'It looks like Luke had someone tell him the police were on the way, and he escaped out the back door with Farrow.'

'Seems to be a habit with Snider,' Monroe muttered. 'I want to know who told him.'

'So do we,' Bullman looked back at Billy. 'However, we think we might have an idea where Mainsworth's going.'

Declan turned to Billy, who placed the mug gently down, turning to face the two new arrivals.

'I'm fine, by the way,' he deadpanned. 'Don't you worry, or ask how I'm doing at all.'

'How are you doing, laddie?' Monroe deadpanned back in response. 'I'm worried about you.'

Billy gave a weak half-smile.

'Doctor Marcos is back in her mad scientist laboratory downstairs, but before she went to follow you on "hunt the dummy" duties—'

'I'm giving you that one on account of being tasered,' Declan snarled gently. 'Next one gets another fifty thousand volts, or whatever it is.'

'Point taken,' Billy didn't look bothered by the threat. 'Anyway, before she went to follow you, she retrieved the plate from inside the lighter. It was a brass one, like local club trophies have, and it had two words "Anne Boleyn" stamped on it.'

He shifted painfully in the chair.

'I told Charlie Mainsworth this, and a few seconds later

she was off downstairs. I'm guessing she worked out pretty bloody quickly what it meant.'

'Tower of London?' Declan suggested. 'Maybe he hid it on the site somewhere? Definitely a safe place.'

'No, I think it was a more personal message,' Billy shook his head. 'A way for Arthur to remember if he forgot, but also for the one he loved, Charlie, to find it if he died.'

He shrugged.

'Problem was, he never told her the message was in the lighter,' he added. 'I don't think he expected to be killed.'

'But once she heard the name, she instantly understood it,' Declan nodded. 'So, what do we know about their relationship?'

'I could just tell you, if you want,' Billy muttered. 'Unless you want to solve it all alone?'

'Can someone find me a Taser?' Declan asked the office sweetly. 'Billy's about to become a two-time winner.'

'Go on, laddie, out with it,' Monroe checked his watch. 'We're approaching an hour left.'

'I listened to the tapes,' Billy said. 'First off, when Ford talked to Bullman and Anjli, she said Arthur would meet up with Chloe during West Ham home matches. She didn't realise at the time it was actually Charlie doing this.'

'And then Laura mentioned in our interview that she was told by someone they'd seen her husband and Charlie at a home game at Upton Park, cuddling up like lovers when they looked like father and daughter,' Declan nodded. 'So it's West Ham related?'

'It was their special spot, alone and ignored among thousands of other fans,' Billy nodded, turning and tapping at his keyboard. On the screen, the image of a football stadium appeared.

'Cooper also had notes from when they spoke to Johnny Lucas, where he said he had a box in the Dr Martens Stand at Upton Park, and he'd meet with Arthur there while he was an informant. Apparently Snider had spots in "the cheap seats."'

'That means up in the Gods,' Monroe replied. 'As high as you could get. And they called it Upton Park because of the location, but the official name was the Boleyn Ground, named after the local club, Boleyn Castle, in 1904. They took it over after the two clubs amalgamated.'

'Anne Boleyn,' Declan nodded. 'So the money's hidden there? Do we know where?'

'Doesn't matter,' Monroe stroked at his chin now. 'Because it won't be there anymore.'

'Why not?' Declan frowned.

'Och, you need to follow more local teams,' Monroe chided. 'West Ham left Upton Park in 2016. They took over the London Stadium after the 2012 Olympics, almost destroying Leyton Orient in the bidding war process, and the old stadium was torn down, and turned into posh housing.'

He looked back at the image of the stadium.

'This all happened after Snider died, of course. And if he hid the money there, expecting Charlie to get the lighter at some point and find it, it's about seven years too late, as they would have removed it with the rest of the stadium.'

On the screen now was a Google Maps image of the current site; no longer a stadium, but now a series of tall apartment blocks, with four running along the middle, and two taller ones on either side.

'He could have been in the same stand as the Twins, that would have made meeting them easier,' Billy said, pointing at the west side of the image. 'Which would be where this building, Chapman House here is, now—' he pointed at the bottom left of the blocks '—or the one next to it, Chamberlain Court, depending on whether they were left, right or centre in the stands.'

'So Snider could have hidden the money somewhere in the upper stands,' Declan mused.

'Surely they would have found the money during the takedown?' Bullman asked, but Billy shook his head.

'They were using giant machinery, taking out tonnes at a time,' he said. 'It'd be like spotting a needle in a haystack, while tossing the haystack to the side.'

He paused as a thought came to mind.

'Actually, maybe not,' he said, looking around at them. 'There was something else that stood out to me during the Lucas interview. He said Snider helped him buy a pub in a roundabout way. But he couldn't have, as he was dead when Johnny and Jackie did that.'

'How do you mean?' Declan pursed his lips as he frowned.

However, it was Monroe who answered this one.

'They bought *The Trooper* pub in Bethnal Green, sometime in 2007,' he said. 'I think it was an old gangland haunt, and it was about to be bought out, turned into a restaurant. They were short of some money, and the Twins came up with it. However, when the war between Johnny and Vickie Lucas kicked off last year, the pub went up in flames. I don't know if they've renovated yet. I don't even know if the insurance covers "arson by sibling war" or anything.'

He grimaced.

'I'm a bloody fool,' he said. 'I should have put them together. When they paid for it, somewhere around a million and a half in total, they did it through third parties, but we knew it was them. I asked them where the money came from, and they said they found it at a football match. We assumed at the time it was criminal activities, or dodgy deals done in their West Ham box during a match, and they were just having a laugh at our expense, but now ...'

'Now it looks like they could have literally found it in Upton Park, right before it was destroyed,' Declan nodded. 'And nobody can prove otherwise, because the money's location was never discovered.'

'Apart from the Twins.'

'Who must have been following him or something.'

'Mainsworth must know this, though,' Monroe sighed. 'What's she playing at?'

'I don't think she wants the money, boss,' Declan muttered. 'I think she wants revenge. And she doesn't care who gets in the way of this, even if it's a DCI she doesn't know.'

'Then we'd better work out what she's doing quickly, before Luke Snider realises this has all been for nothing and starts removing his loose threads,' Monroe straightened. 'Globe Town's on the way to Upton Park. Speak to Lucas one more time, see if he has anything else he can use to help. Then call me, and we'll go to the buildings on the old site and work out where Mainsworth's gone.'

'I'll check into the West Ham Supporters Club records,' Billy said. 'He had a season ticket. They'd give him a set spot.'

'Aye, that helps, And maybe Lucas can remember too.'

'You think that's wise, boss?' Declan frowned. 'Going to face Charlie?'

'I'm the one who knows her best,' Monroe shrugged. 'I think I'm the best option. Anjli's almost back at the unit. Get De'Geer to process our new arrivals and take her with you.'

He stopped.

'Charlie called Luke,' he said. 'Told him to get out.'

'How can you be sure?'

'Because if I was about to throw away my life killing the people who hurt me, I'd bloody well make sure they were all there,' Monroe said. 'We need to find them all, and fast.'

22

PARTY POLITICS

ANJLI HAD ARRIVED AT THE UNIT WITH JENNIFER CARMICHAEL to find Declan waiting at the doorway.

'Change of plans,' he said as he nodded to a couple of uniforms to assist with getting Carmichael out of the car. 'We're off to see Johnny Lucas again.'

'Let me guess, because he's actually more involved in this than we thought?'

Declan grinned.

'You're an outstanding detective,' he said, already walking over to his Audi. 'Billy got us an address of where he is tonight, a fundraiser in Bow. If we put the lights on, we can be there before he finishes.'

Anjli smiled.

'A police car doing the full "blues and twos" won't exactly help his chances for election,' she said.

'Oh no,' Declan deadpanned. 'How terrible for him.'

JOHNNY LUCAS WAS TIRED. HE'D BEEN GLAD-HANDING ALL DAY, and if he was brutally honest, the whole election had been more effort than he'd expected.

In a way, he almost hoped he'd lose, just so he could have a break.

He was in what had been explained to him as a "Boutique Hostel", but to him was just a cheap hotel, albeit in a Georgian, Regency villa, with an attached coach house. The dorms all had oak wood floors, customised bunk-bed pods, top of the line mattresses and cotton bedding and the windows had grand plantation shutters on them. And, as for the private rooms, half the rooms were ensuite, half had shared bathrooms, and most had full-size baths.

This was a better hotel than the Travel Lodge down the road, and completely at odds with his "man of the people, fighting for London" persona. He could already see the headlines, pointing out that even he struggled to find the people he spoke of, in this new, gentrified East End.

He was almost happy to see Declan Walsh enter the back of the large room he stood at the far end of, his banners blazing out his message as he spoke to the press.

'If you'll excuse me a moment,' he smiled. 'I have to speak to an old friend about important police work I'm helping with.'

He stepped off the podium and walked to the two detectives, smiling as he felt the cameras following him.

It had worked for Charles Baker, he thought to himself. *It can bloody well work for me now.*

Declan, meanwhile, had groaned inwardly the moment he heard Johnny Lucas say the words. He'd only just got away from the front pages, and here he was, with a rival to the Government, and therefore a rival to Charles Baker. Declan could almost envision the countless variations of "tug of love" headlines he was about to inspire.

'DI Walsh, DS Kapoor,' he smiled. 'Thank you for coming to see me. However, as you can see, I'm a little busy right now.'

He waved at the press.

'Unless you'd like to endorse me?' he asked. 'There are some donors in the room who I'm sure would be overjoyed at that thought.'

Declan smiled back, but it didn't quite meet his eyes.

'We need to speak somewhere private,' he said. 'I have some urgent questions for you.'

'I'm a transparent person now,' Johnny kept his smile regardless, checking his watch. 'The event is over soon, and the reception should only take—'

Declan leant in close.

'If you don't want me to go on stage right now and ask these questions in front of them, you'll give me five minutes,' he snarled. 'We're running against the clock, and a police officer is about to die.'

Declan stared at Johnny Lucas, and eventually the older man capitulated.

'I'll be back in a moment,' he said to the press, waving Declan and Anjli through a door into a small side corridor. 'Duty never sleeps.'

As the door closed behind them, the smile disappeared.

'This had better be life or death. I heard from friends that Mainsworth was saved,' Johnny said again, this time a little angrier. 'I don't know what your game is here, but sabotaging an election—'

'They kidnapped DCI Farrow today,' Declan said coldly.

'And the body of my father was taken from its grave in Hurley.'

Johnny stopped what he was about to say and looked at Anjli.

'This happened after our chat?'

Anjli nodded, and Johnny straightened, looking back at Declan now.

'What can I do for you?' he asked.

'You took the money, didn't you? In Upton Park?' Declan wasn't dancing around the subject, instead going right for the jugular here. 'There's few people who could have done it.'

'Arthur Snider hid the money in the Dr Martens Stand?' Johnny looked surprised at this, but Declan could tell it was a fake expression.

'Fine, we do this out there,' he snarled, but Johnny grabbed his arm.

'I'm sorry, that came out with the wrong inflection,' he smiled. 'I was agreeing. Arthur Snider hid the money in the Dr Martens Stand.'

'You used it to buy *The Trooper*.'

'I may have, I don't recall. It might have been my "Jackie" persona, and as we said before, I was never in control—'

'We don't give a damn about the money,' Declan snapped. 'We care about a missing DCI, who's been taken by someone who thinks we have it.'

'Yes, I can see how that's a problem for you.'

Anjli stepped forward now.

'You sent Danny Martin, or someone along those lines, to pick up the money after Arthur died, didn't you?'

At this thought, Johnny shook his head.

'Not at first,' he replied. 'Arthur had a season ticket right at the top right of the Stand. South-west corner. It was a terrible view, but he didn't give a shit. He was there to make out with Mainsworth. We never saw her there, but he had two tickets, probably snuck her in later.'

'You met with him at these matches, so how did you not see her?'

'Because he came to us,' Johnny shrugged. 'Me. Jackie. Whatever I was at the time. He'd come to the box and that way I was never seen as looking for him. It was nothing more than a random visit.'

'Kept you clean.'

'Exactly. Anyway, I still had my people keep an eye on him, especially after the Carmichael theft. After all, season tickets weren't cheap, even in terrible locations, and he bought two.'

'You saw where he hid the money?'

Johnny drew a breath in between his teeth, and Declan could see he was trying to work out the most diplomatic way to explain things. Pulling out his warrant card, he tossed it onto a table beside them.

'This is off the record,' he said. 'I don't care about you right now. And neither does Anjli. We just want to save a life.'

Johnny Lucas sighed.

'There was a little alcove in the top corner of the stand, where he had placed a duffel bag and managed to hide it,' he said. 'Nobody ever went that high, and he had access up there by being police. And, he had a season pass, so if he was walking around there, nobody would argue it.'

He leant against the table, almost using it to sit on.

'This way, he could visit the bag whenever he was watching a home match, maybe take a little out for spending money.'

'You saw him?'

'No, but Danny Martin did, and we checked it when he was gone, saw what it was.'

'And you didn't take it for yourselves?'

Johnny smiled.

'I didn't need it, and it was stupidly hot,' he replied. 'Paul Carmichael was still bleeding from its loss, his power base shattered. Never the same again. He was going around London, taking out anyone who even glared at him, like a wounded animal. A war with him would have hurt us, while letting him bleed out hurt The Turk.'

He smiled.

'Also, I didn't want to touch it because we – Jackie and me – knew that down the line, we could use this against him.'

'Blackmail?'

Johnny shrugged.

'Well, having two million quid fall into your lap is great. But having a copper who has two million, and fears being found out, is even better,' he explained. 'We knew we'd get more out of him if he knew we knew.'

He sighed.

'But then he got stabbed. And we realised after a while this wasn't about the money – not entirely, anyway. And not a single bloody person knew where it was.'

'How long did you wait to take the money?'

'Oh, we left it a while, as we were curious. Which one of Patrick Walsh's merry men and women would come and pick it up?'

Declan straightened at this.

'You thought the others knew?'

'Of course we thought that. We had them all in our pocket, remember? Personally, I thought the Scot would come along and pick it up.'

'Monroe?'

'Oh yeah. You know how he was back then. We genuinely thought he'd pop along one day, pick up the money and pass it among the others in his little squad of miscreants. But then, also at the time, we thought it was Chloe that had placed the hit on Snider. We knew she'd been talking to Paul Carmichael. Even so, after he died, nobody picked it up.'

He counted on his fingers.

'We waited around for a good six, seven months. Nobody was doing anything. Then they started talking about revamping the Stand again, and we realised if we were going to move it, it had to be now. So we took it sometime in late 2006, I think,' Johnny chuckled. 'It was only a million and a half, but it was still a nice little bankroll job.'

As he finished, he straightened up, grabbing the lapels of his jacket in the way a barrister might grab the hems of his robes, while speaking in court.

'I will point out to you, though, that we found that money fair and square. We weren't involved in the theft of that money in any way. And Paul Carmichael was a friend of mine. In fact, it was actually after Paul Carmichael passed away that we discovered, by pure chance, this windfall of money.'

He sighed.

'Of course, the pub we bought with it burnt down during the whole palaver with my sister,' he bemoaned. 'Now it's just wasteland. Still don't know what to do with it.'

'And when we spoke, you never thought of telling me about this?' Anjli looked hurt by the betrayal.

'To be honest, none of you asked,' Johnny smiled. 'And more importantly no one actually asked if I knew where it was. I just told you what I knew, answering your questions.'

He looked at Declan, waggling a finger.

'I told her to go speak to Danny Martin. And I'm sure that, as an upstanding citizen, he would have told you everything.'

'While you lie by omission,' Declan growled.

'You say "tomato", I say "I couldn't possibly remember events of fifteen years ago, considering my mental state – a mental state you yourselves helped cure."'

Declan looked at Anjli for a moment before turning back to Johnny.

'You *have* become a politician,' he muttered, his voice cold. 'I don't think it's for the better.'

'Well, I guess we'll know next week,' Johnny started for the door once more. 'But don't worry, when I'm MP for the area, I'll be sure to help up the pay for the police. You do such a good job.'

He opened the door, looking back at Declan.

'I'm sure I'll be seeing you again,' he said.

'Actually, you might see me earlier than you thought,' Declan said, working through what Johnny had just said. 'What time do you finish all this?'

'I'm almost done,' Johnny frowned. 'But these buggers can drink, so I might be here until midnight. Why?'

'Because I think I know a way you can not only help free DCI Farrow, but do something good with that plot of land,' Declan smiled.

'Trying to be my guardian angel now, Declan?' Johnny smiled in response. 'The conscience sitting on my shoulder?'

'Who knows about the purchase?' Declan asked. 'It was cash, so it's off the books, right?'

'Well, we bought it through third parties, but we have all the paperwork.'

'Literally, right?' Declan's smile returned. 'All paper, no

digital copies. Because as a friend recently told me, you can't hack a book.'

'Am I supposed to know what you're talking about?'

'Oh, you will when the time's right,' Declan replied as, with a resigned sigh, Johnny Lucas left the hallway they now stood in and returned to his press conference, likely explaining how he'd save the police or something.

Pulling out his phone, Declan called Billy.

'Boss?' Billy replied, and for a moment Declan thought the old Billy was back again.

'I need the number Anjli found on Jennifer Carmichael's phone,' he said. 'Also, tell Monroe that Snider had seats in the South-West corner, which means it's Chapman House, and we'll meet him there.'

'I'll text you the number, but Monroe's already left.'

'What do you mean, he's already left?'

Billy paused; possibly because he was typing a number to be sent, or more likely because he was caught in the middle of something.

'Five minutes after you disappeared, he decided he couldn't wait around. Got in a car and drove off alone.'

'Send me the number,' Declan replied as he disconnected.

'Monroe's already gone there,' he said to Anjli. 'But he wouldn't know which building to aim at.'

'Unless he knew the seats, but didn't tell us?' Anjli suggested.

'I'd rather not think that,' Declan muttered as his phone buzzed with the number from Billy.

Copying the number, he dialled it, connecting and waiting as it rang.

After a second, Luke's voice answered.

'Hello?'

'Evening Luke, I believe we just missed you.'

'Mister Walsh, I wondered when you'd get my number. I take it Jennifer Carmichael has been taken.' A comment, not a question. Luke Snider was clever enough to read the room.

'Yeah, she's under police arrest,' Declan replied. 'And we were this close to catching you, too. I'm guessing it was Charlie that called?'

'I received a text.'

The voice was uncertain now, and Declan stroked at his chin as he listened.

He didn't know Mainsworth had his mother yet.

'So this is you gloating?' Luke continued.

'Actually, no,' Declan glanced at Anjli as he spoke. 'The meet is still on, it's been changed somewhat. You wanted me to meet you at Bunhill Fields, and I was going to give you the lighter. But as you know, it was a play.'

'I thought as much,' Luke replied, cautious where this conversation was going. 'Let me guess, you spoke loudly in front of my mother, so she would think that was the truth?'

'Yes,' Declan admitted. 'The original plan was to get you to go to Charlotte Mainsworth's house and look for the lighter, all while we were waiting for you. We thought we could gain access to DCI Farrow through Carmichael, while you were doing this.'

'And how did that work out for you?'

'Not great,' Declan said. 'What was it, five minutes? Ten?'

'It was enough to get away. And fear not, DCI Farrow is still with me at the moment,' Luke said with a hint of smugness. 'So I'm guessing you want to apologise or change the deal?'

'Well, we definitely want to change the deal, because the

agreement has changed,' Declan explained. 'Charlie Mainsworth has your mother hostage, and they've gone to find the location of the missing millions.'

'She knows where it is?' There was no concern for his mother in the words, and Declan realised when Luke had first spoken of her, on how it had all been business, that it hadn't been an act.

'Apparently she's always known, it's just that she didn't realise the money was there. It's where Upton Park used to be, on the roof of the south-west side of the buildings that replaced it.'

'Why are you telling me this?' Luke was still suspicious.

'Because an officer of the law is about to take things into her own hands, and kill your mother – probably by throwing her off the roof,' Declan explained. 'I'd rather she didn't do that because that's a dark path to go down. I'd rather we made a swap; your mother for DCI Farrow.'

'And I'm assuming you'd want to arrest me as well?' Luke's voice had lost the mocking edge, and the severity of the situation finally weighed down on him.

'It's over Luke, the money's gone.' Declan pleaded. 'It's been gone for over fifteen years now. Nobody has the money anymore. And I think you've got enough revenge.'

There was a long pause, followed by a low growl down the line.

'This wasn't about the money, Declan,' Luke said. 'This was about that bitch destroying my father's marriage. But I should get something out of this.'

'Then don't punish Henry Farrow because of something that happened twenty years ago!'

Declan slumped.

'To be honest, all I care about is getting Farrow and my father's body back,' he said.

'My mum goes free.'

'Fine. As you said earlier, technically, we have nothing on your mum. We can't prove she was involved. And Jennifer Carmichael's a suitable alternative.'

Anjli held up her phone, the word "SULLIVAN" written on it.

'We still don't know which of you killed Harry Sullivan, though, and all we have you on right now is Charlie Mainsworth's abduction. And even if this goes to trial, there are multiple mitigating circumstances here for everybody.'

'So where do you want to meet?'

'A pub in Bow,' Declan replied. 'I'll text you the address. It's where your inheritance is. I think we can make a deal. And I can bring your mum—'

'No, you promise to save her from that mad bitch. She doesn't need me,' Luke said. 'I'll bring Farrow to this pub, as long as you're giving me what's owed to me.'

'I can do that,' Declan looked off, towards where Johnny Lucas had gone. 'But be aware, Carmichael will come after you for it.'

'I have no fear of Peter Carmichael,' Luke almost laughed. 'I've been sleeping with his daughter for weeks now.'

'This is the daughter you just left in a house you knew we were heading towards, yes?' Declan replied calmly. 'Your dad stole his dad's money, and now you've just got his daughter arrested under accessory to murder. I'm sure Peter will have no issues with you right now.'

There was a long pause.

'Text me the address. And no police.'

'I will. And your mother will—' Declan started, but stopped as he realised the call had ended.

'Right then,' he said, checking his watch. They still had fifteen minutes until twelve. 'Take the car, get to Monroe, and make sure he doesn't do something stupid.'

'What about you?'

'I'm going to go chat with Johnny again,' Declan replied, putting his phone away. 'I have a way to finish this bastard once and for all.'

He sighed.

'And, in the process, guarantee Johnny Lucas next week's election.'

CHARLOTTE MAINSWORTH STOOD IN THE MIDDLE OF THE apartment complex, beside a small garden feature, with Laura Snider beside her.

'So, do you think your son will come?' she grumbled, her head continually on a swivel, expecting to be caught at any moment.

Laura shrugged.

'You probably saved his arse with the message stopping him going to your apartment, but he's never been the greatest fan of mine,' she admitted.

Mainsworth looked around, gaining her bearings.

'There,' she said, pointing at Chapman House, to the south. 'We go there.'

She pulled Laura along, walking over to the main entrance. It was almost midnight, and many of the people inside would be sleeping, but Mainsworth didn't care as she slammed the buzzers with her hand, flicking across all apartments, all floors.

Eventually, one answered.

'Yes?'

'Who am I speaking to?' she asked.

'What? You buzzed me!'

'I repeat, who am I speaking to? This is PC Charlotte Mainsworth of the City of London police,' Mainsworth said, showing her warrant card to the camera. 'I need access to your roof.'

'Oh, um, Dave, Dave Proust.' The voice at the other end was more cautious now. But the door buzzed open and Mainsworth noted the number she'd pressed.

'Stay alert,' she said, pulling the door open. 'My colleagues will arrive soon and need the same.'

'Should I be worried?' the voice asked. 'Am I in danger?'

'Not if you stay where you are,' Mainsworth was already walking through the door, Laura with her.

Stopping beside the elevator, she pressed the button as she pulled out her phone. The number was there; she'd texted it earlier that evening to get Luke out of the house he was in before he was arrested. She felt bad for this, as it meant DCI Farrow was still with him, but she couldn't kill a man in prison, at least not before they dragged her there for killing his mum.

'I heard you took Mum from the cells,' the voice of Luke Snider spoke, the background noise and speakerphone echo revealing that he was currently driving.

'Walsh?' she asked.

'Yeah,' Luke replied. 'Just called. I want my mum freed now.'

'I have an address for you,' Mainsworth stated as the doors opened. 'I need you to—'

'I'm not coming to you,' Luke interrupted. 'The money's long gone from where you are. I'm going to the actual location.'

'That's unfortunate,' Mainsworth said as she pushed Laura into the elevator carriage. 'Because I don't intend to be arrested before I gain my revenge.'

'Mum can take care of herself,' Luke replied. 'And the police are on their way right now to save her. All part of the deal I made.'

'Your deal sounds kinda sucky, Luke,' Mainsworth muttered angrily.

She looked at Laura.

'Say goodbye to your son,' she said.

But before Laura could shout anything, Mainsworth disconnected the call.

'Actually, screw that,' she finished. 'I never got a chance to say goodbye to your husband, so you don't get to say goodbye to your son.'

'So you're going to kill me?'

'Honestly?' Mainsworth pressed the top button as the elevator doors closed. 'I haven't decided yet. But make no mistake, someone dies tonight.'

23

ROOFTOP PARTY

'IF I CLOSE MY EYES, I CAN ALMOST HEAR THE CROWDS,' Charlie Mainsworth said as she stared out over the edge of Chapman house, down the many floors towards the pavement below. 'Oh, that's a long drop.'

There was a noise from the door behind them; a set of stairs accessed the roof from the top level, leading to a single metal door that opened outwards.

Laura looked expectantly towards it, most likely hoping for her son to miraculously come and save her, but instead it was Alex Monroe, emerging from the stairs slowly, his hands out, showing he was unarmed.

'You shouldn't have come, Alex,' Mainsworth muttered. 'This ending wasn't for you.'

'I had to come, Charlie,' Monroe replied. 'You've gone too far. And now it needs to be stopped.'

'I haven't gone far enough!' Mainsworth snapped back angrily. 'That's the problem! All these years I've sat patiently waiting for someone, *anyone,* to give the actual reasons for

Arthur's murder. To find the person who actually did it and bring them to justice.'

She pointed the scalpel – which had up to that point been resting against Laura's neck – at Monroe.

'Did you do it?' she barked. 'No. It took me being *abducted* for you to do it. It took his son trying to *kill me* for you to do it.'

'I apologise for that,' Monroe spoke calmly, moving closer still. 'But now we have enough to put Luke Snider away. Not just for abduction, but for murder, and half a dozen other things.'

He looked around, almost as if expecting Luke to be standing there.

'But at the moment we're still in a predicament,' he continued. 'Because although you have Laura Snider there, he has Henry Farrow – and unfortunately we need him back alive.'

'So what, some DCI from Tottenham is worth more than my lover's memory? Is that what you're saying?'

Monroe shifted uncomfortably at this.

'In this case, it is,' he admitted. 'As much as I hate to say it, we have to look to the living more than the dead.'

There was a long silence as Charlie Mainsworth took the words in.

'Were you a Hammers fan, Monroe?' she eventually asked.

'Aye, a little,' Monroe replied. 'I was more a Rangers fan.'

'Queen's Park?'

'Glasgow, please, lassie.'

Mainsworth nodded.

'See any games? West Ham, that is?'

'A couple, but I can't remember where I sat,' Monroe said, looking around the surrounding roofs. 'Too low to make out landmarks, that's for sure.'

Mainsworth looked down at the roof of the building they currently stood on.

'This is where we watched them,' she said. 'Here or there about. South-West corner, up in the rafters. We would sit up here, and when we did, we were the rulers of the world, looking down on the stadium, on the thousands of people beneath us.'

She choked back a tear.

'Rulers of the world, Alex. And we knew that one day we would rise this high on our own merits. We sat up here talking about the future; we didn't care about the match which was going on. The two of us talked about what we would do together. Did you know we were going to move to America?'

Monroe shook his head.

'He'd spoken of it, but I didn't know he intended to take you.'

'We were going to start a new life, one with the money Arthur had squirrelled away,' Mainsworth replied.

'By "squirrelled away," you mean—'

'Stole? Yes,' Mainsworth smiled wistfully. 'I mean "acquired by whatever means necessary." But then this woman ...'

She stopped, pulling back her anger as she stared at Laura, the scalpel drawing a small pinprick of blood.

'She caused his death more than anybody else.'

'You were having an affair with my husband,' Laura snarled, angering as she listened to the confession.

'Arthur didn't love you, and you knew it,' Mainsworth argued back. 'He told me you'd both been unhappy for years. He didn't want to be with you anymore. And when my mum found out what was going on she tried to stop us from seeing each other.'

Mainsworth turned to Monroe now.

'She shouted at me, I wouldn't listen, and when she realised I was going to run away with him, she came to Laura, and they both worked together on a plan. And then they killed Arthur.'

'Sorry, lassie, but no,' Monroe sadly shook his head. 'For all intents and purposes, you killed Arthur.'

He held his hands up quickly, pausing any reaction from the angry police officer.

'You kept this affair secret for so long, you both knew the moment it came out it would cause problems. And your mum? Aye, she had every right to be annoyed. She was being accused of having an affair with Arthur when she was actually having one with Patrick Walsh.'

He sighed.

'She didn't understand why people thought she and Arthur were seeing each other, but she heard the rumours. There was no smoke without fire and she was a good detective.'

He stepped to the side.

'You could have denied it, you could have found ways of convincing her nothing was going on,' he continued, 'but you didn't. One night, you sat down and told her everything. You wanted to hurt her; you wanted her to know how much you didn't need her.'

His voice was tightening now, the anger barely restrained.

'That night, you told Chloe Mainsworth every single

thing about you and Arthur Snider, and in the process, signed his death warrant.'

———————

'I THINK THIS IS A BAD IDEA, IT'S GOING TO DESTROY MY election chances, and I'm going to publicly nail you to the wall for this if it shits in my face,' Johnny Lucas grumbled as they sat in his car.

'Noted,' Declan smiled winningly. 'But if it goes well, you save a loved police officer, and use a location you've lost money in.'

He looked at his watch.

'Almost midnight,' he whispered. 'I hope Anjli made it okay.'

'You and her doing alright?' Johnny asked. 'Caught a bit of tension there.'

'We're surviving,' Declan was tight-lipped. The last thing he wanted to do was discuss relationships with Johnny Lucas.

'You should be doing more than that,' Johnny replied knowingly. 'She can do better than you, and you know it.'

Declan did know it, and he sighed, but before he could respond to this, he saw a car driving towards them.

'Heads up,' he said as he climbed out of Johnny's car. It was a Jaguar SUV, and it was comfortable, but this wasn't a night for comfort.

The car pulled up under a streetlight, around twenty yards away, and Luke Snider climbed out.

'DCI Farrow?' Declan asked as he walked over towards him. He stopped, however, when Luke pulled a gun from his pocket.

'In the back seat,' he said. 'Perfectly fine, don't worry about him. Worry about yourself if this all goes badly.'

'Where's my dad?' Declan continued.

At this, Luke gave a nervous giggle.

'You've not been home yet, have you?' he smiled. 'We didn't take him far. He's in your back garden.'

He held up a hand as Declan started towards him.

'I knew you'd be staying on the case, so not returning from London. And the coffin was bloody heavy. Did you bury all his medals in it or something? Anyway, we left it in your back garden, by the wall, and left. Well, that is, Jennifer did. I only wanted you to suffer a little. The dead are just skin and bones, so Patrick didn't give a shit.'

He looked around.

'So, where's my money?' he asked.

Declan walked closer, pointing at the burnt-out remains of *The Trooper* pub, now next to them.

'There,' he said.

Luke stared at the building for a very long, very uncomfortable moment.

'What do you mean?' he eventually asked. 'It's in the basement or something?'

'No, he means we bought it,' Johnny Lucas said as he walked over, placing the palm of his hand a couple of feet above the ground. 'Hello, Luke. I remember you being this tall when your dad used to visit us.'

Luke turned back to Declan.

'What the hell is this?' he growled. 'I said to come alone!'

'No, you said "no police," and I think we can both agree Johnny Lucas is as far from that as you can get,' Declan smiled. 'Also, he's the one who had your money.'

Johnny stepped forward.

'He kept it hidden in Upton Park, in the upper stands,' he explained. 'And when he died, nobody claimed it. So, we "liberated" it. Which was lucky, because if we didn't, it would have been lost forever when the place was torn down.'

Luke now turned from Johnny to look at the remains, and then back again.

'You bought a pub?'

'Just over one and a half million,' Johnny nodded. 'Good deal, too. Kept it as a local boozer for years until an unfortunate fire last year utterly gutted it. We weren't able to claim on insurance, so we have to renovate out of our own pocket. It's ... well, it's taking time.'

'This is your money,' Declan said, pointing at the ruins. 'Your dad spent some of it, and the rest went here.'

'You promised me my money,' Luke growled, his gun raising again.

'No, I promised you an inheritance,' Declan looked back at Johnny, who reached into his pocket, pulling out a folded sheet of paper.

'This is the deeds to the land,' he said. 'Worth a million easy to a developer. You can make something out of it, and it's yours, if you release Henry Farrow.'

Luke stared at the paper and then went to snatch it out of Johnny's hands.

'But be aware of one thing,' Johnny kept hold of the end of the paper, halting Luke in place. 'After Paul died, Peter Carmichael never came at me, because he knew he'd never win. It's why his daughter used you; because her father wouldn't act. But the moment Peter knows you have what was stolen, and that you betrayed his own daughter to do it, do you think he'll hold back?'

'Have you ever met Peter Carmichael?' Declan asked, pulling out a phone.

Luke shook his head, paling.

'I'll get Jennifer to speak to him—'

'I wouldn't bother,' Declan smiled. 'She already told us she was using you to get the money. She'll stab you in the back quicker than your father was stabbed.'

Luke's face darkened, and he was about to say something, but Declan, phone to his ear, held a finger up.

'Let's find out, shall we?' he asked, before turning his attention to the call. 'It's me. You can come grab your prize now.'

He disconnected the call and placed the phone away.

'What did you do?' Luke asked.

'Did you kill Harry Sullivan?' Declan asked in response, ignoring the question.

'*What did you do?*'

The answer to the question appeared through the hazy night air a moment later, when another black SUV pulled up, and a large, suited man with two track-suited goons beside him climbed out.

'Luke, let me introduce you to my old and long-time friend, Peter,' Johnny smiled. 'I knew his dad well, you know. Peter, meet Luke Snider, son of the man who ... well, you know the rest.'

The man, now known as Peter, walked over to Luke, whose gun had now dropped to the side.

'Been hearing your name a lot recently,' Peter said, his voice gravely. 'I hear you have something I've been looking for.'

Luke realised at this moment that Johnny Lucas had let go of the deeds to the pub.

'Your dad got his money back,' Luke said softly. 'This is mine.'

'Let's play a hypothetical game,' Peter smiled, and it was the smile of a killer. 'Let's say, for ease, that my dad was Paul Carmichael, and he ran money for the London gangs. And let's say, hypothetically, your father, Arthur Snider, took two million pounds of his money.'

He looked around, taking in the location they stood in, as if for the very first time that evening.

'And then, let's say, your father died, and so did my father, and Johnny and Jackie Lucas bought this shithole with the money. What would you do in my shoes?'

Luke swallowed.

'I'd try to negotiate with them,' he said. 'Explain the money was mine.'

'But you just told me it wasn't my money,' Peter's mouth shrugged. 'You told me it was yours.'

Before Luke could continue, though, the two goons moved to his side, flanking him.

'Now, let's say, hypothetically, I can't go against this man, a man I've worked for, and my dad worked for, but I don't explain why to my daughter, because it's none of her goddamned business. And, hypothetically, she comes to you and you team up. You kill Harry Sullivan, one of the OG of East London, and leave him dumped in a corner like a bloody dog.'

'I didn't kill him!' Luke was rapidly realising the situation he was now in, glancing back at Declan. 'Aren't you gonna do something here?'

'Like what?' Declan asked. 'I mean, you're the one with all the cards right now.'

'And let's say, hypothetically, *you're* Peter Carmichael,'

Peter continued. 'Your daughter has been arrested, and the money you've wanted to regain is now in the hands of the little scroat who not only sent her to the police, but who also kidnapped a bloody DCI to get it.'

He leant in, taking the gun from Luke's terrified fingers.

'The money isn't with the Lucas Twins anymore,' he whispered. 'It's now in the hands of a corrupt little wannabe lawyer with mummy issues, who has nobody left to save his arse when I come for it. Come for *him*.'

With this, he raised the gun, aiming at Luke's face.

Declan, however, took this moment to step in the way of Peter.

'I'm still an officer of the law,' he said. 'And this is something you shouldn't be saying or doing in front of me.'

He looked back at Luke.

'So, let me free DCI Farrow, and we'll get out of your way.'

'You can't do that!' Luke almost screamed. 'He'll kill me!'

'You dug up my dad, kidnapped my police officer and then my ex-boss, possibly killed Harry Sullivan and attempted to blackmail the police?' Declan spun on Luke. 'This is all on you. All of this, everything here, it's the end point of every step you took.'

He waved off vaguely in an eastwards direction.

'Right now, your mother is being held on a roof in Upton Park by the woman you kidnapped and tortured, and my officers, the same ones you also targeted, are trying to save her life.'

He tapped the sheet of paper In Luke's hand.

'All because of this,' he said. 'All because of a stupid bloody lighter and an affair twenty years ago.'

He turned, walking off.

'I'm done here,' he said. 'When the rest of you have

finished with him, scrape him off the pavement and send DCI Farrow back home. I'm off to stop Charlie Mainsworth from being stupid.'

'You can't do this!' Luke screamed out. 'You can't leave me with them!'

Declan stopped, turning back to face Luke, standing in-between the two devils.

'Watch me,' he said.

24

CHEKHOV'S HAMMER

Charlie stared angrily at Monroe.

'She was always telling me I was too young for him,' she muttered. 'She said I was only sixteen, like this was important. I could join the army if I wanted to. I could get married. I could smoke. I could have a child and no one would bat an eyelid, and there she was telling me I was still too young to do what *I* wanted to do.'

She looked at the floor.

'She said I was making a big mistake, I'd regret for the rest of my life.'

'She might have had your best interests at heart—'

'Did she have my best interests at heart?' Mainsworth yelled suddenly, cutting Monroe off. 'When she told his wife about me? Did she have my best interests at heart when she worked with her to arrange a hitman?'

'We didn't arrange the hitman.'

The voice was calm and collected as Laura spoke the words.

'Aye, we assumed as much,' Monroe replied carefully. 'We thought it might be Carmichael.'

'It was Paul Carmichael,' Laura lifted her chin up defiantly. 'We wanted Arthur stopped. So, all we did was tell Paul what you told Chloe.'

'What did I tell her that would lead to this? That I loved him?' Mainsworth stared at Laura. 'I didn't tell you anything.'

'You told your mother you were going to leave. Go to America and start a new life with the money Arthur had. You told her he had millions put aside. What did you honestly think Carmichael was going to do?'

Laura looked at Monroe now.

'He wasn't supposed to die,' she admitted. 'He was supposed to be taken, dragged somewhere and forced to give away the location of the money, but instead he was taken down at the worst possible moment, as Casey Smith stabbed him – not realising at the time he was giving a killing blow.'

Laura pulled away a little from Mainsworth as she tried to turn and face the younger woman, her neck gaining another small nick from the scalpel.

'But everything that happened was because of you, Charlotte,' she said icily. 'Everything that happened after his death, the problems that came afterwards were because you spoke to your mother – because you couldn't keep your mouth shut.'

Laura crossed her arms, glaring across the rooftop at Monroe again.

'She killed him, not us. And I'll be damned if I become the surrogate death for her own bloody conscience.'

There was the sound of footsteps hurrying up the stairs, and Laura smiled.

'Luke's here,' she said triumphantly. 'Now we can finish this properly.'

But her smile faded as Anjli emerged into the night air, slightly out of breath.

'You okay, boss?' she asked, walking over to stand beside Monroe, who seemed genuinely surprised to see her, turning away from Laura to stare at his DS.

'You shouldn't be here,' he said.

'I'm only here for the reports,' Anjli forced a weak smile, waving around the roof as she did so. 'You know how the suits get when they find a report where everyone involved is there, and there's no plausible deniability.'

She pointed at Mainsworth.

'She's a surviving officer who has a personal stake in this, but so are you, sir.'

Monroe grimaced.

'You don't want to be here for this,' he said.

'With all respect, boss, but I think of the two of us, that's you needing to be told that.'

She looked across at Charlie Mainsworth and Laura Snider.

'Your son's not coming,' she said to the latter. 'He's in Bow, believing he's getting his money. He left you to us, expecting us to fix whatever this is.'

She emphasised the last part by waving a hand at both Mainsworth and Laura.

'PC Mainsworth, this woman caused you great pain, and you're probably suffering from PTSD right now,' Anjli stepped closer.

'Come any closer and I slice her throat open,' Mainsworth snarled, waving the scalpel.

'What, this woman's throat?' Anjli smiled. 'Good. She

attacked PC Cooper with a kitchen knife. I couldn't give a shit about her.'

She took another step closer.

'But I do give a shit about you,' she said.

'Why?' Mainsworth muttered. 'You don't know me.'

'No, you're right, I don't,' Anjli nodded. 'But Esme Cooper does, and she vouches for you.'

'Well, she shouldn't.'

'Well, she does,' Anjli folded her arms. 'She said when you put your mind to it, you're a good copper. So, put your mind to it and be a good copper. And even though you tasered Billy, he's not pressing charges.'

She leant in slightly, holding her hand to her mouth as if whispering conspiratorially.

'Apparently, he was a little hungover from something called a bong and accidentally tasered himself.'

Mainsworth straightened, shocked by this.

'He did this for me?' she whispered. 'He doesn't even know me.'

'He doesn't need to,' Anjli shrugged. 'You're Last Chance Saloon. That's all he needs to know.'

Mainsworth looked from Anjli to Laura.

'Give me a reason why I should let this bitch go,' she muttered. 'They left me there. They tasered me and tried to kill me and I can't get vengeance for that?'

'No,' Monroe said now. 'We don't do vengeance. We're the police. But we can give you justice.'

'I'll be arrested too,' Mainsworth replied angrily. 'There's no way I'm keeping my job after this.'

'Charlie, have you seen the Last Chance Saloon?' Anjli laughed at this. 'I mean, really *seen* it? We're all on our third or even fourth strikes here! The Guv there was so screwed we had to blackmail a sitting Prime Minister to pardon him!'

She stopped, becoming serious.

'We can fix this,' she said. 'PTSD. A sting operation to get Luke to reveal himself. A dozen other ideas. And you can go back to being a PC.'

'And if I don't want to?'

'Then bloody quit,' Monroe snapped. 'But stop with all this bollocks already. If you were going to kill her, you'd have done it already, and we all know you'd rather be here with your knife at Luke's neck, anyway. Or even your mum.'

Mainsworth looked away.

'I let her down,' she said.

'No, lassie,' Monroe spoke softly. 'She let you down. We all did, back then. And for that, I'm sorry. I should have been there for you.'

He held a hand out.

'Let me be there for you now,' he offered.

Mainsworth stared up at him, biting her lip as she considered the words.

'And you're capturing Luke?' she asked.

'Oh, I can guarantee you Luke Snider is having an absolutely terrible time right now,' Anjli laughed.

'PLEASE!' LUKE PLEADED. 'HE'LL KILL ME! YOU NEED TO DO something!'

'I could arrest you, I suppose,' Declan smiled, looking at Peter. 'If I arrested him, would you be okay with that? You wouldn't take action while he was in prison?'

'If he gave me the land deeds,' Peter suggested.

'But you have a problem there,' Johnny held up a hand. 'What can you arrest him for? Kidnapping an officer? Kidnapping a DCI? I know I could get someone out in a couple of years for that.'

'He's right,' Declan looked back at Peter. 'If Luke was released in a couple of years, would you go after him?'

'Hell yes,' Peter smiled. 'He's about to have Jennifer put down for murder.'

'That's true,' Declan looked back at Luke. 'Did she kill Harry Sullivan? Because the witnesses only saw you and your mum.'

Luke paled.

'I ... I demand a solicitor.'

'That's your right,' Declan said. 'Although they aren't that common around here at midnight.'

Luke leant his head back and howled in anger.

'It was Mum,' he eventually admitted. 'She killed Sullivan.'

'Can you prove that?'

Luke shook his head.

'I wasn't there,' he replied. 'She told me she did it.'

'Interesting, but easy to disprove,' Declan replied. 'Show me your right forearm.'

'Why?'

'Because when you came to see Monroe, you were scratching at it.'

'I don't know what you mean.'

'Do it, or I'll do it for you,' Peter snarled. 'And you won't like it when I do that, believe me.'

Slowly, Luke removed his jacket and pulled his shirt sleeve back, revealing a thin scratch, a small red line that was now coming up in a vicious-looking bruise.

'The killer of Harry Sullivan left DNA under his nails,' Declan smiled. 'We'll have the DNA match soon. If it was your mum, we'll know. Likewise, we'll know if it was you.'

Luke slumped a little.

'He deserved it,' he muttered. 'He'd been sniffing around for years, looking for the money. And when he turned up yesterday I didn't know he'd been sent by Monroe. I thought he'd been told by Jennifer about the money, and that he was working for... well, him.'

He nodded his head at Peter.

'I tried to shut him up, but in the struggle he tried to strangle me with a length of packing cord he picked up. I took it from him, being scratched in the process, and finished the job. I didn't mean to kill him – it was self-defence, I swear. It was only after that, though, that Mum suggested leaving him as a message. I should have checked his nails first, though.'

He looked over at Peter now.

'I don't want to die,' he said, passing across the papers. 'Here. Let's call this an end between us, yeah?'

He held out his hands, and Declan dutifully cuffed them.

'Open the door,' he said, nodding at the car.

With great difficulty, Luke pulled a remote out of his pocket and clicked it. The car beeped, and Declan walked over to the back door, opening it.

There, dazed and probably drugged, his hands cuffed together was DCI Henry Farrow, his glasses skewed, and his hair wild, as if he'd been sleeping rough, the little tufts at the side giving him the look of a sleepy owl.

'You okay, Guv?' Declan asked as he leant in, uncuffing Farrow.

'This ... is a shite ... stag night,' Farrow forced the words out.

'Stay here, I'll call an ambulance,' Declan smiled, looking back at Luke, now sitting dejectedly on the pavement.

There was a buzz, and Declan pulled out his phone.

FROM: ANJLI KAPOOR

> Mainsworth stood down Laura in custody again coming home how are you?

'Your mum's safe, not that you cared,' Declan said, then nodding to Peter. 'Thanks for coming, Pete.'

'You kidding?' Peter smiled, loosening his tie. 'I've been body guarding that bugger all week, it's been a chance to do something new.'

Luke frowned at this, his face not comprehending the sudden shift in his reality.

'Oh, Luke, I've been remiss,' Johnny smiled as "Peter" passed the paperwork back to him. 'This is Pete. He's one of my trainers at the gym, and he runs security for me when I'm at events.'

'No, he's Peter Carmichael,' Luke shook his head.

'Yeah, no, he's not,' Johnny shook his head. 'Peter Carmichael lives abroad somewhere.'

'But you called him that!'

'Did they?' Declan asked. 'I believe Mister Lucas here simply stated "my old and long-time friend, Peter." And when he spoke to you, he said ...'

'Let's play a hypothetical game,' Pete grinned as he repeated his earlier words. 'Let's say, for ease, that my dad was Paul Carmichael, and he ran money for the London gangs.'

'He never said he was Peter Carmichael,' Declan pulled Luke to his feet. 'He said for you to play a hypothetical game – one that never ended. He didn't even call Jennifer "my daughter", instead simply naming her. I thought you'd have worked it out when he did that, if I'm honest.'

'Yeah, sorry about that,' Pete replied sheepishly. 'It just came out like that.'

'And the deeds?' Luke glanced at Johnny, the look of betrayal on his face almost pitiful.

'Just the menu for a talk I did tonight,' Johnny tossed the papers aside. 'If you'd bothered to look, you'd have noticed.'

Luke sobbed, but Declan realised after a moment it was actually laughter. And, as DCI Farrow finally emerged, shaky-legged from the car, Luke took one look at him and started to uncontrollably belly laugh.

'All this was for nothing,' he said, looking back at Declan. 'You win again, the bloody golden child.'

'You think this is a win for me?' Declan grabbed Luke by his jacket collar. 'You dug up my bloody father! You kidnapped friends! You murdered a man!'

'Declan, as the senior officer here, please, I need to ask you to step away,' Farrow said calmly. 'You're too close to this.'

'Henry, he—'

'I know what he did,' Farrow replied. 'And I'm asking you to stand down.'

Reluctantly, Declan let go of Luke's lapel, stepping back.

Farrow walked up to Luke, stared at him for a moment, and then punched him hard in the face, sending the younger man stumbling backwards, blood streaming from his nose.

'Oh, I'm sorry,' Farrow said with mock realisation. 'You're handcuffed! I thought you had a weapon. My bad.'

Declan looked back at Farrow, who was watching him expectantly.

'Oh, yes, sorry, Guv – absolutely looked like a weapon. My apologies for not mentioning the handcuffs.'

Johnny Lucas started laughing.

'It's never dull with you,' he said to Declan while offering his hand to Farrow. 'We've met, haven't we? Either way, we'll be talking more. In particular during tomorrow's press conference, where I explain in detail how I risked danger to take down a vicious madman, and save a DCI's life.'

Declan glanced at Farrow, who slumped against the car's bonnet.

'Can I sleep first?' he asked, pulling off his wire-framed glasses and cleaning them with a microfibre cloth. 'It's been a really long day, and I'm getting married tomorrow.'

'Of course, Guv,' Declan smiled. 'But I'd suggest calling Liz first. She's worried sick about you.'

And, this suggestion made, Declan called for an ambulance, and a squad car to take Luke Snider back to the cells, while Johnny Lucas had Pete take photos of him beside the now stunned and bleeding Luke.

It was only then when he realised it had passed midnight and was now Saturday.

'Oh, shit,' he blurted. 'You get married today!'

Farrow smiled weakly.

'As I said, shittest stag night ever. Still, at least I was hand-cuffed, so that's a start.'

EPILOGUE

DECLAN HADN'T GONE TO THE WEDDING.

It was well past one in the morning when he brought Henry Farrow back to Liz's house, his ex-wife glaring balefully from the door as the police car arrived.

Farrow had hugged his wife-to-be, said everything was fine and even gave Declan credit for saving him, but as he entered the house, too tired to argue, Liz turned her attention to Declan.

'You know he was targeted because of his relationship with you,' she said.

'I know,' Declan apologised. 'It won't—'

'It won't happen again?' Liz raised a finger to stop him. 'You're damn right it won't happen again. You had Jess in danger. Henry in danger. Hell, you even had me go to friends' houses once to make sure I wasn't in danger. And you know why? One word. Walsh.'

Declan said nothing.

'Tomorrow, I change that for good,' Liz snapped. 'Tomorrow I become Liz Farrow. And if Jess has any sense, she'll follow suit. Because being a Walsh is bad for your health.'

'Liz—'

'Don't you "Liz" me,' she half shouted. 'It's "Mrs Farrow" from now on. You're the father of my child, and you'll always be a part of her life, but you don't have to be a part of mine. We're *done*, Declan.'

Declan looked up at the night sky.

'I got him back,' he said. 'Doesn't that count for something?'

'That's the only reason I'm not taking out a restraining order on you, keeping you away from the whole family,' Liz turned to enter the house. 'I get married in less than twelve hours. And until half an hour back, I didn't even know if my fiancé was alive. You're toxic, Declan. Everything you touch turns to shit.'

'No.'

The word was soft, but set in stone.

Liz paused as Declan leant in.

'You've wanted me out of your life since the divorce and I get it,' he said. 'You wanted Jess to cut all ties with me, and I get that, too. But don't you *dare* say that. Anjli is the best thing that ever happened to me, and I will not have you label her as—'

'I didn't say she was anything,' Liz replied, her tone softening. 'I said everything *you* touch turns to shit. And it will, believe me. You can't help yourself. You love Anjli? Do her a favour and walk away before you destroy her life, too. Don't come later, your invite's been rescinded.'

And, with the door slammed in his face, Declan turned and walked back to the squad car.

De'Geer, the driver for the journey, pretended he hadn't seen anything, and Declan appreciated that.

'I know you heard that,' he said, sliding into the passenger seat. 'I deserved it.'

'No, sir, you didn't,' was all De'Geer said as he started the squad car. 'And in time she'll realise it.'

Declan looked out of the window at the house, at one time his house, as they drove off.

Liz Walsh – no, the soon-to-be Liz Farrow – was taking charge of her own life.

He needed to do the same with his life now.

'DID YOU HEAR ABOUT EDEN STORM?' ANJLI LOOKED UP FROM the newspaper she was reading. 'Apparently, he's now dating his assistant. You met her. Amanda.'

Declan smiled.

'I suggested that,' he said.

'Of course you did,' Anjli mocked gently. 'Look at you, giving relationship advice to billionaires.'

Declan knew better than to argue this and glanced over at Billy. His hair was freshly groomed, probably costing more than Declan had spent in haircuts over the last year, and his three-piece suit looked brand new and bespoke.

'And how are you doing?'

'Not bad,' Billy smiled. 'Getting better over the last couple of weeks, mainly as I've been taking apart Copper Dropper.'

'I thought we were keeping it going?' Declan looked around the office.

Bullman, sitting next to Monroe, shook her head.

'It was tempting, but it's too anonymous,' she said. 'I'd

rather it was gone. And yes, they'll start new ones, but we'll stop those too.'

'Rosanna is furious, though,' Monroe said. 'She always wanted her own account there.'

'I can make her one if she wants?' Billy suggested. 'It'll take a week or two to fully end it. We still have half the IDs on it as anonymous, and I could do with help there.'

He grinned.

'It could be my wedding gift to you,' he said.

'No offence, laddie, but I'd expect a little more than that,' Monroe replied. 'Though she'd love a chance to look around. Ever since it came back as Luke's DNA under Harry Sullivan's fingernails, she's been bored witless.'

Declan grinned. Following the wrapping up of the Snider case, with the bodies being returned to their rightful places and the administrational hassle of all of that, the unit had been unusually quiet. The only moment of high activity had been a week back, when the newest Member of Parliament for Bethnal Green and Bow had turned up to thank Declan for his sterling work in getting them over the line.

Johnny Lucas and DCI Farrow had been all over the papers, detailing how the former had helped with a detailed sting operation to rescue the latter once the police ran out of options, and how he'd also decided to use a burnt-out pub as a new community centre – which of course meant he could now use council funding to fix it up.

It hadn't been the landslide Declan had expected, though – many people remembered Johnny's criminal past, and Declan knew he'd have an uphill battle – but Johnny had started a new journey, and he would be churlish to wish harm on him.

But, apart from that, things had been quiet. They charged

Luke Snider with two counts of kidnapping and one count of murder, while his mum and Jennifer Carmichael had been charged with being unknowing accessories, charges that any good lawyer could get them out of. Arthur Snider's body had been quietly reburied, and only Anjli and Declan had been there for the reburying of Patrick Walsh, a week after he'd been removed.

Declan had spent some time alone at the grave afterwards, talking to his father. He had explained how he understood his adultery, even if he could never accept it, and promised he would do better in his own life, before returning to his house and Anjli.

And to a quiet time at the Temple Inn Crime Unit.

In fact, the only exciting moment in weeks was one that was about to happen, and this was the reason everyone was in the office. Anjli was at her desk, Declan at his, Billy at the monitor station, and Bullman, Monroe and De'Geer were standing around, loitering, even.

As Doctor Marcos opened the door, they all stood up.

'Congratulations!' they shouted out as Esme Cooper brought Charlotte Mainsworth into the office.

Mainsworth, seeing the audience, grimaced.

'Set up,' she muttered.

'Absolutely,' Monroe smiled, walking over to her and shaking her hand. 'We'll miss you. But London's loss is Scotland's gain.'

It had been a quick decision, but apparently one long considered. PC Charlie Mainsworth had been given a new lease of life, career wise, and had received a verbal warning for kidnapping Laura Snider from her cell, but also had received a written commendation for her actions in helping take down her kidnappers and torturers, as part of the same "sting" that caught Luke Snider. But even with her career saved, and a spot waiting for her at the Last Chance Saloon, Mainsworth had decided London was filled with too many memories, especially ones with Arthur Snider's name on. And, a couple of days after the night on the roof, she'd applied for a transfer, in her words, "as far from here as possible."

Monroe had worked his magic, reminding DCI Hendrick in Edinburgh that there was still a debt owed after he helped take down Lennie Wright the previous year, and now, in one week, PC Charlotte Mainsworth was starting her new life in the Edinburgh Police.

As Mainsworth received hugs and handshakes from everyone, Declan stood on his chair, raising his mug of coffee. He'd wanted to do this with champagne, but to be honest, they'd all forgot to go get some.

'Everyone,' he said, using his metal tactical pen to tap against the side of the mug. 'That's not all.'

This hadn't been expected, and the clamour of voices dropped.

'Detective Chief Inspector Monroe, if you will?' Declan toasted Monroe as he, too, climbed onto a table.

'Aye, so we had a wee chat, and spoke to the Guv—' he nodded at Bullman, who leant back in her chair.

'That's me. I'm the Guv. Me.'

'Aye, yes, she is. Anyway, we had a talk, and then we spoke to Scotland Yard, and based on DI Walsh's recommendations, we have agreed, on principle, the following rank changes.'

He looked at Billy.

'Detective Constable William Fitzwarren, you are hereby promoted to the rank of Detective Sergeant,' he said to a stunned reaction, followed by rapturous applause.

But holding a hand up, he then looked over at Anjli.

'Detective Sergeant Anjli Kapoor, for sterling service and going beyond the call of duty, you are hereby promoted to the rank of Detective Inspector.'

'Beyond the call of duty?' Anjli was stunned, but confused.

'Aye, keeping that eejit in line,' Monroe pointed at Declan. 'Both promotions are in accordance with guidelines passed to us by the National Police Promotion Framework, and are currently temporary, twelve month promotions. In the next year, both of you will require a work-based assessment, leading to a professional qualification in police management – but I doubt these will be a problem.'

He raised his own mug.

'Congratulations DS Fitzwarren and DI Kapoor.'

As the others in the office raised their own mugs, or imaginary glasses to this, Declan climbed off the chair, patting Billy's shoulder.

'You deserved this,' he said with a smile. 'Don't let us all down by being a miserable, drunken sod any time soon.'

Billy grinned, but was already being pulled to his feet by Cooper, kissing him on the cheek as she dragged De'Geer into a three-way hug.

Anjli, noting Declan's expression, pulled him aside.

'You didn't get me promoted just to keep me with you, right?' she said, half-joking.

'No,' Declan replied honestly, smiling. 'It was the right thing to do. You've both deserved this rise for a long time, and I've been aware I've kept you back.'

'Who said this to you?' Anjli frowned.

'Shaun Donnal, back during the mistletoe case,' Declan explained. 'Said some things that made sense.'

And they had made sense – Shaun had seen exactly what had happened.

'But while you don't go for DCI, what about the others? The DS over there or the young blond DC who was outside Devonshire House that day? Are you stopping them from progressing by not doing it yourself?'

Declan smiled.

'You still need to pass the tests,' he said. 'I can't do everything for the pair of you.'

'And you?' Anjli asked. 'You'll try for DCI?'

'No, I'm fine here,' Declan replied. 'This was more—'

'Bullshit,' Anjli snapped. 'What's the real reason?'

Declan looked to the carpet.

'It was part of the deal Bullman made with Scotland Yard to get you both through,' he said. 'Getting the two of you promoted on the basis I didn't try.'

'Then I don't want it,' Anjli's face was furious. 'And when Billy hears, he won't—'

'Monroe's fighting it,' Declan shook his head. 'And this isn't about me. Take the win. We can always look at my promotion after yours is official.'

Anjli frowned, watching Declan, as if waiting to see if he was lying.

'I'm not happy about this,' she said. 'There might be ... repercussions at home.'

'Promises promises,' Declan embraced Anjli, kissing her. 'You really did deserve this. Now go call your mum. She'll be furious you've already waited five minutes before telling her.'

Anjli smiled and, pulling her phone out, walked off.

As she did so, Monroe walked over.

'Did you tell her?'

'That she deserved it?'

'No, you bloody idiot,' Monroe growled. 'About your own promotion. Or, rather, lack of one.'

Declan nodded.

'And did you tell her what that means?'

Declan shook his head. The Last Chance Saloon were their own boss for a lot of the time, but they still worked to the beat of the City of London police. And, more importantly, their budget.

A budget that didn't have funds for two DIs in the unit.

'I have until the end of the financial year to work it out,' Declan smiled. 'Maybe I'll get that promotion after all, and we can work together in your office.'

'Aye, that might happen,' Monroe sighed. 'But until then, tell Anjli. Because if you haven't sorted this out by the start of April, which is just over six weeks, by the way, and if the budget doesn't change, either you or Anjli will have to transfer out.'

With that ominous deadline given, Monroe walked away and Declan stared at the laughing Anjli, on the phone now, telling her mother the good news.

If she found this out, she'd kill him.

Maybe I should have taken the Edinburgh job instead of Mainsworth, he thought to himself as he walked back to the crowded office area. *Although she'd still hunt me down, even up there.*

It was fine. He was sure of it. After all, he had six weeks to fix it.

And six weeks was a long time in the Last Chance Saloon.

DI Walsh and the team of the *Last Chance Saloon* will return in their next thriller

KILL YOUR DARLINGS

Order Now at Amazon:

mybook.to/killyourdarlings

ACKNOWLEDGEMENTS

When you write a series of books, you find that there are a ton of people out there who help you, sometimes without even realising, and so I wanted to say thanks.

There are people I need to thank, and they know who they are, including my brother Chris Lee, who I truly believe could make a fortune as a post-retirement copy editor, if not a solid writing career of his own, Jacqueline Beard MBE, who has copyedited all my books since the very beginning, and editor Sian Phillips, all of whom have made my books way better than they have every right to be.

Also, I couldn't have done this without my growing army of ARC and beta readers, who not only show me where I falter, but also raise awareness of me in the social media world, ensuring that other people learn of my books.

But mainly, I tip my hat and thank you. *The reader.* Who once took a chance on an unknown author in a pile of Kindle books, and thought you'd give them a go, and who has carried on this far with them, as well as the spin off books I now release.

I write Declan Walsh for you. He (and his team) solves crimes for you. And with luck, he'll keep on solving them for a very long time.

Jack Gatland / Tony Lee,
London, February 2023

ABOUT THE AUTHOR

Jack Gatland is the pen name of *#1 New York Times Bestselling Author* Tony Lee, who has been writing in all media for thirty-five years, including comics, graphic novels, middle grade books, audio drama, TV and film for *DC Comics, Marvel, BBC, ITV, Random House, Penguin USA, Hachette* and a ton of other publishers and broadcasters.

These have included licenses such as *Doctor Who, Spider Man, X-Men, Star Trek, Battlestar Galactica, MacGyver,* BBC's *Doctors, Wallace and Gromit* and *Shrek*, as well as work created with musicians such as *Ozzy Osbourne, Joe Satriani, Beartooth, Pantera* and *Megadeth.*

As Tony, he's toured the world talking to reluctant readers with his 'Change The Channel' school tours, and lectures on screenwriting and comic scripting for *Raindance* in London.

An introvert West Londoner by heart, he lives with his wife Tracy and dog Fosco, just outside London.

Locations In The Book

The locations and items I use in my books are real, if altered slightly for dramatic intent. Here's some more information about a few of them...

Temple Church has been used in several of my books, including *The Lionheart Curse*, and it's one of my favourite places to visit. That said, it does, as I mentioned in the story, suffer from connections to Dan Brown's work. If you're near Temple Inn at any time, it's well worth a visit.

Box 57 at the Royal Albert Hall is a real place, and I booked it at Christmas to watch the Royal Albert Hall's Christmas Carol show. The boxes are really quite narrow, and very red. The food, however, is amazing, and you can see the stone crown of the Royal Box directly below you if you peek over, just as Declan does.

The Boxing Club near Meath Gardens that Johnny Lucas has turned into his Election HQ doesn't exist, and neither do the Twins - but the location used is the current **Globe Town Social Club**, within **Green Lens Studios**, a community centre formerly known as Eastbourne House, that I would pass occasionally in my 20s.

The Morpeth Arms on Millbank is a real pub, and has real cells underneath. You can even visit them on a quiet weekday lunchtime, if you ask nicely. The other notable feature of the Morpeth Arms is its "Spying Room." This is on the second floor of the pub, decorated in a 1920s style and themed after Mata Hari, the infamous dancer and double agent. The windows, which happen to look out upon the British Intelligence Service building across the Thames, are adorned with binoculars so pub patrons can spy on the spies. MI6 and FBI agents are said to occasionally call in for a pint.

The Clerkenwell Catacombs also exist, under the more official name of *the Clerkenwell House of Detention,* north-east of Clerkenwell Green. Its history stretches all the way back to 1617, including its destruction by fire in the 1780 Gordon Riots. The prison was demolished in 1893 to make way for the Hugh Myddleton School, but beneath the playground, however, significant remnants of the older buildings remain. If you watched Guy Richie's first *Sherlock Holmes* movie a few years ago, you would have seen these, as the catacombs doubled for the tunnels under Westminster in the last act.

And finally, **Upton Park** *was* pulled down and turned into apartment blocks, with West Ham moving stadiums as Monroe and Billy explain in the story - and we've done our best to make sure the rough area was used correctly!

If you're interested in seeing what the *real* locations look like, I post 'behind the scenes' location images on my Instagram feed. This will continue through all the books, and I suggest you follow it.

In fact, feel free to follow me on all my social media by clicking on the links below. Over time these can be places where we can engage, discuss Declan and put the world to rights.

www.jackgatland.com

www.hoodemanmedia.com

Visit Jack's Reader's Group Page
(Mainly for fans to discuss his books):
https://www.facebook.com/groups/jackgatland

Subscribe to Jack's Readers List:
https://bit.ly/jackgatlandVIP

www.facebook.com/jackgatlandbooks
www.twitter.com/jackgatlandbook
ww.instagram.com/jackgatland

Want more books by Jack Gatland? Turn the page...

THE THEFT OF A **PRICELESS** PAINTING...
A GANGSTER WITH A **CRIPPLING DEBT**...
A **BODY COUNT** RISING BY THE HOUR...

AND ELLIE RECKLESS IS CAUGHT IN THE MIDDLE.

JACK GATLAND

PAINT
— THE —
DEAD

A 'COP FOR CRIMINALS' ELLIE RECKLESS NOVEL

A NEW PROCEDURAL CRIME SERIES WITH
A TWIST - FROM THE CREATOR OF THE
BESTSELLING 'DI DECLAN WALSH' SERIES

AVAILABLE ON AMAZON / KINDLE UNLIMITED

THEY TRIED TO KILL HIM...
NOW HE'S OUT FOR **REVENGE.**

NEW YORK TIMES #1 BESTSELLER **TONY LEE** WRITING AS

JACK GATLAND

THE MURDER OF AN **MI5 AGENT**...
A BURNED SPY **ON THE RUN** FROM HIS OWN PEOPLE...
AN ENEMY OUT TO **STOP HIM** AT ANY COST...
AND A **PRESIDENT** ABOUT TO BE **ASSASSINATED**...

SLEEPING
SOLDIERS

A **TOM MARLOWE** THRILLER

BOOK 1 IN A NEW SERIES OF THRILLERS IN THE STYLE OF
JASON BOURNE, JOHN MILTON OR **BURN NOTICE,** AND
SPINNING OUT OF THE **DECLAN WALSH** SERIES OF BOOKS

AVAILABLE ON AMAZON / KINDLE UNLIMITED

EIGHT PEOPLE. EIGHT SECRETS.
ONE SNIPER.

THE
B⊕ARD
ROOM

HOW FAR WOULD YOU GO TO GAIN JUSTICE?

NEW YORK TIMES #1 BESTSELLER TONY LEE WRITING AS

JACK GATLAND

A NEW STANDALONE THRILLER WITH
A TWIST - FROM THE CREATOR OF THE
BESTSELLING 'DI DECLAN WALSH' SERIES

AVAILABLE ON AMAZON / KINDLE UNLIMITED

JACK GATLAND

THE LIONHEART CURSE

HUNT THE GREATEST TREASURES
PAY THE GREATEST PRICE

BOOK 1 IN A NEW SERIES OF ADVENTURES
IN THE STYLE OF 'THE DA VINCI CODE'
FROM THE CREATOR OF DECLAN WALSH

AVAILABLE ON AMAZON / KINDLEUNLIMITED

Printed in Great Britain
by Amazon